D1736214

A
PRINCE
SO
CRUEL

INGRID SEYMOUR

PenDreams

To all of those struggling with their inner demons

CHAPTER 1

The Fae realm was supposed to be safe for humans. Yet, here I was, backed into a corner, facing three snarling males.

My heart hammered out of control, and my messenger bag hung heavily from my shoulder. It was full of the healing ingredients I bought at Yalgrun's Wares a moment ago, supplies I couldn't get back home.

Just a few hours ago, I'd left my condo in St. Louis, walked to Forest Park from my house on Art Hill Ave, and traced my transfer rune on the wooden railing of Steinberg Bridge. The Fae rune was a symbol assigned only to me, which granted me passage to Elf-hame, specifically to a trading post in the small, bustling town of Pharowyn, a town I'd visited safely a thousand times.

But now, in front of me, was the evidence that the sense of security I'd felt during my previous visits was as false as my nonna's teeth. If only I'd sensed something was wrong, I might have returned home and wouldn't be facing the chilling looks of the three very tall, very buff Fae who were eyeing me as if I was about to become their next meal.

Suddenly, I felt as if I were in no-man's-land and not the fairyland that maintained a diplomatic relationship with my realm.

"What do you want?" I demanded, as my back hit the wall behind me.

They didn't respond.

I tried to run out of the tightening circle they'd formed, but the male to my right—a Fae whose pointed ears were quite visible thanks to his platinum-blond cropped hair—blocked me.

"I'll scream if you don't let me pass," I threatened.

The male on the left smirked. He had skin the color of mahogany and eyes like warm honey. His face was framed by a couple of long braids that fell from his otherwise short, coiled hair. A glint in his gaze told me no one would help me, no matter how loudly I screamed.

I cast a glance through the gap between my assailants' muscled arms and caught a glimpse of a woman on the other side of the street. She had paused and was looking at me as if I deserved whatever was coming my way.

Really? Why?

Did she think I was a trouble-making human? Was I? Maybe I'd inadvertently done something wrong, committed some faux pas I wasn't aware of. I mentally retraced my steps since I'd arrived and couldn't find anything.

After tracing my rune on the bridge, I appeared in a quaint tavern at one of the many tables assigned for that purpose. Appearing and disappearing wasn't exactly what happened. No one could really do that. What the rune did was break the membrane between one realm and the other, transferring one's reality to a Fae location that occupied the same time and space. It was all very technical, and I'd learned all about it in high school, though I'd forgotten most of it. Healing magic was my jam, mages like my brother, Leo, could concern themselves with those other details.

It was early on a Saturday morning, and the tavern had been buzzing with an assortment of *Skews*, which was what humans with no supernatural abilities were called back home—not that the Fae used those terms. To them, there was the Fae, and then there was everybody else. The point was that the tavern was crawling with people from my realm, as well as the Fae servers who worked there.

I got up from the table where I'd appeared—they were supposed to be left empty to allow others to transfer by using their own runes—and took a seat at a small, round table for one.

A slight Fae, thin as a rail, rushed toward.

"May I serve you, respectable lady?" he asked in a lilting accent. He wore a green tunic with carved buttons and cropped brown pants. His bare feet were stuffed in thin leather shoes that molded to him perfectly. Two small horns protruded from his forehead, and a garland of wild flowers rested on them.

"Good morning, *Abin Cenael*," I said, calling him *respectable sir* in return. "I would like a cup of jasmine tea and a honeyed bun with goat cheese."

He inclined his head. "Serving you is my pleasure. You won't have to wait but a minute."

In seconds, he was back with my breakfast, which I'd enjoyed immensely, though it was now souring in my stomach. After that, I'd done my shopping and headed back toward the tavern with the purpose of returning home.

No, I hadn't done anything wrong.

Despite the female's mean stare, I couldn't help the plea that rose to my lips. "Help me."

She huffed in disgust and pranced away on hooved feet that clattered against the cobblestones.

My eyes flicked back to the males. Who were they? Guards? They certainly were armed to the teeth with swords and daggers. Whatever they were, they appeared lethal and authoritative—not the kind of males anyone would want to cross, especially to help a visiting human.

The one in the middle loomed over me, all seven feet of him. He had long, red hair swept to one side and green eyes that sparkled like emeralds. He wore an elaborate gold-trimmed leather jacket, unbuttoned at the front to reveal a tattooed torso lined with heavy muscles. The hilt of his sword peeked above his head, promising violence.

I fought the urge to lower my gaze, and instead, held my head high. He raised a perfect red eyebrow, appearing mildly impressed by my pluck.

"I will turn you all into horny toads if you don't get out of my way," I lied, pretending I was a witch and putting a growl in my voice, though I wasn't sure it was very convincing. My normal day consisted of communicating with sick children, who always brought out the sweetest side of me. I wasn't used to dealing with Fae a-holes.

The platinum-haired guy inclined his head and spoke with a purr. "You will find the horny part easy to do, I think. In truth, you probably only need to worry about the toad part."

"Shut up, Silver," the redhead snapped, without breaking eye contact with me. "You're coming with us." He grabbed my elbow.

"No, I have a date I can't miss. I need to get home immediately."

This part wasn't a lie. I had dinner plans with Ethan Malone, a pediatric neurosurgeon I'd shared a spark with in the cafeteria line. We both worked at Children's Hospital, and I'd seen him doing rounds many times. He was hard to miss in those blue scrubs that matched his eyes and hugged his perfect butt. I'd been content with looking at him from afar, afraid he would turn out to be an arrogant jerk like most of the other residents, afraid the spark would die after the first date due to lack of chemistry.

He seemed nice and didn't bat an eye when he learned I was a healer and not an MD. Maybe the fact that he was a talented neurosurgeon would mean he wouldn't be intimidated by my Skew healing abilities. He was a *Stale,* a regular human with no magic, and normally Stales in my field resented healers. They said we had it easy, which wasn't true. I'd gone to college too and worked hard to learn biology, chemistry, anatomy, child psychology, and a slew of other things.

I didn't want to miss that date. I'd been looking forward to it. I hadn't been lucky in love like my sisters. They talked about sizzling physical attraction and unconditional feelings, but I'd never felt that after my first boyfriend in college, and I was beginning to think it wasn't in the cards for me.

The Fae dude didn't care about my date, though, and tugged harder on my elbow.

I screamed. "Unhand me, you pervert."

"I'm not a pervert, I'll have you know. That particular title belongs to *that* one." He threw a sidelong glance toward the male he'd called Silver.

Silver—whose name seemed appropriate given his hair color—rolled his eyes. "A much better title than *asshole with the stick up his ass*."

The third guy sighed and gave a pointed look at the redhead's hand around my elbow. "Let her go, Kryn. You know what he said." His voice was nice and melodic.

My ears perked up. *What* who *said?*

From the sounds of it, someone had sent them to collect me, but I had no idea who. Other than Yalgrun—the store owner where I shopped—I didn't know anyone else.

Reluctantly, the asshole with the stick up his ass, Kryn, removed his large hand. I shook myself and made as if to walk away. The males didn't budge.

"Let me pass," I demanded. "I'm due home, and if I'm one minute late, my boyfriend—he's a badass vampire, by the way—will come looking for me." I didn't have a boyfriend, badass or otherwise, but I had to try something.

"You need to come with us, please," the dark-skinned guy said.

Silver huffed. "Good luck using the nice approach with this one, Jeondar. I can spot the feisty ones."

"We're wasting time." Kryn looked annoyed.

"Please, Daniella," Jeondar said, my name on his lips making me shiver, "come with us."

"Quietly or not," Kryn added.

"My name isn't Daniella. You have the wrong person," I said, barely managing to keep a straight face.

Silver blew air through his nose, looking amused. "Personally, I think she'll choose *or not.*"

Jeondar smiled sweetly. "Don't make this harder on yourself." He offered me a hand forward, as if to guide me down the sidewalk.

But I knew that if I went anywhere with them, I was done for. I would never go home or see my family again.

I shook myself. "All right, I will..." I threw my messenger bag at Jeondar's face and ran, ducking under his arm.

It wasn't even worth the try. I'd barely taken two steps when pain exploded on the left side of my face, and I started going down, though strong arms scooped me up before I hit the ground.

"Shit, Kryn," Jeondar said angrily. "You didn't have to do that."

The world around me whirled, and then I was hanging upside down, my arms and head dangling. Kryn had draped me over his shoulder like an old coat. Shadows gathered around my vision. I fought not to pass out.

"He won't be happy you hit her," Jeondar said.

"He can get over it."

"She has a nice ass." Silver laughed.

"I wish Cylea would have come instead of you," Jeondar complained.

"Agreed," Kryn said. "She wouldn't let a dick get in the way of getting her work done."

Silver huffed. "That's because she doesn't have one."

My head swam, and the shadows took over as I spiraled out of consciousness.

CHAPTER 2

A loud *bang* slipped through the heavy waters of my unconsciousness. I struggled to break the surface, my head dazed and
throbbing with pain.

The *bang* was followed by a deep growl and a string of words that
sounded garbled to my pounding ears. I clawed at my consciousness
until I got a hold of it and pushed my head above the haze that
surrounded me.

I winced, coming to. I was lying on my right shoulder, my hands
twisted awkwardly behind my back. I tried to move, only to discover
I was tied up.

With some effort, I cleared my blurry vision and stared directly at
a soft rug, its fibers tickling my cheek. A bit further, there was a fire
pit made of smooth rocks arranged in a circle. A few logs smoldered
in the center, a gentle warmth emanating from them. Beyond the
pit, there was an opening that let in a slice of daylight. It was just a
narrow slit, the flap of a tent.

"Calm down. She's fine," a male voice said outside the tent. It
sounded familiar, even though I'd only just heard it. It was Kryn,
the asshole that decked me, the one responsible for the splitting
headache and the pain now traveling down my jaw.

"Don't talk to me like that," a second male growled in a deep voice
I'd never heard before, and never wanted to hear again.

A shudder traveled down my body at the savage rumble, my instincts telling me to stay far, far away from whoever that was.

"You mistreated her," he rumbled again, sounding like a thunderstorm getting ready to tear the world apart.

"She'll be all right. We've made sure she's comfortable." This was Jeondar, the dark-skinned male with the melodic voice. He sounded respectful and reassuring, unlike Kryn.

Comfortable, my ass. My arms were twisted behind me, and my wrists felt raw.

"It won't happen again," Jeondar promised.

"You'd better make sure of it," that growling male again.

Was it the other one? Silver?

No, I didn't think so—not unless he was some sort of Fae shifter, and he'd morphed into a huge lion with a boom box instead of a voice box. Though, to my knowledge, shifters couldn't speak while in their animal form. My half-sister Toni sure couldn't when she turned into a wolf. But maybe it was different for the Fae. I'd studied their kind in high school and college, but never in depth. Elf-hame was more vast and varied than my own realm. God only knew all the creatures that could be found in this land.

I listened a little longer, but everything went quiet. After a couple of minutes, I struggled to a sitting position. My shoulders and head screamed in pain as I reclined against the wooden pole I was tied to.

Just the effort of sitting up left me panting. I inhaled deeply for a minute, and once my breathing evened out, I called on my healing powers, focusing on the pain and tightness around my jaw. The spot where Kryn punched me felt swollen and was probably bruising already.

The first chance I got, I would kick him in the balls. I didn't care if he decked me again.

Without being able to use my hands to direct my healing magic, it took longer than normal to repair the damage the asshole Fae caused. I cursed under my breath, frustrated. Normally, an injury like this would require no time to heal, but it took at least ten minutes for my headache to finally go away.

Damn! I didn't know I had become so reliant on the use of my hands to channel my powers. Of course, I'd never been kidnapped and tied up before. My siblings were the ones who normally got themselves into this kind of trouble. I was the sensible one, the one Mom trusted to get the other three in line.

Mom... She would freak out when I didn't show up tomorrow evening. Once a month, I went home, and we cooked together. Some decadent Italian dish that she wished to pass down to her kids, the way Nonna passed it down to her.

First, Mom would try to call me, and when I didn't answer the phone, she would call Toni. My sister would try to calm her down, and that might last for a day, but by the next morning, Mom was sure to involve the police—not that it would do any good. I hadn't told anyone I was coming here, and even if they figured it out, what then? Our police had no jurisdiction here, and at best could use diplomatic means to inquire about my whereabouts. But based on the fact that no one had helped me when those assholes assailed me, it wasn't hard to guess what would happen if anyone came asking questions about one of the many human visitors who crossed the veil into Pharowyn to purchase goods.

I glanced around the tent. It stood tall, thick fabric draping down from the twelve-foot center pole, many rugs layered below to cover the ground. To my left, a large, gilded chest sat next to a table topped with an ornate metal pitcher and matching cups. A sleeping area made out of thick blankets, furs, and pillows was behind me. Male clothes lay strewn on top, and a pair of tall boots rested at the far end. Folding canvas chairs were pushed against the right side. I thought for a long moment, wondering where I was. Everything looked expensive, but there was no clue as to who had taken me, why, and most importantly, where.

Was I still in Pharowyn?

God, I hope so!

But what if I wasn't? Would I know where to go if I escaped?

I shook my head. Though the questions needed answers, I couldn't just sit here, waiting for them. I had to break out and take my chances. But how?

One idea occurred to me. It would be painful, but I couldn't think of anything else. Drawing in a shaky breath, I pulled on my restraints, testing them out. They were tight, but I was ready to scrape my skin to the bone, dislocate my thumbs, or whatever it took to slip away. It would hurt like hell, but I could heal myself afterward.

Clenching my teeth, I pulled harder, focusing on my right hand. The rough rope bit into my skin as I worked my wrist from side to side and tugged as hard as I could. I swallowed the whimper that rose to my throat, then stopped to take a break and ease the pain for just a bit. I'd managed to slide the rope down my wrist about an inch. I could do this, even if I turned my joints and ligaments into pulp. I inhaled deeply, trying to focus on getting home instead of the pain.

I'd gotten mentally ready to start tugging again when someone pushed the tent flap to one side and walked in. I froze.

Jeondar stood on the other side of the fire pit, frowning at me. He held a metal plate and a cup in his hands. He smiled knowingly but said nothing. Instead, he walked to the table that held the pitcher and set down his load. Reaching behind his back, he pulled out a large knife and walked in my direction.

Stomach sinking, I pressed my back to the pole and watched him warily. He came around, took his sharp knife to the rope, and cut it. He brought my right hand forward and carefully removed the remnants that still circled it. Through narrowed eyes, he noticed the bloody marks around my wrist. Again, he didn't say anything. He just huffed and walked back to the table.

I busied myself by removing the rope from my left hand.

"I brought you some food," Jeondar said. "You must be hungry."

Ignoring him as he approached, I placed my left hand over my bloody wrist and quickly healed the wound. Skin and tissue knitted themselves, and the pain ebbed slowly until it completely disappeared.

"Impressive," Jeondar said as he set the plate and cup in front of me. The meal consisted of roasted meat and vegetables, and something that looked like red wine.

Despite myself, my stomach rumbled loudly enough for Jeondar to hear.

He chuckled. "Eat. I promise it's good."

I tore my eyes from the food and glowered at him. I wanted to pick up the food and throw it at his face, but I doubted he would bring me more, and I needed to keep my strength. However, I wasn't going to eat while he was here, so I crossed my arms and continued glowering.

"Where am I?" I demanded.

He ignored my question and sat on one of the chairs, crossing his ankles. I didn't think he would answer, but he surprised me by saying, "A few miles north of Pharowyn."

A few miles. That was not bad. I could jog and make it there before nightfall. It wasn't too late in the afternoon, judging by the amount of sun spilling through the tent flap. But what if he was lying? What if we were south of Pharowyn? Either way, that didn't change my situation. I had to escape.

"Why?" I asked. "Why did you take me? What do you want with me?"

Jeondar shrugged. "You'll find out soon enough. It's not my job to tell you."

His honey-colored eyes lowered to the food, then met mine again.

He wanted me to eat. He probably would not leave until he saw me take a bite, so I picked up the plate, grabbed the two-pronged fork that rested on top of it, and speared a piece of what looked like beef. The meat practically melted in my mouth, and I had to fight the urge to close my eyes and savor it. Instead, I swallowed and followed it with a piece of eggplant, which was perfectly seasoned. He hadn't lied. The food was delicious. The wine too. Full and not overly sweet. It slid down my throat easily, quelling my thirst.

I stared at the fire pit, ignoring Jeondar altogether. After a few more bites, I was starting to think he was waiting for me to finish so he could tie me up again, but in the end, he let out a heavy sigh and walked out.

Hurriedly, I set the plate down, and the first thing I did was trace my transfer rune on the rug, praying it would take me back home. Nothing happened. The rune would only work in Pharowyn. Shit! I rose to my feet and, crouching low, inched toward the tent flap and tried to peer outside, but the view the slit offered was limited, and all I could glimpse was grass and a few trees about twenty yards away.

I craned my neck, trying to see if there was a guard stationed out front, but I couldn't tell. I had to assume there was. They wouldn't leave me unattended. Turning, I faced the back of the tent, then walked its perimeter, looking for the best place to sneak out. I checked around and found that the bottom of the tent was tucked securely under the layered rugs.

Dammit!

There would be no escaping through the sides or back. I whirled inside the tent, eyes roving around as I tried to think of how to escape without being noticed. A new idea occurred to me. I searched the tent once more and spotted my messenger bag on one of the canvas chairs.

Thank the witchlights!

I rushed there and pulled out a bundle of herbs. I quickly unwrapped it from the piece of tan cloth that held it together. Yalgrun sold the strongest aeradonus. A pinch was enough to create a very effective bronchodilator. I used it to treat my chronic asthma patients. One more thing about aeradonus... it smoked like crazy when it came in contact with fire. I'd discovered that the hard way when I accidentally dropped a bit of it into the open flame of my gas stove. It was so bad it triggered the smoke detector and I had to open all the windows and turn on the fan to clear the mess.

I took the tan cloth and checked the contents of the metal pitcher on the table. I sniffed it and was relieved to find out it was water. I poured some on the cloth, which I then wrung and secured around my head, covering my nose. I then checked the compass function on my smartwatch to figure out which way Pharowyn lay.

Heart pounding out of control, I slung the messenger bag across my torso, threw the bundle of aeradonus in the fire pit, and crouched next to the tent flap, my eyes squeezed shut.

A pungent smell like a combination of menthol and camphor quickly filled the tent. The smoke rose, building a huge cloud overhead, searching for a way out. Soon, the entire space was swimming in a thick haze. I fought the urge to cough, pressing a hand tightly to my mouth.

"There's smoke coming from the tent," someone yelled outside.

Footsteps sounded around the tent, and the flap was thrown open as several people rushed in. I couldn't tell how many, but as soon as they cleared the exit and started coughing, I slipped out and took off at a full pelt, heading south.

The messenger bag bounced at my hip as my arms and legs pumped. A line of trees stood several yards ahead, and I ran faster, eager to hide behind their foliage. I was almost there when a shape dropped from one of the many branches overhead and landed in a crouch in front of me.

"Going somewhere?" the female Fae asked with a wicked grin.

CHAPTER 3

I skidded to a halt as the tall female stretched to her full height, blocking my escape. I started to run right, but she was there in the blink of an eye. I turned left. The same happened.

She *tsked* and shook her head, a curtain of light blue hair swinging around her stunning face. She had clear blue eyes to match her hair, as well as indigo-painted lips and tattoos running along her pale collarbone. She wore a cerulean tunic that hung off her shoulders and was cinched around her waist by a leather corset. Under the tunic, she wore matching leggings and a pair of knee-high boots carved with the same intricate patterns as her corset. A sword hung from a belt at her side.

"Creative, this one," she said in a husky voice, and the three ass-holes who took me from the trading post rushed out of the tent and joined us. They were wincing and coughing, and the sharp smell that clung to them was enough to make me wince.

The female wrinkled her nose. "Are you all right?"

Silver nodded, wiping tears from his eyes and clearing his throat. "She must've used something from her bag." He pointed at it.

"Who's grand idea was it to leave it in the tent?" Kryn's emerald eyes flicked toward Jeondar.

"They're *her* things," Jeondar argued, sounding hoarse until he cleared his throat. "I was trying to be nice."

"I warned you it wouldn't pay off to be nice. I told you I can spot the tricky ones a mile away." Silver shook his head.

Kryn cursed, mumbled something about stupidity, and walked to a large fire pit. There, he reached into a bucket that sat on the ground, scooped water out, and rubbed his face. The others followed him and did the same, while I stood seething, and wishing death on the entire bunch. If only I had some ability that could help me fight them, but my Skew skills were useless in a fight. I couldn't shift into a wolf like Toni, use telekinetic powers like Lucia, or blast fire from my hands like Leo. My siblings could have put up a fight. Me, I couldn't even outrun my captors.

Dammit all to hell.

The blue-haired female circled around to me, assessing me from the top of my head to the tip of my flats, her predatory manner sending a shiver up my spine.

"So this is she?" She didn't appear impressed.

Silver came around, water dripping from his chiseled jaw. He extended a hand in my direction. "I see you've met Cylea. Good. Now, give me your bag."

I clung to the strap, wrapping both hands around it.

"Give. Me. Your. Bag," he repeated.

Kryn huffed. "Just take it."

Silver took a step forward, but Jeondar moved in front of him.

"I will keep your bag safe," he said, putting a hand out.

Cursing inwardly, I pulled the strap over my head and handed it over.

"Thank you." He inclined his head respectfully and gave Kryn a raised eyebrow. "See, you *can* accomplish things through good manners."

"We would still be arguing with her in Pharowyn if I'd left it up to you." Kryn marched toward the tent and threw the flap wide open to let the smoke out. He shielded his nose and mouth with his hand and mumbled, "How long is the stench going to last?"

Not long, I knew, but I didn't contribute that bit of information. Instead, I glanced around, trying to assess my situation a little better. We were in a small clearing, with two smaller tents positioned a distance away from the larger one I'd just escaped. Nine horses stood nearby, tied to a long, low branch and stamping the ground.

The trees around us were thick and tall, blocking the view of what might lie beyond. One thing I could tell, however, the sun was quickly going down, and nighttime would be here soon. My chest tightened at the thought. I felt that the longer I stayed here, the smaller my chances of going back home.

"Take a seat here while the smoke clears." Jeondar pointed to a log next to the fire pit.

I didn't want to sit, didn't want to do anything these people said, so instead, I started pacing like a caged lioness. I wanted to rail, curse their mothers, but I knew it wouldn't accomplish anything. No matter how haughty and badass they acted, they were not in charge. Someone else was, and he wasn't here.

"Arabis?" Kryn asked the blue-haired female, Cylea.

Arabis? My ears perked up. Was this the person in charge?

"She's already gone with…" her eyes flicked toward me, "… him."

Nope, not her.

Silver set to work by the fire pit. A black round pot, like a witch's cauldron, hung over the embers. He poured water in and walked to a saddlebag that rested on the ground. He came back holding a pouch from which he took out different herbs that went into the pot. He rubbed his fingers together and sniffed them, enjoying the scent the herbs had left behind. It was a familiar motion, something I did while I prepared remedies with various ingredients. It was strange watching him move lithely around the fire, despite his muscular frame. He looked like a ballerina pretending to make soup on a stage, twirling among prop trees. The Fae were graceful beyond measure, male and female alike. If not for my circumstances, I might have enjoyed the performance.

I watched all of this out of the corner of my eye, still pacing while I pretended not to be aware of what was going on around me. Maybe they would get distracted, and I would be able to slip away. Maybe I could still make my date. I huffed at the pathetic thought. Ethan would think I stood him up and whatever chances I might have had with him would disintegrate. He could have his pick of women. Why would he bother with someone who got herself kidnapped right before her first hot date?

"When is *he* getting here?" I blurted out. "I need to know what's going on. Now."

Everyone ignored me, even Jeondar.

"You all are useless. Clearly. Little peons to some asshole." I figured that would make them mad, but they weren't taking the bait. "Where is he? Prancing around the woods?"

"Somebody gag her, please," Kryn said. He was brushing one of the horses, a tan one with a long red mane like his.

Jeondar pointed at the log once more. "Why don't you sit down? Patience is a virtue, you know."

"And not kidnapping people is common decency," I retorted.

Sitting close to the fire, supervising Silver's cooking, Cylea snorted. I thought I detected a hint of sympathy in her eyes, but if it was ever there, she concealed it quickly.

"Believe me," Jeondar said, "if there was a different choice, you wouldn't be here."

"There are a million different choices, you asshole."

"Not for *him*."

Cylea cleared her throat as if warning Jeondar. He pressed his lips together and joined Kryn. He focused on a white horse, patting its neck tenderly and pulling something from his pocket—a sugar cube?—to feed the animal.

I must have paced for an hour before I got tired and finally sat down in front of the fire. By now, Silver's soup was bubbling. He'd thrown in meat and vegetables at some point, and the smell that wafted from the pot stirred my hunger. I'd only taken a few bites from the meal Jeondar offered me earlier, and my breakfast of honeyed bun and tea was long gone. So when Silver passed around bowls full of soup, accompanied by bread, I ate without complaint, even as the sun kept going down and I despaired.

"We should be on our way," Kryn complained as he tore pieces of bread and threw them into his soup.

"Yes, we should," Cylea agreed with a sigh. "But under the circumstances, it will take twice as long to get there."

Jeondar shook his head, looking sad and concerned. The sky was a blend of dark blues and purples, and the fire was starting to cast dancing shadows over everyone's faces. Silver got a couple of logs and set them on top of the embers. Jeondar leaned forward, stretched out a hand toward the logs, and in an instant, they caught and started to smolder.

My eyes snapped to his amber gaze. He was no regular Fae. He had control over fire. I wondered if others also processed special skills.

Witchlights, I was more outmatched than I'd imagined.

Silver had just finished gathering everyone's bowls, when the sound of metal against metal, like two swords glancing off each other, reverberated through the woods.

Jeondar jumped to his feet immediately and gestured with one arm. "Get back in the tent."

The others stood too, their expressions alert as they spread out through the clearing, hands hovering over their weapons.

"Now!" Jeondar ordered when I remained sitting on the log.

Something about his expression told me this wasn't the time to be contrary, so I did as he said. He followed close behind me and lowered the tent flap as we entered. He set out to light a few lanterns with his bare hands, making the interior look cozy and welcoming, even if it was a prison. The smell of aeradonus hung pleasantly in the air.

"Make yourself comfortable," he said. "Get some sleep."

As if.

"What's going on out there?" I asked.

"Nothing you should be worried about."

I crossed my arms. "You look worried."

"We're just taking precautions."

"Against what?"

Jeondar shook his head. "Like I said. You don't need to worry about it. Now, you should rest."

I huffed and glanced around. My eyes landed on the pile of blankets, furs, and pillows.

"Not there," he snapped. "Anywhere else is fine."

I hugged myself as a shiver raked through me. This must be *his* tent, and that must be where *he* slept. It made sense. He was the one in charge, and this was the biggest tent.

Asshole! He was determined to ruin my life.

Fuming, I walked to the opposite corner from *his* bed and sat on top of the plush rugs. I grabbed a cushion from one of the chairs and laid my head down, my back pressed tightly against the side of the tent. My eyes followed Jeondar as he placed a chair in front of the exit. He sat there, facing me to ensure he could watch me closely.

Damn Fae male.

I closed my eyes simply to avoid his piercing gaze, though I kept my ears tuned to every tiny sound. A long time passed as I lay there listening to what was mostly silence. Jeondar might as well have been a statue for all he moved. The Fae had that quality same as vampires. They could go for hours without moving a muscle. Whereas I kept tossing and turning, feeling every lump under the rugs.

At some point in the night, a howl sounded in the distance, a sound so guttural and deep that it shivered over my bones. My eyes sprang open to find Jeondar frowning, his pointed ears tilted toward the fading echo of the mournful call.

I squeezed my eyes tightly, wondering what was out there that could make Fae warriors look so wary. There were many more howls through the night, each one making my arms wrap more tightly around my torso, each one driving my drowsy sleepiness away.

CHAPTER 4

T he sound of birds singing cheerfully woke me up the next morning. I sat up straight, heart pounding as I realized I'd drifted off at some point near dawn. Jeondar was gone, and for a moment, I thought I was alone in the tent until I heard light snoring coming from the back.

I jumped to my feet, scanning the bundle of blankets and furs. Someone was there. I could make out the shape, though nothing else. At some point, *he* had come in, walked right by me, and gone to sleep. All while I was lying down unaware, helpless.

I staggered out of the tent, blinking at the bright morning sunlight.

Kryn stood guard next to the tent. "Good morning, healer," he said with that annoying smirk of his. "Slept well?"

"Fuck you," I snapped, unable to help myself.

"Such a filthy mouth."

I flipped him the bird.

"And hand."

"Oh, go to hell."

"I think I'm already in what you humans call hell, judging by the she-devil raining curses on me."

"She's not a devil," someone said behind me, "just an excellent judge of character."

I turned to find a petite female sitting by the fire. She had golden brown hair, much like my own, though her eyes were blue, the same clear shade as Cylea's. She wore a form-fitting one-piece suit made of supple green fabric, trimmed with gold around her waist and collar—the color complimenting her golden skin perfectly.

"Don't listen to him. He's a prick," she said with a welcoming smile. "My name is Arabis Perven. What is yours?"

No one had bothered to introduce themselves until now. They'd all treated me like a prisoner, while this female was acting as if I were a guest instead. I distrusted her immediately, especially since she was the one who had been gone with *him* yesterday.

"I'm sure you already know my name," I said. "Like everyone else."

"Yes, but..." She twirled a dainty hand in the air. "I figured it wouldn't hurt to be polite. But I understand how unpleasant this must be for you. Are you hungry, Dani?"

"I only allow my friends to call me Dani."

Despite my standoffish demeanor, Arabis kept a pleasant smile on her face as she ate dry fruit and nuts from a small bowl. I glanced around, searching for the others. I spotted Silver feeding the horses, but the others were nowhere to be seen.

"They went by the stream to wash," Arabis explained, as if reading my thoughts. "You may want to do the same later. I have some clothes that I think will fit you."

"I don't want your clothes."

"Oh, they're not mine. You're tall and curvaceous, two attributes I'm not blessed with."

Where would she have gotten clothes that fit me? Cylea was taller than me, so they couldn't be hers either. But "*why*" was the more important question. Had they planned this to the extent of procuring clothes for me?

"Who is that in there?" I pointed toward the tent.

"He'll be up soon, and you'll meet him. In the meantime, you should eat."

"I don't want to eat," I burst out, collapsing on the log across from Arabis. "I just want to go home. I don't belong here."

Arabis's forehead parted with a deep frown. "I'm sorry," she said, her tone sounding sincere. "We all wish there was another way."

I glared at her, puzzled. She sounded like Jeondar, regretful and apprehensive.

With a sigh, Arabis stood and started walking toward the tent. "I'll wake him up. I think you've waited long enough to learn why you're here."

"He needs to sleep." Kryn blocked the entrance to the tent.

"He has slept enough. Get out of my way."

Kryn stood nearly two feet taller than Arabis and was twice as thick, yet the withering look she gave him was enough to send him stomping away from the tent.

"Whatever you say, *Abin Manael*," he said the last couple of words in a sarcastic tone.

The words meant *respectable lady*, a term I'd heard many times in Pharowyn. It was the way the servers addressed females at the tavern, the term Yalgrun had used with me before he knew my name. Did Kryn not consider Arabis respectable or a lady? The guy certainly seemed to have a stick up his ass.

Suddenly feeling a mess, I pulled my hair from its ponytail and ran my fingers through it, smoothing out the knots that had formed during yesterday's struggles and a night of restless sleep.

Arabis was gone for nearly twenty minutes. When she reappeared, she inclined her head toward the tent.

"He will see you now," she said with a reassuring smile.

I stood, my heart pounding. Now that I was about to come face-to-face with the person responsible for my situation, I didn't feel ready. Deep inside, I harbored the hope that this male was someone I could reason with, someone who would let me go once I explained why it was imperative that I return home. But what if he wasn't?

Gathering my composure, I lifted my chin and walked into the tent. As my eyes adjusted, I spotted a tall figure standing at the back of the tent. He was facing away from me, strapping a belt around his waist and adjusting the large sword at his side.

As I fought to keep my breaths steady, I took in his wide shoulders, and the midnight blue hair falling to his shoulders and held back by a few thin braids. He wore a flowing shirt, rolled up to his elbows, and tight high-waisted pants. An aura of power emanated from him, his presence filling the tent's every corner, the same way the smoke had.

I stood in front of the fire pit, waiting for him to turn and face me. He cracked his neck and took a deep breath before spinning around and...

Holy fuck.

Time seemed to slow down as I took him in, recognition flooding me despite the shadows in the back of the tent. My gaze slid over his features, taking in every detail, searching for something that would prove my eyes wrong, something that would make it clear that the person standing in front of me *was not* the person I thought was standing in front of me.

It was impossible.

Impossible!

I'd never meant Prince Kalyll Adanorin, so the chances that this was all a product of my imagination were high. Maybe inhaling all that aeradonus had messed up my head.

He placed a fist on his chest and gave a small bow. "Good morning, Abin Manael."

Midnight blue hair. Cobalt blue eyes to match. An intricate pattern of tattoos running down the right side of his face and neck.

These were all traits I knew belonged to the Prince of the Seelie Fae. The eldest son of King Beathan Adanorin and Queen Eithne Adanorin. Yet, this *couldn't* be him. This had to be some sort of impostor or doppelgänger.

"My name is Kalyll Adanorin," he said. "And I must apologize for your current... predicament."

I shook my head, still unable to believe what my eyes and ears were telling me. I had seen pictures of the prince. Even in my realm, he was known. He had visited on diplomatic missions and had been on television, magazines, newspapers—not often, but enough to make him recognizable. And not only that, the guy was legendary. Stories were told about his prowess as if he were Alexander the Great or some shit. Moreover, my sister Toni knew him.

"You're... really the prince?" I asked, my words halting.

"I am. I know it must seem unlikely that I'm responsible for your abduction from Pharowyn, but, regrettably, I am." His words were almost as halting as mine. He appeared embarrassed, contrite even.

The hope I'd been harboring surged to the surface in an instant.

"You must have a good reason," I said, doing my best to sound sensible—though prince or not, he had no right to do what he'd done, and he deserved vitriol, not civility. Still, it was to my advantage to keep things as diplomatic as possible.

"I assure you, I do." He took a step closer, the shadows receding from his face, and the light spilling through the entrance illuminating his features.

My breath caught. The pictures I'd seen of him didn't do him justice. He wasn't only handsome. He was striking. His face was chiseled to aching perfection. His straight nose, razor-edged jaw, high cheekbones, and devastating lips were a sculptor's dream. Thin eyebrows rose at an angle, framing those azure eyes and giving him an impish appearance that seemed to promise untold pleasures.

But it was his imposing aura that stole my breath more than anything else. I could see why they said his enemies trembled in his presence. He felt like contained momentum, a leashed tornado ready to destroy the world at the least provocation.

He wasn't the only one who felt leashed, though. Anger simmered in my gut at the prick's entitlement. The pretty boy had wanted something, and he took it. The hell with diplomacy.

"Well, I don't give a rat's ass about your reasons. You need to let me go. Now."

The prince's eyebrows went up in surprise at my change in attitude. He quickly recovered and gestured toward a chair. "Why don't you take a seat so we can talk?"

"What part of *'let me go'* don't you understand? You're breaking the treaty between your realm and mine."

As long as they behaved, humans and Fae were supposed to come and go between realms at their leisure and without being bothered. That was the law.

"I'm well aware of that, Ms. Sunder," he said, with no small amount of chagrin.

"Then release me."

"I can't."

"What is it that you possibly want from me? I'm nobody."

His eyes glinted. "Hardly."

He held my gaze, making me feel exposed, as if he saw more than I would ever be willing to show him.

"I require your special talents, Daniella. May I call you Daniella?"

"No."

"Dani, then." He smiled, disarmingly.

"Only my friends call me that, and you're not one of them. On the contrary."

He winced at that. Tiredly, he sat on one of the folding canvas chairs. A brighter shaft of light illuminated his features, revealing dark circles under his eyes. Wherever he'd been last night, he hadn't been sleeping.

"You have healers in Elf-hame," I said. "Why would you need me?"

"Because you're the only one who can help."

I frowned. There was no special skill I possessed that a good Fae healer would not. Unless…

Witchlights.

He couldn't be talking about what I thought he was talking about. I had recently delved into some obscure materials that dealt with demons and how to heal them. The materials had been conveniently placed in my path by a powerful demon who foresaw the need for my skills to save his own life. Did the prince have a demon pet in need of healing?

"If you need me to heal somebody, you could have just asked." My words were still laced with biting anger.

If someone had told me that I would one day be standing in front of a Fae prince yelling at him, I would have laughed in their faces. First of all, I'm not the yelling kind. Negative emotions are not conducive to healing. Second of all, yelling at powerful people was also not conducive to long free lives. I was sure the prince had a dungeon where impertinent people he decided not to cut down with his sword spent their miserable days.

"Very true," he said. "However, I know you would have refused."

I shook my head. "You clearly know nothing about me. I've never refused to help anyone in need of my help."

"I know more about you than you might suspect," he said, his voice low and deep, his eyes knowing.

My very bones shivered. How could he know *anything* about me?

He's been stalking you, my logical mind whispered.

I thought back to the last few days. Had I noticed anything strange? Anyone following me? I didn't think so. I had stuck to my routine, getting up early to go jogging, walking to work, eating a quick lunch at a nearby restaurant or the hospital cafeteria, staying at work later than was wise, then going home to crash into bed. Rinse and repeat.

I considered for a moment longer, anger simmering. I wanted to keep screaming at the entitled jerk, but I knew it wouldn't accomplish anything. Instead, I took a calming breath.

"Who do you want me to heal?" I asked in a clipped tone. "Bring them so I can be on my way."

"It's not that easy. If it were, you wouldn't be here."

"So, what will it take for you to let me go home?"

"That's exactly what I would like to discuss with you." He gestured toward a chair once more.

Deep breaths, Dani.

Realizing that I wasn't going anywhere until I let him speak, I sat down, folded my hands over my lap, and resolved to listen without interruption. The quicker we got this done, the sooner I could get back to my life.

The prince pushed to the edge of the flimsy chair, his large frame balancing precariously. His intense cobalt eyes roved over my face, making me feel as if he were categorizing every detail. There was power in his gaze, a combination of confidence and strength that I found compelling in males, except those of the kidnapping variety.

"My friends and I are embarking on a journey to Mount Ruin," he said.

Oh, shit. I didn't like the sound of this already. I bit my lower lip to hold back a protest. I didn't need to jump to conclusions. This journey and the ruinous mount had nothing to do with me. Nothing.

He went on. "The journey will take several days and will be arduous. Mount Ruin is located one thousand miles from where we now stand. It is there, and only there, that your skills will be needed."

I shook my head. "No, no, no. Just no."

He lowered his eyes to the ground, as if embarrassed by the distress he'd caused.

"This can't be. Whatever it is, there has to be another way."

"I'm afraid not."

"You can't do this. You can't snatch someone, uproot them from their life, and force them to do your bidding. I'm not one of your subjects."

A muscle ticked in his jaw, and it was clear to see that my words cut straight to his sense of right and wrong. He knew that what he was doing was terribly wrong.

"It wasn't an easy decision." He rose, his tall frame looming over me. "But it is made."

I jumped to my feet, refusing to be dwarfed by him. "I'll lose my job, my house, everything I've worked so hard to build. There's this little girl who needs me. Her name is Muriel. She needs me. I'm the only one who can heal her."

"I promise you will be compensated," he said coolly. "Handsomely."

"I don't give a shit about your money or how fucking abundant it is. I have a life that I enjoy, little patients to take care of. I had a date last night with someone I really like, but that went out the window thanks to you. I have a family who will go crazy. They're probably going crazy right now. If you have a heart, if you have a shred of integrity, you will let me go."

"Trust me, Ms. Sunder, I considered all these things and weighed every option. I knew you would not abandon your life willingly, hence the extreme measures I was forced to take. If there was any other way, you would not be here."

"You bastard. The spoiled little prince has to have his way, no matter who he squashes in the process."

His eyes narrowed and his jaw clenched tightly, the first sign of anger that had registered on his features. "This is not about me, I assure you. The future of my people rests in the balance, and I would do anything to spare them the misfortune that would come their way if I don't act. One life, your life, is nothing compared to that."

Tears burned in the back of my eyes, but I didn't cry. Not in front of him. "I see. My life means nothing to you, then?"

He opened his mouth as if to argue, then shut it again. What could he respond without contradicting his earlier statement?

The hope I'd harbored died. There was a deep hollow left in my chest as it expired, and even though I tried to remain strong, my eyes filled with tears that quickly spilled down my cheeks.

When the prince noticed, he made as if to come closer, but stopped himself. "I know it fixes nothing, but I'm sorry."

I hugged myself and turned my back on him, biting back a sob.

He stood behind me for a long moment while all I heard were his even breaths. "We leave in an hour," he said at last, then strode out of the tent.

CHAPTER 5

I curled in one corner of the tent, hugging my legs and crying silently into my knees.

Mount Ruin. One thousand miles away.

How long would it take to travel that distance on horseback? I had no idea. To distract myself from the pain crushing my chest, I did some mental math, trying to calculate how long it would take me to jog that distance.

I could run a mile in fifteen minutes, so like ten days, if I was a robot and could run nonstop. But realistically, I could probably only do four to five miles a day without killing myself. So two hundred days, then.

How much faster was a horse? Three times? Four times? Five times?

I decided on four. That meant fifty days instead.

If I returned home after that long and told everyone I'd been kidnapped by the Prince of the Seelie Fae, they would understand, right? They would pat me on the back and say, *"So sorry that happened. Here's your job back, and no worries about the mortgage and bill payments you missed. Here is your beautiful home, which you so adore."*

And my family... they would survive that long without me. They might tear down the heavens and the earth looking for me, maybe murder a few unhelpful people in the process, but they would not be any worse for wear.

You'd better double that time, Dani, logical me said.

I was assuming there would be no detours, no mishaps, but that was hardly how things worked, right? Even back home, I could get a flat tire, run out of gas, encounter a group of hungry vampires that didn't care to follow the law. Surely, there were comparable calamities that could assail us here. A sick horse, a band of crazed trolls, a constipated prince.

Bastard. Bastard. Bastard.

Light spilled into the tent as the flap was thrown open. I glanced up. Arabis stood there, looking all around, a bundle resting in her hands. Finally, she spotted me in the corner.

"There you are." She deposited the bundle on a chair, came close, and kneeled in front of me. Her expression was sympathetic. "I'm sorry it has to be this way. I promise you, this isn't easy for Kalyll or any of us. If there was any other alternative..."

"Spare me," I bit back.

She ignored my animosity. "Think of it as an adventure vacation. It could be fun, and we won't let anything bad happen to you."

"Anything bad?"

She nodded enthusiastically. "We're all good in a fight. Kryn can be an asshole, I admit, but you can just ignore him. Jeondar is my favorite, and Silver and Cylea aren't bad either."

"There will be... fighting?"

Arabis pursed her lips and moved her head from side to side as if weighing my question. "We try to avoid fights. Well, Kryn doesn't, but we already established that he's an asshole, so... But you don't have to worry about that. Forget I even brought it up."

"I can't stay here. Please, help me get back home." She was the nicest one, so I had to try.

"I wish I could, Dani, but this is bigger than all of us."

Bigger than all of us. The future of my people rests in the balance.

Was it true? Something major at play? Whatever the case, I couldn't bring myself to care. Their concerns were not mine. All I cared about was my simple life, my family, and the children who depended on me. It had been stupid to ask Arabis for help. None of them cared about my small existence. I was little more than an ant they could step on while gallivanting around during their quest.

I was on my own here, and on my own, I would keep trying to find a way to escape.

Arabis stood and walked back to the bundle she'd left on the chair. "We have to get on our way before it gets too late. Here are some clothes you can change into. They'll be more comfortable for riding, and will help you... not stand out. I'll be back in a few minutes."

She left, closing the tent flap behind her. My clothes were dirty and sweaty, and my flats weren't the most practical by any means, so even though it irked me to go along with anything my captors said, I unpacked the bundle and inspected what Arabis had brought.

A pair of knee-high boots rested on top of a folded tunic and a pair of leggings. The boots' leather was supple and adorned with flower carvings on the folded cuff at the top. There were no undergarments, and I didn't like the idea of keeping the dirty ones, but I didn't have a choice.

Walking back to the corner, I quickly took off my flats, jeans, and T-shirt and slipped into the Fae garments. The leggings were soft and stretched nicely, hugging every curve. They were brown and complemented perfectly by the tan tunic, which fit loosely around me and came to mid-thigh. An embroidered pattern of vines went around the collar, skilled needlework that could not be found in my realm.

Soon, Arabis returned and smiled contentedly when she saw I'd changed. She took my dirty clothes and bundled them under her arm. "We'll save this, so they'll be waiting for you on your return. Now, follow me."

She exited the tent, leaving the bundle behind. I went after her and found everyone waiting outside already on top of their horses, the prince sitting a distance away on a massive black stallion, his back stiff, his eyes staring straight ahead. Jeondar welcomed me with a smile. Silver and Cylea simply waved, and Kryn ignored me, picking dirt from his fingernails.

The two smaller tents had been taken down and appeared to be packed atop two of the horses, along with other supplies.

Arabis gestured toward a small, spotted horse that looked like a giant Dalmatian. "This is Dandelion. She's a sweetheart and will do right by you. Do you know how to ride?"

I shook my head and glanced around, considering running for my life. Once they took me far from Pharowyn, it would be a lot harder to find my way back home. But what chance did I stand racing against five Fae on horseback? Zero to none.

"It's not hard at all. You'll get used to it in no time. You'll see. Just put your right foot here." She pointed at the stirrup. "Then swing your other leg up. You can hold on to the horn, here." She pointed at a protruding handle on the saddle.

I did as she instructed, and without making a fool of myself, managed to get on top of Dandelion. It seemed I should have been scared on top of such a large animal. I was a city girl, used to car rides, and most daringly... bicycles, but as I surveyed the camp from my vantage point, I felt nothing.

Mounted on a horse, it might appear as if my chances of escape had increased, but quite the contrary. The likelihood of falling ass-first into a thorny bush if I attempted to do anything other than slowly trot was distinct—not that Arabis ever let go of the reins. In fact, she held on to them even as she mounted her own horse, a tan creature with a black mane that was a bit smaller than mine.

Once we were all mounted, the prince urged his horse forward, and in no time, we were out of the clearing, riding over an expensive plain carpeted with luscious grass and colorful wildflowers. Above us, a deep blue sky stretched far, uninterrupted by clouds, its fringes obstructed by massive mountains that appeared blue-gray in the distance.

After a couple of hours on top of Dandelion, bouncing on the hard saddle, my backside began to hurt. I twisted this way and that, trying to get comfortable, but it was impossible.

"It gets easier," Arabis said with a smile, noticing me squirm.

"If you say so."

Despite my rude response, her smile didn't disappear. If her niceness was an act, she put on a good one. I didn't like to be rude. If this was genuinely her personality, she seemed like the kind of person I would get along with, but a friendship with her or any of these people offered no appeal. All I could think of was home, my mother's warm hugs, my conversations with Toni as we talked for hours about work, men, and what an overprotective pain in the ass Mom could be sometimes. Then there was my little sister, off in college, who often needed my help. Would she be all right? Would she call me for help and fare badly without me?

When the sun was straight overhead, we stopped under a copse of large trees, the mountains in the distance looking just as far away, despite the few hours on horseback.

Stiffly, I got off my horse, my ass feeling as if it'd gotten a good spanking. I rotated my hips, wincing, and realizing I was a fish out of water in this place. It felt good to stretch, but it felt even better when I released a wave of healing magic right down my spine and the pain receded.

"We'll eat something, let the horses rest, and be on our way again," Arabis informed me.

"I need to..." I glanced toward an area flanked by several tall boulders, "you know."

"Of course, I'll go with you."

"Go with me?"

"To make sure you don't try to escape again." She smiled. "Jeondar told me what you did yesterday. Very clever."

"Where am I going to escape on foot? I don't even know where we are."

She shrugged. "I'm sure you can figure it out. You're smart." She flung her thick, golden brown hair behind a shoulder and marched toward the rocks.

I followed, fuming. Was I to have no privacy on top of everything else? I walked behind the largest boulder and stared at Arabis with a raised eyebrow. She didn't turn away.

"I can't pee with you watching."

She rolled her eyes and turned around. "Fine."

I did my business as quickly as I could, feeling utterly humiliated. When we got back, Silver offered us strips of dried meat, fresh apple slices, a large chunk of cheese, and bread. I ate, discovering that the ride had stirred a ravenous hunger in me. I practically inhaled the food, enjoying every morsel. Even the apple was better than any variety I'd tasted at home.

The entire time that we sat under the shade of one of the trees, the prince stayed a distance away, eating by himself, then pacing in front of his horse while the animal pawed restlessly at the ground. They both reminded me of me yesterday, caged lions that saw no way out. He caught me watching and threw a nasty look in my direction.

Back at you, buddy.

"Is that where Mount Ruin is?" I asked, pointing toward the distant mountain range we seemed to be heading toward.

Kryn sputtered a laugh. "Not even close." He was reclined against a tree, his long legs stretched before him as he chewed on a blade of grass.

"We're heading toward the Summer Court first," Jeondar said. "My home," he added proudly.

"The Summer Court?" I echoed.

Jeondar nodded.

"How long will we stay there?"

"Kalyll has to pay his respects to the Summer King and discuss... matters of importance with him. It should only be a few days."

A few days added to my sentence. *Damn it!*

"How long will it take to get to Mount Ruin from there?" I asked, fearing the answer.

"There's no telling," Silver offered. "Three weeks."

Kryn huffed. "That's if we even get there."

"Shut up, Kryn," Arabis barked. "We don't need your negativity."

"It's not negativity, sweetheart. I'm a realist."

"I've told you a thousand times not to call me sweetheart." Arabis's blue eyes flashed with annoyance.

Kryn smirked, as if satisfied that he'd made her angry.

Her eyes rolled upward, making her appear aggravated for letting him get to her.

A flash of quick movement caught my eye, and I glanced toward the prince. He had stepped a few yards away from his horse and was performing a set of movements that looked a lot like a martial arts form.

"Oh, no, he's at it again," Cylea said when she noticed him.

"At least he ate," Arabis put in.

The prince went through a series of steps, an apparent dance. Every motion of his legs, arms, and hands was precise. After he struck each pose, he held it for a few seconds, then struck a new one. Despite myself, I couldn't help but admire his grace and agility, which spoke of the many hours he must spend training. For the first time, I wondered how old he was. He looked to be between twenty-five and thirty, but I knew the Fae aged slowly after reaching maturity. For all I knew, he was hundreds of years old. He had to be in order to have legends written about him, didn't he?

When he was done, he removed the heavy leather vest he wore over his shirt and cast it to the ground. The shirt followed, revealing more tattoos down the right side of his body that connected with the ones on his neck and face. The patterns were intricate and certainly done by a skilled artist.

Cylea wiggled her eyebrows. "So it's one of *those* days."

The prince walked to his horse and retrieved a large sword, a weapon that, from the looks of it, few people would be able to lift. It appeared extremely heavy, and standing up straight, would reach the prince's hip.

He twirled the weapon over his head as if it were a toothpick, the blade slicing through the air and making whistling sounds as it sliced into an imaginary foe. The large muscles in the prince's torso flexed as he started a new dance, this time with a partner, one that I didn't doubt was his favorite. Within minutes, his large muscles were slick with sweat.

"My oh my." Cylea sat up straighter, admiring him.

"You know well he's not on the menu," Silver pointed out.

"That doesn't mean I can't admire the banquet."

Arabis slapped her arm. "Have some respect for your future king."

"You suck the fun out of everything." Cylea batted a hand in her direction.

Kryn's sharp green eyes were glued on the prince. After an intent moment, they flicked toward Arabis. She ignored him. Spitting the blade of grass, he rose to his feet. Methodically, he removed his tunic and discarded it at the base of the tree. His pale torso was long and lean, with well-defined muscles in all the right places.

"Not this again," Jeondar complained.

Kryn ignored him and, after retrieving his sword from a scabbard cinched to his saddle, he walked toward the prince, swirling the sword in a one-hand maneuver that seemed to defy all laws of physics. When the prince noticed him coming, he turned to face him, his weapon held at the ready and a wicked smile stretching his lips.

"One of these days, he's going to get himself killed," Jeondar said.

"It might be today." Silver stood and reclined against a tree to watch as if we were at the theater.

Arabis abandoned her food and moved closer. Her expression was pinched, betraying her concern.

Metal sang against metal as their swords met. It all seemed to start like a graceful exercise where each got a chance to attack while the other one defended. Next to Kryn's seven-foot height, the prince should have looked small, but it was the opposite. Kryn was muscled but in a leaner way, while the prince had more bulk, sporting the anatomy of a super athlete. And at six-three, he was no dwarf.

Gradually, their sparring grew more intense and soon started looking like a real battle. The prince's blows were vicious, and it seemed like a miracle when Kryn blocked them and his sword didn't split in two.

Looking worried, Arabis moved even closer to the scuffle, her brow etched with a deep frown and her blue eyes fixed on the males.

"I think that's enough," she pronounced when the prince sliced his sword close to Kryn's face, barely missing his nose.

The males didn't listen and continued slicing and stabbing. The prince growled, doing his best to cut his opponent right down the middle. Kryn blocked the blow just in time while the prince bore his entire weight on the sword, his face twisted in rage. My heart skipped a beat when I thought I saw the prince's eyes turn entirely black, but it happened so fast that I decided I must've imagined it.

Kryn pushed away, panting. The prince was on him again before Kryn could recover, knocking him off his feet with a swipe of his powerful leg. Kryn landed on his back with a heavy *thud*, and the prince slammed a foot on the fallen male's chest. He raised his sword, evil intent in his eyes.

"Let him go, Kalyll," Arabis commanded in a deep and firm tone that didn't seem to belong in such a tiny frame.

The prince ignored her, and instead, pointed the tip of his weapon at Kryn's neck and stabbed.

I gasped, jumping to my feet.

Arabis's voice boomed like a thunderclap. The air around her wavered, and the ground shook, pebbles bouncing on its surface like tiny balls. The trajectory of her projected shout was almost visible and seemed to hit the prince in the back of his head.

The prince froze, and for an instant, so did everyone else.

"Did he...?" Cylea couldn't finish her question.

Kryn was immobile, and from our angle, there was no way of knowing if the prince's sword had wounded him.

Arabis was the first to move, taking a halting step forward. Her clenched fists trembled at her sides.

"Kalyll," she said quietly, her sweet voice barely a whisper, nothing compared to the violent scream she'd let rip from her throat just seconds ago.

The prince took a step back, pushing off Kryn's chest. He twirled his sword—its tip bloodied—and casually walked away, leaving his opponent on the ground.

Arabis rushed to Kryn, falling to her knees by his side.

We all approached, our steps hesitant.

Kryn's eyes were closed and blood stained his neck.

"Gods," Arabis nearly sobbed, pressing a hand to her mouth.

Kryn opened one eye, his mouth stretching slightly to one side. "I'm all right, sweetheart. No need to fret over me."

"You blasted piece of carrion." Arabis slammed a small fist on his chest.

He recoiled, looking as if he were fighting the urge to burst out laughing.

"I should have let him kill you," Arabis shouted, and if her fury were fire, she would have left a trail on the ground as she stomped away.

Kryn sat up, chuckling, his green eyes glinting with mischief. A trail of blood slid from his neck down to his chest.

Jeondar shook his head, turned on his heel, and walked away. Silver and Cylea exchanged a glance.

"Honestly, you're deeply disturbed," Silver said, running a hand through his cropped platinum hair. "I thought you would lose your head for sure. Literally, I mean."

"She wouldn't let that happen," Kryn said, glancing toward Arabis.

Cylea *tsked*. "I wouldn't count on that if I were you. She's about had it with you."

Kryn rose to his feet and dusted himself off. "You know she loves me," he said, sounding like a conceited butthole.

There certainly seemed to be something going on between them, though I wasn't sure I would call it love.

I didn't know what made me offer, probably habit, but I pointed toward Kryn's neck and said, "I can heal that for you."

He blinked and peered at me as if he'd forgotten I existed. He shook his head. "This is nothing. It'll heal on its own. I'm Fae." He walked off, the words he didn't say echoing in my mind. *I'm Fae, not a weak human.*

"And you keep him around, why?" I asked.

Silver chuckled. "I constantly ask myself the same question. He's good in a fight, but little else."

Pushing at a strand of hair as blue as the sky, Cylea said, "And there'll be plenty of those to come, and then you'll be glad he's here."

"Arabis," I said, pointing at my throat to indicate what she's done with her voice, "what was that?"

"She's a Susurro," Cylea said, as if that explained everything. "Don't you have them in your realm?"

I shook my head. Or maybe we did, and I just hadn't encountered one.

"Her voice can command anyone to do whatever she wants."

I frowned as a shiver ran over my body. That was a scary skill.

Silver leaned closer and said, "She could order you to slit your throat, and you'd have to do it."

My shiver redoubled, making me tremble visibly.

Cylea elbowed him. "Stop. You're scaring her. Don't listen to Silver. Arabis would never do something like that. She's too nice."

"The skill is wasted on her, I'd say," Silver put it. "Don't you think?"

I glanced toward the prince, who was getting dressed by his horse. The real question was: why had it taken a Susurro to get the prince to stop killing one of his own?

CHAPTER 6

As we got back on the horses and started toward the mountains again, I kept glancing over my shoulder, judging the distance we'd already traveled, picturing my home growing smaller and smaller with each step.

How can I go back?

After watching the vicious way the prince and Kryn had fought, the idea of escaping now seemed not only unlikely, but ludicrous.

I'm Fae, not a weak human.

Weak. It was a word I'd never used to describe myself. I had always thought of myself as strong and capable. I wasn't the oldest of my siblings—Leo was—but I might as well have been. He was always irresponsible and careless and was gone as soon as he turned eighteen, which left me to take care of my sisters, who also seemed to share some of Leo's cavalier attributes. I was their confidant and the mender of their little bruised hearts and knees. Mom and Dad were there, and they did a great job raising us, but Toni and Lucia always sought me, which Mom was happy to allow, especially after Dad died. She was more of a dictator kind of parent, one who set rules and boundaries and expected them to be followed.

But to my captors, I wasn't strong or capable, and I had to admit that, among them, I didn't feel that way either. Every escape plan I came up with ended with me back in their clutches without any of them breaking a sweat to stop me. Yet, considering what this journey seemed to have in store, I knew I would regret it if I didn't at least try. I just needed to wait for the perfect chance to try again. So I kept a close eye on our surroundings, memorizing every landmark that would lead me back to Pharowyn and marking a few hiding places since I wouldn't be able to run there directly. They would expect me to do that and would catch me easily if I didn't get creative.

"What are those woods called?" I asked Jeondar, pointing toward the right.

"That's South Crosswood," he replied affably. He seemed happy to explain. "These woods run all the way north alongside the Emerald Plains." He pointed at the flatlands to our right, which surely deserved the name due to its intensely green grasses. "Further up, the forest's name changes to Mid Crosswood, then North Crosswood, but it's all the same. The Zundrokh Barrens lay to the west of the woods, desert land, as you might well guess."

I nodded and stored the information away in case it came in handy later. I couldn't help but admire the majestic view and inhale the clean air. Elf-hame was pristine, idyllic, the way my realm must have been a thousand years ago. It was a paradise, unless you found yourself kidnapped.

Like earlier, the prince rode his horse in front of the procession. He was angry and broody, barely directing a word to anyone, the manners and civility he'd displayed this morning gone completely. I figured he must be worried about what waited for him at the end of the road, whatever that might be. Either way, I didn't care. I only cared about ensuring I wasn't there when he arrived.

Arabis rode next to me, constantly looking up at the sky as if she expected some giant bird to swoop down and scoop her up.

I craned my neck and looked through the few clouds that had moved in from the south, from Pharowyn. She noticed my eyes flicking between the sky and her.

"I'm just checking the time," she informed me.

I looked at my smartwatch. "It's 5:25 PM."

She huffed. "Humans and their gadgets."

Clearly, she didn't seem to think much of gadgets, not even accurate ones.

"Have you ever been to my realm?" I found myself asking, curiosity getting the best of me.

"A few times, yes. It has its charms."

"Such as." I had no idea what a female Fae might consider charming.

"Fashion, for instance. So many pockets and varied colors."

I frowned, wondering if she was being sarcastic.

"I also find automobiles and planes interesting means of transportation."

"Interesting?"

She glanced toward the sky again, then nodded. "Fast and damaging."

Now I knew she was being sarcastic.

"What's in Mount Ruin, Arabis?" I asked, doing a one-eighty with the conversation.

Her features darkened. "I don't know exactly."

I had the feeling she was lying, but was also telling the truth. Odd.

I squirmed in my saddle, cursing at the pain that had quickly returned to my backside. With this sort of thing, healing myself was a bad idea. If I kept doing it, my muscles would never adapt to the demands of riding a horse. Though, I didn't plan on getting used to it. If I could help it, I would never ride a horse in my life again.

Arabis checked the position of the sun for the *nth* time.

"It's 5:30," I informed her, my tone mocking. "Is a hot date waiting for you wherever we're going?"

"You think you're funny," she said, her delicate mouth stretching to one side as she tried to repress a smile.

I almost smiled too, but when I realized that Stockholm syndrome seemed to be taking root, I curved my mouth into a frown instead and resolved *not* to like her.

Despite the horses' legs moving without stopping for hours, the mountain range in the distance only appeared marginally closer. I told myself it was a good thing because if we'd reached it, my chances of escape would be null, and I would be stuck with these strangers for who knew how long.

It was still daylight when Arabis rushed ahead to the prince's side and spoke to him.

The others slowed down and started guiding their horses toward the line of trees that framed the plains on the right side, South Crosswood. I'd thought we would keep traveling—the Fae were legendary for their endurance—but maybe they needed to stop for the sake of the horses. I doubted they were doing it for my sake. I was only a prisoner. I wasn't complaining though. My trek back to Pharowyn would already be long enough as it was.

Jeondar, Cylea, Silver, and Kryn quickly set up camp, unpacking the horses, starting a fire, and setting up one of the tents. It all happened in record time as I watched sitting on a wide rock, evaluating the area and tracing an escape route in my mind. I didn't know yet how I would manage to get away without being noticed, but I would figure it out.

Once more, the prince stayed away from us, though this time Arabis was with him. I wondered if keeping his distance was some princely thing that didn't allow him to mix with the rubble. Whatever the case, it was to my advantage. One less pair of eyes to worry about—two if Arabis stayed with him.

"I'll be back soon." Cylea had wrapped the flowing ends of her tunic around her waist like a belt and wore a bow and quiver at her back.

Silver glanced up from where he tended the fire. "Get us something good."

She merely waved a couple of fingers as she disappeared through the trees. I assumed she was going hunting for our dinner.

Kryn was again reclining against a tree, looking bored, while Jeondar and Silver moved busily around. Lazy bastard. It seemed he considered himself too important to help. I wondered exactly who he was. Royalty like Kalyll Adanorin, perhaps. Yep, another entitled jerk. Oh, how I hated them. They were exactly the type of male I always tried to avoid, even among my kind. They didn't make good friends, boyfriends, or even acquaintances. They were experts at *assholery*, first-rate narcissists.

Not long after she left, Cylea returned with a bunch of bunnies tied together by the legs and slung over her shoulder. Three in the front and four in the back—one for each of us. I glanced away from the poor dead things. If I looked at them much longer, I wouldn't be able to eat dinner.

Jeondar was securing the tent to the ground when he paused and frowned. I followed his gaze to find that the prince was gone, same as Arabis. I searched all around but didn't see them anywhere. Only their horses remained, unsaddled and tied next to each other.

Rubbing the back of his neck, Jeondar shook his head. Were the prince and Arabis an item? Of their own accord, my eyes flicked toward Kryn. It was clear to me that he had a thing for the petite Fae, but if he was jealous that she'd disappeared with the Seelie Prince, he gave no sign of it.

"The tent is for you." Jeondar now stood beside me, though I hadn't noticed his approach. "You'll be comfortable there."

"Comfortable and contained," I pointed out—no doubt someone would be stationed right by the entrance all night.

He sat next to me, resting an arm on his bent knee. We watched Silver and Cylea cook, moving around the fire in a well-orchestrated partnership. No doubt, they'd done this before, many times.

"How do you all know the prince?" I asked. "Are you related in any way?"

"Arabis is a distant cousin. She's the only one who grew up in Elyndell, the Seelie Fae capital. But the rest of us aren't related and grew up in different courts. One from each. Silver is from the Winter Court. Cylea from the Spring Court. Kryn the Fall Court, and as I said before... I'm from the Summer Court."

I frowned, wondering if there was any significance to the fact that there was a representative from each court. I had to dig deep into my memory banks to remember the Fae history I'd been taught in high school. Seelie and Unseelie Fae didn't get along. They had a vast track record of wars and feuds. Though in the past century, they'd been living in relative peace. Had any of my knowledge become obsolete since I graduated high school nearly five years ago? I decided to find out.

"The Winter Court and Fall Court align with the Unseelie Fae, don't they?

"Traditionally, yes." Jeondar nodded.

"And the Spring and Summer Courts with the Seelie Fae, correct?"

"Correct. Geography is partially responsible for that." He pointed toward the now dark mountain range in the distance. The sun had gone down. "The Sunder Mountains split our territory."

"The Sunder Mountains," I echoed, remembering that fact, which had faded into memory. I'd gotten a kick out of it in class when I learned that my last name matched the name of the famed Fae mountains. I nodded as additional knowledge bubbled to the surface. "Yes, I remember. The Seelie Court is on the south side of the range, the same for the Summer and Spring Courts. And the Unseelie Court, along with the Winter and Fall Courts, lie directly north."

"I'm impressed by your knowledge. You know more than I know about your realm."

"They made us study it in high school."

"Really?" He seemed bewildered by that.

"There is a Fae Studies degree in college for those who remain fascinated by the subject. Many humans dedicate their lives to studying your kind."

I wondered if there were Fae who were equally fascinated by us. It didn't seem like a distinct possibility, not considering how haughty and holier-than-thou they always acted. They believed themselves superior in every way, and even when they visited or lived in our realm, they seemed to look at us down their noses. Like Kryn and the prince.

"Interesting. I wouldn't mind talking to one of them." Jeondar's comment seemed genuine. "I've heard of a settlement on the way to Mount Ruin where a number of humans live. It's called Fylahexter. Perhaps some of these *fascinated* people you mentioned couldn't resist the allure and came to stay."

"Interesting. *I* wouldn't mind talking to one of them myself."

Jeondar chuckled. "Perhaps you will."

The comment quickly brought me back to reality. It might be interesting to talk to the humans living in that settlement, but not if it didn't happen on my terms.

"Dinner is ready, I think." Jeondar stood, stretching.

Roasted rabbit, cheese, bread, and wine were passed around, along with fig preserves that went perfectly with the meat. The prince and Arabis never came back from wherever they'd gone, but no one seemed to worry or wonder about it.

My watch vibrated, telling me it only had ten percent battery power left. I cursed inwardly and set it to "save battery" mode, wishing I'd thought to do it earlier. I noted it was 6:30 PM, early for dinner. I was used to eating closer to eight or nine, but my appetite didn't complain. Riding a horse was more physically demanding than I'd imagined.

"Are you going to show us a good time in Imbermore, Dear Jeondar?" Silver asked, sucking on a bone. "We've been too long on the road and I... desire some company."

I could only imagine what type of company he was referring to.

Jeondar's mouth twisted sideways. "This isn't a leisure and pleasure trip such as you're used to."

"Pity," Kryn put in.

Cylea poked at the fire with a long stick. "Of course you would say that." She glanced in my direction. "They're worse than dogs, the two of them. They would fuck a dragon egg if it came with a hole for them to stick their cocks in."

Jeondar let out a hearty laugh while all I could do was feel the blush of shame on my cheeks. I was no prude, but I didn't know these people, and in my experience, jokes of this kind were not thrown out until there was a certain level of familiarity. Though I'd never had any Fae friends, so maybe they were different.

"You and I can go shopping," Cylea declared, pointing at me. "What do you say? Imbermore has some of the best silks in the realm."

"Is that a tradition here?" I asked. "Taking your prisoners shopping?"

Jeondar raised a dark eyebrow as he cut a sliver of rabbit meat with a small knife, brought it to his mouth, then distractedly stabbed the knife into the ground.

Cylea batted a hand at me. "You're not a prisoner. You're a... fellow traveler on a journey to save the realm."

"A what?"

"You're going to scare the boots off of her." Silver's face and platinum hair seemed to glow under the light of the fire.

"She needs to know why she's here," Cylea argued.

"That's up to Kalyll to divulge, not you," Jeondar said, his expression stern.

She rolled her eyes. "I hate the secrecy."

Jeondar shook his head. "You know it's necessary, and we can't trust just anybody."

"Yeah, yeah." She seemed tired of it, as if it were something she'd been dealing with for a while.

Just anybody.

I caught the not-so-veiled insult in Jeondar's words. I wasn't to be trusted. They didn't feel they owed me an explanation, even if they were uprooting me from my life, destroying everything I'd worked so hard to attain.

"You can shove your secrets up your ass," I spat.

Kryn, who had mostly stayed out of the conversation, chuckled quietly. The others peered at me with wide eyes. I'd been a good girl today. They probably thought they'd squelched my spirit, and maybe I should have let them believe that, but I was tired of their pompous asses.

No one responded to my comment. Instead, they set out to gather things up. While they were distracted, I snatched Jeondar's knife from where he'd left it. As quickly as possible, I slipped it under my tunic and crossed my arms, trying to look angry rather than nervous.

The fringes of the small camp dissolved into darkness where the light of the fire couldn't reach. Still, there were no signs of the prince or Arabis, and still, no one seemed concerned about it. Like Arabis, Jeondar glanced up at the sky as he stood next to the fire, his brown skin looking golden. I checked the time. It was 7 PM.

"You should go in the tent." He offered me a hand to help me stand, but I ignored it and stood on my own, hoping the knife wasn't visible under my tunic as he ushered me into my makeshift cell.

Past the flap, the tent was cozy and, suddenly, felt more like a safe heaven than a prison. There was a lantern that cast a warm glow over a comfortable pile of blankets and furs. Best of all, no one was staring at me. I quickly sat down and hid the knife underneath me.

Resolved to wait until everyone was asleep, I waited.

CHAPTER 7

Even though I was exhausted, I didn't lie down and risk drifting off to sleep. I was worried that, despite my precarious situation, my body would betray me if I got too comfortable. Instead, I sent a wave of healing magic over my muscles to ensure I was in the best shape possible. I had to be if I was to outrun anyone tonight. Though, hopefully, it wouldn't come to that. Hopefully, no one would notice me when I slipped away.

I vaguely wondered where my messenger bag was. I wished I could get it back, or at least my phone and the emergency charger I kept there, but those were trivial things that I could easily replace when I got back home.

A howl broke the relative silence, sending a wave of panic crashing into my chest. I wrapped my arms around my body, rocking backward and forwards and telling myself I would not get eaten by some Fae beast I had no name for.

Gradually, the sounds around the camp subsided, though the howls continued, making the hairs on the back of my neck stand on end every time. I put out the lantern to indicate I'd gone to sleep and listened intently for a long while before I retrieved the knife, moved to the back of the tent, and slowly, taking advantage of the howling, carved a hole large enough for me to slip out.

Once outside of the tent, I crouched low, my heart hammering so loudly I was sure it would not go unnoticed by sharp Fae ears. The moon was hidden behind a cluster of clouds, which was a blessing. When no one came, I slunk toward the trees, each step careful and premeditated. I was no survivalist, but I knew sloppiness would get me noticed, especially with nature-savvy Fae as my sentries.

It was painful going until I felt safe enough to start moving at a faster pace. I quickly checked my watch to make sure I was headed generally south and kept on, constantly glancing over my shoulder, trying to peer through the darkness with my too-weak human eyes. My only relief was that the further I went, the further away the howling of that creature got. *Thank the witchlights!*

I walked for hours, pacing myself. I wanted to run, but I knew I would get farther if I walked steadily. A few times, I walked to the edge of the woods to make sure I was still walking parallel to the plains we'd traversed on horseback. The moon had left the clouds behind, painting the faraway mountains and grass with silver light. It was a breathtaking view that I had only but a few seconds to admire before weaving back into the forest.

My watch informed me that dawn would be here soon. My captors would discover I was gone, then would come after me—I had no doubt. This meant that, before long, I would need to find a hiding place, somewhere that could conceal my presence from their keen senses.

As the sky grew lighter, my nerves redoubled. On horseback, they would catch up with me in no time. My only hope was to remain hidden. I wanted to keep going, to run as fast as my legs would allow me, but I knew it was unwise.

Instead, I slowed my pace and scanned my surroundings. I dismissed a couple of too-obvious places and settled for a mostly rotted tree trunk overtaken by moss and lichen. I settled in its hollow center, gathering dirt and moss around my body, hoping to disguise my presence from sensitive eyes and noses. I left only a small gap for my eyes to peer out, then lay still.

As time passed and no one came, I felt foolish and started thinking I could get closer to Pharowyn if I just kept going, but my patience prevailed and I stayed in place. I could sit next to a sick patient for hours, watching their vital signs, applying healing spells at regular intervals, hoping and praying for the smallest sign of recovery. This was no different, except it was my life on the line, not someone else's.

A few times—as my tired muscles settled, sighing in relief—I almost drifted off to sleep, but a swift pinch here and there helped me remain awake.

I could almost sense the sun rising in the east, swallowing away the shadows and inviting dawn to paint the sky with a palette of colors that only nature possessed.

The sound of a breaking branch reverberated through the woods. I froze, biting the inside of my cheek and breathing as silently as I could. Steps disturbed the dry foliage, someone approaching.

Was it my captors? Or an animal that would sniff me out and eat me for breakfast?

Witchlights!

Maybe I would've been better off if I'd stayed with the prince and the others. I didn't know exactly what roamed in these lands, but I'd read enough that I was aware that all manner of creatures lived in Elf-hame, many of them putting my realm's wildest beast to shame.

The steps came to a halt. Something was nearby, and it wasn't one of my captors. I could tell by the ragged breaths that it huffed in and out, each accompanied by a low guttural sound, the growl in the back of an animal's throat.

I prayed I'd rubbed enough moss over my skin to camouflage my scent or that I was upwind from where the creature stood.

More steps, and then the beast's back came into view. I peered at it from my mask of moist lichen and nearly screamed.

The beast was unlike anything I'd ever seen. It resembled a wolf, an apex predator, but it was larger, three times larger than any of the wolves in my realm, even the powerful alpha werewolves like my sister's boyfriend.

He—the creature was undoubtedly male—walked on four legs, but instead of paws it had what looked like a mix between talons and hands, extremities that could grip and tear things up to shreds. Sharp black claws tipped each digit. They sank into the supple ground as the beast's weight settled. Nearly black fur covered the creature, fur that, for the most part, was short, except at the head and tail. In those areas, it was abundant, giving the creature a mane and something like a horse's tail.

But the strangest thing of all was the tendrils of darkness that floated around it like ribbons made of mist, and the thick shadows that puddle beneath him.

Keep moving. Keep moving. Keep moving.

I willed the creature to leave. To never look back and—

The animal turned around, and I got a full glimpse of its savage face.

Its features were angular and cruel, framed by a mane of dark hair that would be more appropriate on a lion than a wolf-like creature. Dark blue eyes shone as they roved around searchingly. I held my breath, trying not to imagine its three-inch fangs ripping into me. Its considerably long, pointed ears angled away from its head, a trait undoubtedly Fae. They twitched at the small sounds of a scampering rodent.

My lungs burned, but I didn't dare breathe. If I but blinked, I knew the creature would find me, and that would be my end.

The beast turned and began walking away, methodically sniffing the ground as it went, its strange talons kicking up dirt. When he was twenty yards away, I allowed myself a tiny, silent breath. At fifty yards, when all I could see was its furry tail up in the air, I forced my body to release its tension, though whatever small amount of relief I gained was quickly gone as a snake slithered into my field of vision.

It was moving alongside my body, its forked tongue tasting the air. Its head had a triangular shape, and its body was bright red, which meant that, most likely, it was venomous.

Once more, I found myself holding my breath and tensing from head to toe. The snake traveled south toward my feet, and I prayed inwardly that it would pass without noticing me.

I didn't know how or why it realized I was there, but I knew the moment it sensed another creature lying right next to it, the moment it coiled back to attack.

In that same instant, my survival instincts had me kicking, jumping to my feet, and leaping away from the hollowed-out husk of the fallen tree trunk. Moss, lichen, and dead leaves flew all over, and miraculously, I escaped the snake's bite.

But it was like jumping from the frying pan straight into the fire.

Heart in my throat, I glanced up to find the wolf-creature eating up ground as it barreled toward me.

I ran, my instincts taking over. I didn't dare glance back, but I knew my speed was no match for this beast, and I might as well be standing still. Yet, the adrenaline pumping through my veins would not let me do anything but fight for my life.

The sun had risen a fraction, barely breaking the dawn, and I could see far enough to tell that—ahead of me, past the thick tree trunks—the terrain stopped and backed to what looked like empty air.

It wasn't the plains that bordered the forest—I was running in the opposite direction—it was something else, an area just as expansive, but... different. Something in the back of my mind told me that danger lay beyond. Briefly, I had the ludicrous idea of fighting the beast with Jeondar's knife, but I kept going.

I dared a quick glance over my shoulder. The beast was merely ten yards away. My heart attempted to launch itself out of my chest and seemed to propel me forward, giving my legs additional strength to cover the remaining distance to the edge.

Arms windmilling through the air, I leaped.

CHAPTER 8

I didn't know what I expected, but it wasn't to quickly hit the ground and go rolling end over end on what felt like the banks of the sandy beach. I tumbled head over feet, shoulder over shoulder, sand blasting my face and filling my mouth.

When I finally came to a stop, my head was spinning, and I didn't know which way was up. I sat there blinking, spitting, and wiping my eyes.

What looked like a desert stretched as far as the eye could see. The Zundrokh Barrens that Jeondar had mentioned. It had to be.

A guttural growl of rage had me jumping to my feet. As I glanced back, I saw the beast at the top of the ridge from where I'd leaped. For a second, I thought it might be my lucky day, and he might be allergic to sand, but a small voice inside my head told me something different: that if a ferocious animal like that chose to stay up there, maybe it was because something worse lurked down here.

The beast's eyes held to mine. I flipped him the bird, which proved to be a huge mistake.

He leaped after me anyway.

"Shit."

I turned and ran.

Suddenly, I was in a worse nightmare, one of those where you try to run fast but your legs are useless. My feet sank into the sand as I tried to push away, slowing me down to a near crawl.

"Oh, God! Please!"

I'm dead.

The thought struck me with certainty. In moments, there would be nothing left of me. Maybe a few drops of blood that would soon sink into the dry sand, but that would be it. And no one would know what happened to me—not even my captors.

Why didn't I just stay with them? What made me think I could brave this unknown realm?

I glanced back just to find the beast soaring through the air, its terrible talons extended and aiming straight for my neck.

Below me, the sand seemed to give way, and I sank even further. The beast overshot me, sailing above, completely missing me. A ray of sunlight pierced through the trees we'd left behind, hitting the sand and blinding me. I shut my eyes as the sand underneath me trembled and then lurched. I fell to all fours and hit something hard. I screamed and tried to stand again, but then I was sliding again, this time in the opposite direction. I got a hold of something and stopped myself. *What the hell?*

Sand slipped away in rivulets as whatever I was standing on rose to the surface.

What is this?

The answer my brain provided was shit. *You've landed on a sandworm from Dune,* it informed me.

No, no, no.

But maybe a sandworm would have been better because this creature seemed worse. It had extremities that could snatch me. Case in point, the huge freaking pincers that were rising from the sand to loom high overhead. Worse yet, it seemed I'd landed on its face, and I was holding on to one of its nostrils or something.

With a scream, I let go and pushed back.

Two completely black eyes rose from the hard tan shell. They rested on long stalks that slid out like periscopes out of submarines. Thinking quickly, I sidled next to one of them, hoping to remain unnoticed. Each stalk was about my height, which gave me an approximate indication of the animal's sheer size. It had to be huge. A crab-like beast the size of a school bus.

A skittering vibration came from the animal, making my teeth rattle. Something wet sounded behind me. I turned slowly to find the other huge eyes staring straight at me. They moved independently. *Fuck!* My skin crawled, and my stomach tightened into a knot.

A pair of huge pincers came at me from the side. I jumped out of the way just in time. They snapped shut with a loud clunk that made my ears hurt.

I reached for the knife at my back and brandished it around just as the second pair of pincers came at me from the opposite direction. I ducked and rolled over my shoulder, knife still in hand. The crab let out a high-pitched screech that clearly displayed its frustration.

The pincers came at me again. This time, as they snapped open and shut, I barely managed to get out of the way. I grazed the thing with my knife, but it was like trying to wound a wall. Possessed by insanity, I jumped on one of the pincers and wrapped my arms around it.

The creature brandished its limbs about, trying to dislodge me. I thought of letting go. If I did, I would soar through the air and land on the sand. I would be okay, right? Except that wolf thing was still out there and would probably snatch me as a yummy little morsel as soon as I hit the ground.

Witchlights. What had I gotten myself into?

The crab paused its thrashing for a moment. My breaths were loud in my ears. A moment later, the pincer I was attached to started moving slowly toward a barbed slit under the crab's eyes.

Oh, shit.

The creature was planning to have its first taste of human.

No way.

I jumped off, the knife raised above my head. I stabbed the weapon right in the middle of one beady, black eye and landed on my feet. The creature screamed in agony. I slapped my hands over my ears. The crab thrashed underneath me and, as I staggered sideways, one pincer came toward me so fast I knew I was done for.

I'd given it my best try. I'd fought valiantly, but today was to be the day I said goodbye. I thought of my family: my sisters, my brother, my mother. I would never see them again, and it made my heart hurt more than anything. I wouldn't see my siblings grow into old age. I would never meet my nieces and nephews, if any came. I would never be Aunt Dani, who healed every scrape, every fever. I had sometimes daydreamed about that, more than I daydreamed about having my own kids.

I thought of little Muriel in her sickbed, and the bright hope in her eyes as I assured her I would find a way to cure her.

Damn you Kalyll Adanorin. Damn you.

The pincer scissored shut.

I closed my eyes.

Something whistled through the air, fast as a rocket. There was a loud crunching sound, followed by a growl, then another high-pitch screech.

My eyes snapped open.

As if I conjured him with my thoughts, the prince stood in front of me in a crouch, his sword embedded in the crab's pincer as slimy yellow blood streamed down the weapon. The *goo* slid over the hilt and reached his hands. He winced as his skin sizzled.

Another growl and the prince pulled his sword free. Moving swiftly, he wrapped a hand around my wrist and dragged me along as the crab buckled and tipped to one side. He pulled me close as we fell flat on the crab's hard shell and aimed our bodies toward the back of the creature. We slid along its length and landed on the sand.

Before I had time to process anything, the prince wrapped an arm around my waist and hauled me to my feet. We ran up the slippery dunes toward the forest above. He practically carried me up as the crab screeched and thrashed in agony.

A moment later, the prince stabbed his sword into the verdant ground and pulled us up to the top. I fell to my knees and crawled away from him, my chest heaving, my entire body trembling. I sensed as he climbed to his feet and turned around to watch the creature below as it continued to shriek, while all I could do was hold myself to make sure I didn't fall to pieces.

CHAPTER 9

Tears I didn't know how to stop flowed freely. Stupidly, I said in a long sob, "The poor beast is going to die and it's my fault." I'd stabbed it in the eye. *Oh, witchlights.*

The prince's feet shuffled as he faced me. "What? Do you mean the *decayana*?"

I pulled at my hair and continued sobbing.

"It was going to kill you, Ms. Sunder. You had to fight for your life. It's just natural."

I resisted the urge to throw up, wiped my tears clean, and slowly stood. I turned to face the dunes and watched the animal. The decayana, as the prince had called it, buried itself in the sand, its shrieks becoming muffled until they completely stopped, and there was no sign left of it, except for a slight disturbance in the sand.

Dunes upon dunes stretched before us. I scanned them, searching for the wolf beast, but there was no sign of it. Had it been devoured by the sands? Something told me it had escaped. I peered warily at the forest behind us.

"Thank you," I said, the words nearly choking me.

I expected the prince to yell, to tell me what a foolish thing I'd done and how, if I'd stayed put, none of this would've happened. I thought he would blame me for delaying their journey and say that I deserved almost being devoured, first, by a wolf, and then, by a giant crab.

But he only inclined his head with the grace of a prince. "You're welcome."

His hands flexed as he stretched out his fingers. I noticed the angry welts that covered them, some blistering, as if he'd dipped his hands in boiling water. The decayana's blood had done that. It must have been like acid.

I took a step forward. "Your hands."

He shrugged one shoulder. "They'll be fine. They're already healing."

And indeed, they were. The smaller welts were closing, red, tender skin knitting over them, but the bigger ones would take some time to repair themselves.

"Allow me." I reached for his left hand and held it gently in mine. Rough calluses scraped against my palm. His hand was large and made mine look almost like a child's. I hovered my free fingers over the welts, releasing my healing magic. I watched as the injuries disappeared, leaving smooth skin behind.

I did the same for his other hand, then quickly released it. He flexed his fingers, turning them this way and that.

"Now it is I who needs to thank you." His azure eyes met mine and held them. For a moment, it felt like gravity pulling me down. There was something hypnotic about him, a certain power that seemed to erase every thought from my head, perhaps a skill of the many the Fae were known to possess.

I took a step back, not without difficulty. "There was a beast that chased me," I found myself saying. "It could still be here."

"A beast?" he echoed, narrowing his eyes. "Other than the decayana?"

I nodded.

"I didn't see it."

I glanced all around. "Where is your horse?"

"I... didn't have time to tie it down. He must've wandered off."

"Where are the others?"

"I rode... harder and faster than them. I'm sure they'll catch up soon, but we should head toward the plains."

He pulled his sword from the ground and, after carefully cleaning the blade in a patch of grass, sheathed it behind his back. He started walking, heading east. He ran a hand through his hair, which was in disarray. Feeling self-conscious, I pulled my own hair out of its ponytail holder and ran my fingers through it, too.

As I lingered back, the prince turned. "C'mon, we need to..."

He halted and scanned my face and the length of my hair. His scrutiny made me even more self-conscious, and I quickly gathered my long hair into a knot so tight that it made me wince.

"I'm coming." I marched in his direction and walked past him. I felt his eyes on me, but didn't glance back.

We walked in silence as he set a clipped pace. He stopped a few times as I lagged behind and asked me if I was all right. I was exhausted—I hadn't slept all night, and I'd fought for my life against two monsters—but I didn't complain. I just nodded and kept going, marveling at how gentle and different the prince seemed from the male who fought Kryn yesterday.

As I refused his help to cross over a bubbling brook and skipped from rock to rock on my own, I found myself asking a question.

"Prince Kalyll—"

"Please, call me Kalyll."

For some reason, that unsettled me somewhat. I'd been thinking of him as *the prince* this entire time. I hesitated, then decided he was no prince of mine, and I could call him that when and if I wanted to, just not now.

"Can you be honest with me and tell me something?"

He reached the other side of the brook and waited for me before speaking. "As honest as my duty allows, Ms. Sunder."

"How long will this... quest take?"

He lowered his eyes and shook his head, the thin braids of his hair swinging from side to side. "I cannot say with certainty."

"Give me a range, why don't you?"

He grunted as he thought about it.

"For what you've done, I deserve an answer, at least." I pressed him.

"That and much more." His gaze dipped lower still, and I felt the embarrassment rolling off him in waves. "It won't be long. Five weeks, maybe."

I sucked in a breath. "Long enough. Muriel won't make it."

One of Kalyll's fists tightened. "Muriel?"

The brook gurgled beside us as I thought of her bouncy curly hair and smooth dark skin, those deep brown eyes always holding a spark even when her disease got the best of her.

"She's one of my patients," I answered absently, wondering how she was doing this morning, if she was asking where I was. She had become very attached to me in the past few weeks. "She's very ill, has a rare disease that causes her organs to shift inside her body even while she remains in her human form. She's a coyote shifter, only five years old. I was working on a way to help her, and I think I was close to figuring it out. I could feel myself getting closer and closer to the answer."

"I'm sorry."

"Are you?" I spat, even though I could feel his sincerity. "She'll be dead in five weeks." I threw the words like an accusation in his face.

He flinched but said nothing.

"There are better, faster ways to travel than on horseback. How about that?" I was referring to travel through magical means. He was wealthy enough for that.

"It is not a possibility at the moment."

I huffed, disgusted, feeling like a thousand spiders crawling inside my stomach.

"I wish there was a way I could make it up to you, but I know it's impossible." He turned and kept walking, his shoulders stiff, his midnight blue hair swinging around his face as he lowered his chin.

I batted a stray tear and followed him, resignation setting itself heavily on my shoulders. I would not be going home in time. If I returned and managed to get my job back, all those little faces that looked up at me from their small beds every morning would be replaced by new ones. Most of them would be at home with their parents, healed and enjoying their lives. Others would be gone after losing their battle against the cruel illnesses that plagued them, like little Muriel. Their families would be devastated and would take a long time to think of life as a worthwhile pursuit, if they ever managed. They would blame me, I imagined. The healer who promised to do everything in her power to save their children, and then just disappeared.

I pressed a fist to my mouth and bit back the tears that kept rising. I'd lost other patients before, hadn't I? This was no different. Except it was because I wasn't meant to be here. I was meant to be by their side, leaving no rock unturned until I found a way to use my skill to save their lives.

But thanks to Kalyll Adanorin, they would die.

Damn him.

An hour later, we'd reached the plains and were walking alongside the forest, headed north. Once I got my emotions under control, I started wondering how much harder the prince had ridden ahead of his friends. There was no sign of them on the road. Also, there was no sign of his black stallion.

"Are you sure your friends aren't looking for us in there?" I pointed toward the woods.

"They'll find us," he assured me, appearing unconcerned. "As a matter of fact," he squinted into the distance, "I see them."

"You do?" I strained my eyes but saw nothing except for the grass-lined path stretching for miles, leading toward The Sunder Mountains. I wondered if he was pulling my leg or if this was the famed Fae eyesight I kept hearing about.

"Stormheart is with them."

"Who?"

"Stormheart, my stallion."

A few minutes later, Kryn was galloping in our direction, mounted on his tan horse and dragging Stormheart behind him. His gaze bounced between us, curious and concerned.

"You... found her," he said, sounding surprised. They'd likely convinced themselves that I'd become fodder for one beast or another during my foolish escapade.

"Yes, she's safe and sound," Kalyll said.

I waited for him to add further detail, to tell them he saved me from a decayana right before it cut me in half, but instead, he took Stormheart's reins from Kryn and patted the animal along its long neck. He whispered something in a language I couldn't understand. At first, the horse pawed the ground, appearing angry, but quickly relaxed into his touch.

"Um, what happened?" Kryn asked, eyeing me as if he wanted to yell and point out my stupidity. Though the prince's presence gave him pause.,

"I found her near the edge of the Zundrokh Barrens." The prince mounted Stormheart in one swift motion.

Kryn's eyebrows rose nearly to his hairline. "Not a hospitable place at all." He shook his head at me. "A decayana could've made breakfast out of you in no time at all. Not to mention the other things that roam this forest."

"I wouldn't be so sure about that." Kalyll extended a hand in my direction, offering help to pull me onto his horse.

I stepped back. The horse was big enough for three people, but I wasn't riding with the prince. No way. His hooves were big enough to do my head in, and he didn't have a friendly expression on his long face.

"No, thank you. I'll walk." I marched past Kryn, who scratched the back of his neck, looking supremely irritated.

"We don't need any more delays." Kryn turned his horse around and galloped away. He was clearly pissed. Like kidnappers had a right to expect compliance from their victims. Fat chance.

"Glad to annoy you," I sneered at his back as he retreated.

Kalyll chuckled.

"This is funny to you?"

He put his hands up. "I'm sorry. I just enjoy seeing the way you get under his skin."

I huffed.

"We're still several miles from the group. We'll catch up faster if you ride with me."

"I have no interest in going faster."

"Your feet will hurt."

"My feet are fine. Thank you."

"All right. Then take Stormheart, and I'll walk."

"Nope. I don't trust that horse."

"What? Stormheart? He's a sweetheart."

I shrugged. "He looks nothing like a sweetheart to me, but if you say so."

Kalyll jumped off his horse and joined me in my walk. He dug in his saddlebags and produced a piece of something that looked like a multi-grain cracker, except thicker.

"You must be hungry."

I took the offered piece without a word and started chewing on it, enjoying its heartiness and honey-sweet taste.

"Why didn't you tell Kryn what happened with the decayana?" I asked.

"Because he would find a way to make fun of you even though you fought the creature beautifully."

I glanced sideways at him, wondering if *he* was making fun of me, but he appeared serious, with not a hint of mockery in his expression. He thought I had fought beautifully. I'd never thought of myself as any sort of fighter. When my siblings and I were little, I was always the one breaking the brawls between them, always the pacifist. I exercised a little—for my health, not for any other reason. I did a variety of things, changing them up constantly. Aerobics, pilates, swimming, aerial yoga... anything to keep me from getting bored. I figured all of those things contributed to a certain level of agility and flexibility, but they had nothing to do with fighting. Maybe my survival instincts were just... fierce.

Way to go, Dani.

I blew air through my nose. "I would be dead if you hadn't shown up."

"Who knows? But it's a good thing we didn't have to find out."

A moment later, Arabis came galloping down the road, pulling Dandelion behind her. "Hey, Dani."

"Hey." I took the offered reins.

"Glad you didn't get eaten by a decayana or... anything else." Her eyes flicked to Kalyll.

"Me too, I guess." I climbed on my horse at the same time that Kalyll climbed his.

"Let's try to regain the ground we've lost." The prince pulled ahead, all business, leaving us behind as Stormheart's hooves tore up the ground.

"You all right?" Arabis scanned me from head to toe.

"Just a little humiliated, but otherwise unscathed."

"I was worried about you."

I grunted. I doubted she was worried about me. It was their quest, whatever it might be, that mattered to them. If only they would tell me how I was supposed to help them. Maybe knowing would make all of this easier to accept, but everyone's lips were sealed because they didn't trust me.

"Did you happen to see a decayana?" she asked. "I've only seen illustrations."

I debated whether or not to tell her I had actually been on top of one, fighting for my life, but I was too tired to get into it, so I shook my head.

"Shame. Did you... see anything else?"

I thought of the wolf with its shining blue eyes and taloned extremities. A shudder slid down my back, and something told me being cut in half by the decayana would've been a luckier fate than anything the wolf might have done to me.

"I didn't," I lied and ate the rest of my thick cracker, spurring the horse forward. I was on this quest for good, so now my new goal was to get it over with.

CHAPTER 10

W hen we caught up with the rest of the group, Silver inclined his head in welcome. Kryn ignored me. Cylea frowned, looking annoyed, and Jeondar greeted me with a quiet *Abin Man-ael*. Very few words were exchanged as they turned their small procession around and started heading toward the mountains again.

Kalyll set a steady pace, and by midday, we were back at the place where we camped the night before. Unlike the previous day, we didn't stop to eat lunch, and judging by the dirty look Kryn threw in my direction as he tore into a piece of dry meat, the increased pace and lack of rest were entirely my fault.

After the sun reached its apex, Kalyll pulled ahead and remained at a distance from the rest of the group. The stiff line of his back told me he was in a mood. He was probably tired and cranky, also thanks to me.

The steady, rocking movements of the horse started lolling me to sleep. I splashed a little water on my face from a canteen attached to the saddle. I didn't want to fall off the animal and add insult to injury. I felt humiliated enough as it was. As I blinked, doing my best to stay awake, I noticed Arabis nodding off on top of her horse. A few minutes later, she was completely asleep, her chin resting on her chest, and her body swinging gently from side to side as her mount marched steadily up a rolling hill—one of many that lined the plains on the north end, a prelude to The Sunder Mountains in the distance.

I was amazed by her ability to stay in her saddle. If that were me, I was sure I would've fallen and cracked my head open on a rock. Wherever she'd gone with Kalyll last night, she hadn't gotten any rest. Add to that my escape attempt, and it was understandable why she had started to snore lightly. A smile stretched my lips of its own accord. She looked adorable, petite, almost like a child. Her face was fine and delicate, grazed with the beauty that only the Fae possessed.

As the afternoon sun beat on our backs, I lagged behind, though Jeondar brought up the rear, probably to make sure I didn't try anything stupid again.

Kalyll was a small figure ahead of us, which seemed to undulate with the heat that reflected off the ground. Kryn repeatedly sighed, acting like a teenager assailed by boredom. He twisted backward onto his saddle, then reclined his back on the horse's neck. He rode that way for a bit, his brilliant green eyes flicking back and forth between Arabis and the plains we'd left behind.

"Do you think we'll miss the Summer Solstice Ball?" Cylea asked Silver. They'd been riding side-by-side the entire way, talking in quiet tones, almost without stopping.

I tried to listen a few times, but they kept referring to people and places with strange names, and I quickly lost track, especially since it all sounded like gossip—not anything that could help me get an insight into my situation.

I yawned and rubbed my eyes, wondering if we would stop early this afternoon, the way we did yesterday, then deciding that we probably wouldn't stop since my shenanigans had cost us at least half a day of travel.

Kryn sat up and started digging in one of his saddlebags. He came up with a feather, which he held up in front of his face as he smiled. At some silent signal from him, his horse slowed its pace until he was parallel with Arabis. Still sitting backward on the saddle, he stretched out the feather, placed it under Arabis's nose, and tickled her.

Arabis wrinkled her nose.

"What a juvenile," I said under my breath.

He bared his teeth and rolled his eyes at me, then did it again.

This time, Arabis sniffled and shook her head slightly. Still, she didn't wake. Kryn persisted, this time tickling her cheek. She swatted at her face as if she thought a bug was bothering her. She sighed and continued sleeping.

Kryn leaned forward to tickle her one more time, but before he reached her, she moved with the speed of lightning, punching him straight in the nose without even opening her eyes, then slapping his horse in the butt. The animal careened forward, Kryn cursing as he cradled his nose in both hands. Someone other than a Fae would have probably gone tumbling from their mount, but Kryn rode forward in his backward position, shooting daggers at Arabis and at the rest of us who were laughing our asses off.

"He deserved that," I said.

"That fool deserves more than that," she assured me.

"Why does he have it in for you? I mean... I think I know why, but..." I trailed off, realizing I was prying.

She didn't seem to mind, however. In fact, she shifted in her saddle, making herself comfortable and appearing as if she appreciated the distraction.

"Kryn and I met when we were children. His family was visiting Elyndell on The Starlight Festivalas most royal families often do."

So Kryn came from a royal family too. No surprise there. He acted as if he'd been raised with a silver spoon up his behind.

"During The Starlight Festival, there is a full week of events that include lavish dinner parties, balls, various events that anyone can attend, and competitions of agility and strength. Only the adults participate in those, but the children sure like to pretend they're part of the contests. I was doing just that in one of the training fields, practicing with a wooden sword, when Kryn showed up, all cocky and tall and handsome. You've seen him." She crossed her eyes, making a funny face.

I laughed.

She went on. "He got his own sword and joined us. His skill is almost on par with Kalyll's. That's because he started wielding the sword when he could barely wipe his bottom. At seven years old, he was already good. Really good. He put everyone on their backs in a matter of seconds. When he got to me, I dared scrape him with the tip of my fake weapon. The other children jeered, and that made him angry. He took it out on me. He maneuvered me into a mud puddle and viciously threw me in."

"Witchlights. He was already a jerk at such a young age?"

"If you knew his father, you wouldn't hold it against him too much. I didn't. Though, the next time I saw Kryn... I did hold what he did then against him."

"What did he do?"

She looked as if she was about to tell me when Jeondar trotted to her right side, his amber eyes reading the sky. "Do you think we should stop?"

Arabis blinked, looking surprised. She also glanced up at the sky. "Gods, I lost track of time. Yes, we should stop. Excuse me, Dani, but I must join Kalyll."

She shook the reins and was off. I watched her go, then glanced up at the sky. It was around 5:30 PM, the same time we stopped to make camp yesterday. I was glad that we'd soon have food and rest, but I couldn't help but wonder about the rigid schedule, and why did Arabis need to drop everything to join the prince. The image of that fierce cry she'd issued to stop Kalyll from cutting Kryn down flashed through my mind for some reason. The prince certainly listened to her. In a way, it seemed he needed someone to keep him in line when he lost his temper, and Arabis appeared to be that person.

"Is something wrong with the prince?" I asked Jeondar before I could stop myself.

His head jerked in my direction. "What makes you say that?"

I shrugged, unable to put into words the ideas that were forming in my head.

"There's nothing wrong with him." Jeondar shook his head. "He... just gets a bit moody and irritated when he's under too much stress."

"And this situation is stressful?" I glanced around at the placid rolling hills dotted with colorful wildflowers, and at the backdrop of snow-capped mountains. If I didn't want to go home, I could very well make myself believe this was paradise.

"He has a lot on his mind. There is unrest brewing in some parts of the realm."

"Is that so?" I frowned, thinking that any sort of brewing unrest couldn't bode well for me.

Jeondar nodded.

"He knows I can't heal brewing unrest, right?" I joked in hopes of drawing out even the smallest bit of information about my involvement in this situation.

He smirked and raised an eyebrow, understanding full well what I was trying to do. "Let's make camp, Ms. Sunder. I think we could all use some food and good rest tonight." He gave me an accusatory glare.

"You can't blame me for trying, Jeondar."

"I don't. In fact, it gives me hope."

I opened my mouth to ask what in the world he meant by that, but he was already urging his horse forward, heading to a cozy-looking clearing in between two gentle hills.

In no time, there was a fire going, and the tent from which I'd escaped last night was erected. We had a dinner of mixed nuts, dried fruit, and some sort of bird Cylea fell from the sky with her arrows. Delicious wine accompanied the food, and I drank my share until

Silver took away the skin that held it and declared that I'd had enough.

Same as last night, Kalyll and Arabis were nowhere to be found.

"Where did the prince and Arabis go?" I asked Cylea this time, hoping she might be more forthcoming than Jeondar.

"That's *their* business, don't you think?" she responded in a tone that insinuated the two were rolling in the hay under the stars.

It wasn't unlikely. They were two adults of mating age—as the Fae called it—even if they were distant cousins. *Ew.*

"I heard you and Silver talking about... a ball?" I tried a different tactic.

At this, Cylea's face lit up. "Yes. It's in ten days, at the summer palace. It's a grand celebration. There's food, drink, dancing, delicious gossip." Her husky voice grew a little high-pitched with excitement.

She definitely seemed like a girly-girl. She liked parties, shopping, gossip—things that didn't seem to go with all the hunting and horseback riding. I shook my head, chiding myself. It was silly to try to apply stereotypes to anyone, especially stereotypes from my realm.

"But tell her what you're really excited about," Silver teased as he added another log to the fire.

"Lyanner Phiran will be there." She fluttered her eyelashes several times.

I frowned, wondering if I was supposed to know who this Lyanner was. Was he some famous Fae whose name was known in my realm? There were a few that were sort of celebrities. Of course, most people knew of Prince Kalyll Adanorin. They also knew of his parents and of the Unseelie King. There were portraits of them in museums and online. There were also a few Fae who were Hollywood actors and actresses, and some legendary few whose legends had crossed the veil between realms due to their accomplishments. But as I searched my memory, I couldn't recall anyone named Lyanner Phiran.

"I don't think she knows who he is," Silver pointed out.

"He's only the best dragon trainer in the realm," she informed me. "They call him the Drakeansoul."

I swallowed. Dragons? Like the decayana and that wolf, they were a thing? A thing I didn't wish to encounter. I'd had enough of Fae creatures for a lifetime.

"He must be something else," I said unenthusiastically.

"I've always wanted a dragon," Cylea clapped. "And he's the one who can get it for me. Besides, he's extremely interesting, not to mention handsome."

"He looks like a goat," Kryn put in. His nose had been swollen just a moment ago, but with his fast-healing body, there was but a small red lump left on top of it.

Cylea pushed her blue hair behind her shoulder. "Of course, you would say that. You've always been jealous of him."

"Jealous? Of Lyanner Drakeantroll? Don't make me laugh." He waved a hand in the air as if to dispel a bad smell. "He's an over-reaching nobody."

"As opposed to an underachieving *somebody*." She pronounced the last word as if she meant the exact opposite. "He made a name for himself through his skill, while others unmade theirs through sheer uselessness."

Kryn's green eyes narrowed and a muscle jumped in his jaw. It seemed Cylea had struck a chord. He brooded for a moment, and then seemed prepared to unleash a venomous retort, but in the end, he held back, remaining broody for the rest of the night. He didn't seem to be having a good day, but he brought it on himself with his arrogance. I couldn't say I felt sorry for him.

After a while, Jeondar escorted me into the tent. This time he carried two lengths of rope, which he held up as he pointedly stared at my wrists.

"Seriously?" I protested.

He nodded.

"But I won't be able to sleep. It will be uncomfortable."

"You brought it upon yourself, Ms. Sunder."

"I promise I won't try to escape again."

He gave me an expression that seemed to ask, *do you think I'm gullible?*

"Fine." I extended my wrists, which he tied in front of me, leaving a long line of slack. After that, he proceeded to tie my ankles together.

"Lay down with your head that way." He pointed toward the front of the tent.

I did as he said and stared up at him from my prone position.

"Good night." He grabbed the slack he'd left around my wrists and took it with him.

As he exited, my arms were pulled overhead by the rope. "Hey, that hurts!"

"No, it doesn't," he called from outside.

"Dammit," I cursed under my breath. I was tied like a dog on a leash.

I tossed and turned for several minutes, tugging on the rope. Jeondar tugged back every time. I thought I would be unable to sleep, but once my frustration ebbed and exhaustion took over, my eyelids fluttered closed and I drifted off.

There were vivid howls in my dreams, which quickly turned to nightmares featuring a massive, savage wolf with taloned fingers.

CHAPTER 11

O n the tenth morning after my kidnapping, we found ourselves halfway to The Sunder Mountains. I had never traveled so many miles outside of a car or plane, and I had no idea how to judge distances. The mountains appeared considerably bigger, but they were still a fair distance away.

The forest had flanked our right from the moment we left Pharowyn, but now it curved to form a barrier in front of us, which according to Jeondar was called Mid Crosswood and we would have to cross in order to reach the Summer Court, his home in the city of Imbermore.

I was tired of being on the road, even if I'd grown used to being on horseback and my butt didn't hurt anymore. Still, I longed for a hot shower and a proper bed, and a night's sleep that involved no ropes and no infernal howling from wolves. The ropes rubbed my wrists raw, and the howls triggered terrible nightmares that featured a decayana with talons instead of pincers, talons that managed to catch me and squeeze me until my insides popped out. Not fun.

Jeondar was securing the pack horses while Silver made sure to put out the fire.

As I fed Dandelion the core of an apple, Kalyll talked to Kryn a distance away. They seemed to be joking about something, and a wide smile illuminated the prince's face. He didn't smile often, especially after his mood grew somber as the morning wore on, a daily occurrence that caused him to pull ahead of our party and ride up front by himself. Then at night, he and Arabis disappeared, never having spent one night around the fire with the rest of us.

Now, he laughed at something Kryn said, and as he shook his head, looking amused, caught me staring. His dark blue eyes captured mine with that hypnotic quality they possessed, one I'd begun to suspect might be some sort of magical skill.

With a quick word of dismissal to Kryn, he approached me, never breaking eye contact. He had a certain swagger as he walked, but it wasn't an affectation. No, it was something that had its roots in self-assurance and strength—two things he possessed in spades.

"How are you this morning, Ms. Sunder? Did you sleep well?"

"No, I did not." I bit out the words, feeling rude, then reminded myself I didn't owe good manners to my captor. "Jeondar ties me up every night, and it's very uncomfortable."

He grunted deep in his throat. "I suppose, at this point, that's an unnecessary precaution. You won't try to escape again, will you?"

"I almost got myself killed last time, so I guess not. I'm resigned to the fate you have imposed on me. I only hope that when all of this is said and done, you'll return me where I belong."

"I assure you," he inclined his head respectfully, "I look forward to that moment."

His words bounced inside my head. They could be interpreted to mean that he couldn't wait to be rid of me, but his polite demeanor told me he simply wanted to do the right thing. My gaze roved around awkwardly. He could be so proper and respectful that he made me feel brutish in contrast.

I thought for a moment, realizing that at this rate, the five weeks—or however long I ended up spending in Elf-hame—would be miserable, except it didn't have to be that way, did it? My philosophy had always been to make the best out of any situation. There was much I could learn in Elf-hame to improve my skills. In the past, I'd even contemplated spending some time here researching Fae healing techniques. And now, here I was, whether or not I wanted it. Why waste the opportunity?

Straightening, I swallowed my anger and pride and said, "Perhaps, if you and your friends will agree, we can call a truce. I realize that trying to escape is futile. For better or worse, I'm stuck here."

The prince winced at the last part, but seemed attentive to my offer.

I continued. "So I promise not to cause any trouble and help in any way I can, if you all promise to treat me with respect, quit tying me up at night, and be more forthcoming about why I'm here."

Kalyll pressed a fist to his chest and inclined his head. "This offer is very gracious of you, Ms. Sunder, and I appreciate it. If you have been ill-treated, I apologize. I will make sure to talk to our companions to impress the importance of being agreeable." He threw a sideways glance at Kryn, probably trying to figure out how he would make the jackass behave. "As far as being forthcoming about your presence here, I promise that after we visit the Summer Court, I will explain."

I wanted to ask why he couldn't tell me now, but I suspected the reason. He didn't trust me enough not to divulge his secrets there. But who would I tell? I didn't know anyone there. Still, he'd mentioned his quest had something to do with protecting his people, so for all I knew, his secrets were matters of state, and if we were in my realm, there would be a manila folder somewhere, marked with a red "TOP SECRET" stamp—just the kind of thing somebody without clearance would never get their eyes on.

So, since I definitely didn't have that sort of clearance here or anywhere else, I nodded. "That seems fair. Do we shake on it?" I offered him my hand.

He glanced down at it and gave me a slow smile. He wrapped my hand in his large one and gave it a firm, but gentle, squeeze. He seemed as if he wanted to say something else, prolonging the handshake until it felt awkward and his touch became all I could focus on.

At last, he let go. "You're an admirable woman, Ms. Sunder."

He walked away, leaving me speechless. Admirable? No one had ever called me that. And a prince of Elf-hame admiring me? My cheeks flushed with heat, and I turned away to hide my reaction. I occupied myself with Dandelion, making sure the saddle was tied securely, the way Jeondar had shown me a few days ago.

Seriously, Dani? You're blushing?

I wasn't the blushing type. My brother and his best friend had been total players in high school, and from them, I learned all the moves that drive girls crazy. Together, they'd written the handbook on *How to Make a Girl Blush and Lose Her Panties in Under Ten Seconds*, and I'd studied it with care, so by the time I was of "blushing age," I was practically immune to all the tactics utilized by men. Flattery, longing stares, purred words, posturing, alpha feats, all of it.

The thing was... Kalyll was simply being himself. He wasn't trying to use his male charms on me. He was too preoccupied with other matters to worry about something as vain as flirting.

Chiding myself, I climbed on Dandelion and watched Kalyll talk to everyone in hushed tones. From the looks they threw in my direction—especially Kryn's sideways glare—I knew he was telling them about the truce we'd established.

After they were done talking, we got on our way. We reached the edge of Mid Crosswood an hour later. There, Kalyll paused and scanned the trees warily. The foliage was much thicker here than it had been further south, and the forest floor seemed dark and ominous. Dandelion stamped the ground, and a little tremor ran through her, which transferred to me in turn.

I patted her neck. "Good girl," I said, a gesture that was meant to calm not only her but me as well.

Kalyll seemed to notice my reaction and allowed a reassuring smile to grace his handsome face. He urged his stallion in my direction with a gentle jerk of the reins.

"May I ride by your side, Ms. Sunder?"

"Sure," I blurted out, suddenly feeling flustered.

"Thank you."

We started forward, allowing the horses to set an unhurried, though steady, pace.

"Such thick canopy," I said, examining the branches and leaves overhead.

"Yes. These trees—Imperial Maples, they are called—are known for their abundant foliage."

"They're beautiful, though this gloom is kind of ominous."

"Not in vain. There are creatures that live here that I don't wish to encounter."

I picked at the leather reins with a fingernail. "Are you trying to scare me?"

He chuckled, a deep rumble in his chest that made the hairs on my arms stand on end. There was such power in his voice, such deep confidence that I couldn't help but find it infinitely sexy.

Oh, Dani. You'd better watch yourself.

"Is there no other way to get to the Summer Court?" I asked.

"There is, but it would add several days to our journey."

"And you're... in a hurry."

"We certainly are. I don't think I overstep if I speak for you as well."

"No, you don't."

We were quiet for a bit, and despite the gloomy atmosphere that surrounded us, the sound of clumping hooves behind us, the calls of various birds overhead, and the gurgling of a nearby brook slowly eased my nerves.

"How is your sister, Toni?" the prince asked. "I trust she is well."

"She is. Thank you for asking."

"Is she still with Jacob Knight?"

"Yes. They've been rebuilding her agency."

Toni had a mate tracking agency, which had been destroyed during a battle that Kalyll himself had been part of.

"I'm glad to hear that. I know it caused her no small amount of distress to see it damaged. I know you care about your job as much as your sister cares about her agency," Kalyll said, taking me by surprise. "I understand that you're very good at what you do and that you love working with children."

"I do," I responded in a small voice as I thought of little Muriel and my other patients.

It was very thoughtful of him to realize that. Lots of people never seemed to notice the things that were important to others. So many seemed to think that because they valued fancy cars, jewelry, expensive clothes, and the like that others also should care about those things. Caring about the well-being of others or a job well done was foreign to many people.

"What made you choose this path?" he asked.

"I guess there wasn't much of a choice, really. When you're a Skew, your skills seem to define you, no matter what, especially a skill like healing. Since I was little, my instincts drove me to heal a scrape, a bruise, a swollen bug bite." I smiled, remembering how many times I played doctor with my little sisters.

"I understand." He looked me deep in the eyes and nodded. "I don't have a special skill or a calling like that and often wonder how different things would be if I did. I, however, have a duty, but those are two very different things."

No special skill? He was like a mage with the sword, so maybe he didn't need one.

There seemed to be a certain sadness in his statement, as if his duty weighed on him. It wasn't hard to imagine how inheriting the responsibilities of an entire kingdom could make someone feel that way. Duty had nothing to do with the drive or the need to do something. Duty was about being required to act, even when there was no desire to do so.

Yes, duty could easily be a burden.

I wanted to ask him if he would like to renounce being a prince, but that felt like a very private question, and despite our truce, we weren't on friendly enough terms to get personal.

"I don't think I need to ask why you chose to treat children," he said. "They are so much cuter."

I laughed.

Suddenly, thunder crackled overhead, spooking the horses and making everything around us rumble. Quickly, Kalyll had his hand over my reins, saying something under his breath that calmed the mare instantly.

"Are you all right?" he asked, his fingers brushing mine as he pulled away.

"Yes. That was very loud."

"I suspect we'll have heavy rain before long."

"How fun," Kryn said behind us.

"You're in serious need of a bath," Arabis said. "You should welcome the rain."

"The only bath I want to take is a hot one, inside a giant tub and, preferably, with a nice, soft lady by my side."

Kalyll cleared his throat in warning, his eyes flicking in my direction for a second.

"It's all right," I said. "I'm used to this type of banter. It helps people stay sane, I think."

"Kryn can get out of hand sometimes."

I shrugged. "It doesn't bother me. I have an older brother who can sometimes be as crude as raw steak."

I didn't want Kalyll to think I was a prude, even if he was, though I doubted that. The prince appeared to be good friends with the haughty redhead, and since Kryn didn't seem like the kind to sacrifice his hubris for anyone's sake, I suspected Kalyll was well acquainted with this brand of coarse shenanigans.

As part of our truce, I had asked for respect, so maybe Kalyll thought that meant good-mannered conversation, but far from it.

Kalyll's prediction of rain was on point. A few minutes later, it started pouring, and despite the thick canopy above, in a matter of seconds, I was sodden down to my underwear. My hair was plastered to my face, and my hands shook from cold as I held onto the reins.

I thought we might stop to seek shelter, but to my dismay, Kalyll pressed forward. I glanced at the others to see if they seemed as miserable as I felt and had to do a double-take when I looked at Silver.

Something like an invisible bubble surrounded him, and he was completely dry—not a hair of his platinum head dampened in the least.

Unable to help myself, I stared.

The bubble's edge stood out as if traced in white chalk, but as I looked more closely, I realized it was something else.

"Is that... ice?" I asked, slowing my mare to walk beside him.

He smiled and nodded.

"Are you a mage?" It was what we called Skews with magic in my realm.

"I'm an elemental," he said. "Water."

He was turning the rain to ice before it had a chance to hit him. As the droplets hit the bubble, they seemed to sing, creating a high-pitched melody.

I wanted to ask if he wasn't powerful enough to protect everyone from the rain, but that would've been rude, so I held my tongue. I didn't assume he would save everyone the discomfort if he could. The way this bunch got along wasn't exactly amenable. In fact, it was similar to the way my siblings and I interacted. Leo would have likely let our asses freeze in the rain, while he inwardly laughed and called us wimps.

It was almost midday when the rain finally stopped. My teeth chattered so badly, I feared I would fall from my horse and into a muddy puddle. I tried to clench them, but I couldn't contain the spasms.

Kalyll noticed, frowned, then directed a quick nod at Jeondar, who approached, a sympathetic expression on his face.

"Allow me." He extended a hand in my direction.

Heat emanated from his fingers, warming my skin like the flame of a well-tended fire.

"Let me know if it gets too hot," he said, the glorious heat continuing to emerge from his fingers.

His amber eyes glowed as if a flame rested in the depths of his pupils. His expression was placid, as if he, too, were enjoying the warmth.

In no time, the comfort spread to my very bones and my teeth stopped chattering. My clothes and hair dried considerably, so that I stopped feeling and looking like a soggy stray.

"Thank you, Jeondar. That was wonderful."

"Glad to be of assistance, Ms. Sunder." He bowed his head.

"Um, you can call me Dani," I said. It seemed only fair since I called him by his first name, and he treated me well enough, aside from the ropes.

He seemed surprised for an instant, then bowed again, this time smiling. Ahead of us, Kalyll glanced over his shoulder again. He was frowning as if bothered that I'd extended a courtesy to Jeondar that I hadn't extended to him. Tough deal. He was the orchestrator of my misery. I would continue to be Ms. Sunder to him.

We went on, the horses' hooves making sucking sounds on the muddy ground. With my worries about dying from hypothermia relieved, I suddenly noticed I was hungry. Given the delay I'd caused by trying to escape, we hadn't been stopping for lunch. Resigned to many more hours of riding, I moved to grab some dry meat from my saddlebag. As I leaned to the side, something flew past me, barely missing me. I gasped as a heavy thud sounded on the ground.

"We're being attacked," Kryn shouted just as a rock struck Cylea's back.

She let out a curse, jumped off her horse, and pulled it behind a tree, taking cover.

The next thing I knew, Kalyll was pulling me off Dandelion and dragging me away.

"No," I protested, reaching for the mare's reins. We couldn't leave her to be pelted by rocks.

Kalyll kept pulling with no concern for the animal. My feet skidded over the muddy ground, my body weight nearly toppling us as I pitched to one side. The prince was fast, and hooking an arm around my waist, managed to right me. His back slammed against a tree trunk, and I slammed against his hard body, my nose smacking the leather armor that covered his chest. It took me a few seconds to gather myself and realize I was standing in the circle of Kalyll's arms, one of my thighs ensconced between his thighs, my hands flat on his chest.

He felt as firm as the tree behind him. Not only that, his body seemed to vibrate with power, which thrummed right alongside my front like a vibrating force ready to erupt.

I swallowed, my eyes slowly lifting to his.

CHAPTER 12

K alyll was scanning my face with an intense expression that I felt in my bone marrow. His eyes seemed darker than normal, and something about him seemed almost... feral. His lips trembled and parted for an instant, giving me a glimpse of pointed fangs. His virile scent filled my senses, a combination of leather, rosewood, and his own musk. My chest tightened the way a mouse's must when confronted with a hungry cat.

Had those fangs been there before? Why hadn't I noticed them? Maybe it was because he barely smiled.

His darkened eyes lowered to my mouth and lingered. A thrill went straight to my core, surprising me with its intensity. What the hell? He tightened his hold around my waist, pressing me harder against him.

Something dark moved around the skin of his eye, then Cylea let out a curse and it was gone. Her bowstring tensed as she prepared to shoot an arrow.

"Don't," Kalyll growled.

In the blink of an eye, he grabbed me by the shoulders, whirled, and pressed me against the tree.

"Stay right here, and don't do anything stupid," he scolded me like a child, using a much deeper voice than I'd ever heard from him.

The heat of shame rose from my neck to my cheeks.

It seemed the prince had held in his discontent with my *stupid* escape attempt for politeness' sake, but now his true feelings came out. But what did the jerk expect? That I would sit meekly like a damsel in distress and do nothing? Too bad because that was not who I was.

Letting me go, he turned his attention to the branches overhead. I glowered at his profile, hating the way my eyes immediately trace the perfect edge of his jaw.

"I'll take care of it," he snarled.

Cylea rolled her eyes, looking annoyed, though she slowly released the tension in her bow.

A rock flew right past Dandelion's head. She spooked, and I expected her to run to get away, but she stayed put, probably too well-trained to do anything else. I moved to grab for her reins, but Kalyll pressed his forearm flat against my chest, right over my boobs, and held me in place.

"I told you to stay there. Are you deaf?" he spat.

So much for treating me with respect. I pushed his arm away. "Don't touch me, you asshole."

Ducking under his arm, I ran toward the mare, snatched her reins, and pulled her toward the shelter of the trees.

"I guess you *are* deaf, stupid woman," he growled.

My mouth fell open. Whatever happened to his impeccable manners? It seemed they were all an act, and now he was showing his true colors.

"And you're a heartless prick," I retorted.

Somewhere behind one of the trees, Kryn laughed.

A growl rumbled in Kalyll's chest as he pointed a finger straight at my nose. He was about to say something when another bombardment of rocks pelted the ground close to his feet.

"I'll deal with you later," he said, then was gone.

My eyes roved all around, trying to find him, but there was no sign of him. Had he turned invisible? Or could he move *that* fast? Then

I noticed something hanging in the air, a slight dark haze. Did the prince have a special skill, after all? He'd said he didn't, but clearly, he'd been lying.

As I scanned the trees, I pinpointed everyone's hiding spot. No one looked really concerned. In fact, Kryn was leaning casually against a narrow trunk, green eyes scanning the foliage above.

The branches above us rustled. One cracked and fell right where Dandelion had been standing. I patted her neck, relieved she hadn't been harmed—not thanks to *His Jerkness*.

"You're okay," I whispered.

Judging by her wide-eyed expression, which showed a line of white around her warm brown irises, she was terrified. I soothed her some more, my own heart pounding.

More branches rustled and cracked, then there was a high-pitched cry like that of a child, followed by a, "Let me go, you despot."

Suddenly, a dark shape fell from the trees and landed a few feet away from where I stood with my horse. It was Kalyll, holding a small someone by the neck. Unceremoniously, he threw the person on the ground, and in one swift motion, pulled out his sword and pressed it to their throat.

"No." I jumped from where I stood, pushed him, and fell to my knees protectively in front of what was, indeed, a child. "Don't you dare hurt her. She's just a child."

"How dare you interfere?" Kalyll raised his weapon and pointed it at me instead.

"You can threaten me all you want, but you'll have to go through me to get to her," I spat.

"My pleasure." He moved his arm, ready to lop my head off. The darkness I'd noticed moving around the skin of his eyes returned, this time revealing itself as veins that seemed to pulse with black blood.

"Kalyll, stop." Arabis's preternatural Susurro voice resounded through the trees, directed straight at the prince.

He stopped immediately, blinking, his eyes clearing. He looked between the child and me, then took a step back.

"I... I'm sorry." He looked confused and lost.

Arabis came closer, wrapped an arm around his elbow, and pulled him away.

I sat frozen for several long seconds, trying to understand what had just happened, except there was no time to think about it because the child scrambled to her feet and shot straight through the trees.

"Hold it there, little scoundrel." Silver stepped from his hiding place and snatched the kid by the scruff of the neck.

The girl, who couldn't be more than seven years old, kicked at the air. "Let me go. Let me go."

I got my first good look at her. Her skin was brown, and her bushy hair a bright green, like leaves in the spring. She had pointed ears and huge green eyes that made her look like a scared fawn. Her nose was small as was her mouth, which looked like a tiny rosebud. She wore a sort of crown made from wood with a green gem in the middle of her forehead. For some reason, she reminded me of little Muriel.

Silver glared. "Not until you explain why you're attacking unsuspecting travelers on the king's land."

"This is not the king's land. This is my people's land." She hissed, then a thorny branch sprang from her shoulder and poked Silver's arm.

"Ow." He dropped her and rubbed his arm.

She started to run again, but Jeondar appeared in front of her. "Where are your people? Why are you alone?"

"Because you killed them, you monsters."

Jeondar frowned, looking confused. "What happened, child?"

He kneeled in front of the strange girl, a type of Fae I'd never seen before, and had no name for it.

"You know well what happened," her voice broke, an undeniable pain in every note.

"I am sorry, but I don't."

"You lie. You lie like all of them." She sank to the ground, looking defeated, and began to cry.

"Oh, the poor dear," Cylea said.

"We have just come from Pharowyn in the south," Jeondar explained in a gentle voice. "We don't know what happened. Is your family... where are they?"

"They're all dead," she sobbed. "All of them."

Seeing the agony in her expression, a knot formed in my throat. Jeondar exchanged a glance with Silver.

"What is your name?" Cylea asked.

The little girl shook her head.

"I am Jeondar, and these are my friends. Silver, Cylea, Dani, and that one over there," he pointed at the narrow tree behind me where the arrogant redhead was still reclining, "that one's Kryn. You can trust us. We mean you no harm. I promise." Jeondar placed a fist on his chest.

The little girl sniffled. "I'm Valeriana of Mid Crosswood," she answered, all the fight gone out of her.

"Why don't you tell us what happened?" Cylea said.

Valeriana shook her head adamantly.

"We might be able to help if you tell us," Jeondar said.

The girl doubled down, wrapping her arms around her body. I recognized her behavior all too well.

"Valeriana," I kneeled on the side opposite Jeondar, "it's fine if you don't want to talk about it, but we're here for you."

She glanced up at me with her huge green eyes. She blinked several times as she took me in. She inclined her head, frowning at my rounded ears.

"What are you?" she asked, curiosity getting the best of her.

"I come from the human realm," I told her, unsure of whether or not she knew about it.

"Human?"

Apparently, she didn't.

"I can tell you a bit about it if you want."

Kryn peeled away from the tree and strolled toward us. "We don't have time for this. We should get back on the road before..." He let the words hang and glanced toward Kalyll and Arabis, who were standing a distance away, talking in hushed tones.

I understood immediately what he's left unsaid: *before Kalyll gets angry again.*

Jeondar grunted and rose to his feet. "I think you're right."

"But what about the child?" I asked.

No one said anything.

I added, "We can't leave her here—not if her family is..."

Kryn huffed. "We're not childminders."

"Dani's right," Jeondar said. "She shouldn't stay here by herself. We can bring her to Imbermore. We can find someone there to take care of her."

Valeriana jumped to her feet, fists shaking at her sides. "I'm staying here. I can take care of myself and kill those wretches that murdered my family. They'll come back. They always do."

It broke my heart to see someone so young full of hatred and desire for vengeance. Yet, it wasn't hard to understand her. If someone were to hurt my family...

I thought for a moment about what to say to convince her, then spoke, "You're entitled to revenge, but you're small right now, and it might be hard to do what you want. When you're bigger, it would be easier to accomplish anything you set your mind to, don't you think?"

She didn't answer, but I could tell by her expression that she didn't disagree.

"So maybe the best way you can honor your family right now," I went on, "is to make sure you make it, to make sure you give yourself the chance to get big and strong. But it's up to you."

Jeondar nodded thoughtfully. "I agree with Dani. You look like a smart little dryad, Valeriana, so I think you'll make the right choice.

I promise that I will find someone to care for you in Imbermore. I know people, and we can find a clan of your own kind for you to join."

The girl took two steps back, sniffling. It seemed she'd decided to stay.

Jeondar inclined his head. "May the sun warm your path in your travels."

Everyone walked back to their horses and mounted. I reached for Dandelion's reins, glancing at Valeriana over my shoulder, wishing there was something I could do for her. If only my healing powers worked on broken hearts.

Before mounting, I glanced her way one last time. Her head was hanging low as she peered sadly at a trampled cluster of wildflowers at her feet.

Jeondar had called her a little dryad, which meant she was a tree nymph who lived among nature.

Pushing away from Dandelion, I approached her again. Slowly, I kneeled by the patch of crumpled yellow flowers. I extended my hands over them and let my healing powers flow. I felt as the little broken stalks and petals mended, then I stepped away.

"Such beautiful things should never be harmed," I said.

One big tear slid out of the corner of her eye and cut across her cheek.

I climbed on Dandelion and urged her forward, keeping my eyes straight ahead, knowing that if I glanced back, I would refuse to leave. The other ones had ridden ahead, but Jeondar was waiting for me. He gave me a sad smile as our horses plodded ahead, falling into step.

CHAPTER 13

"Do you know who could have harmed that girl's family?" I asked Jeondar after several minutes of riding in silence.

"I can very well guess."

"Fucking Mythorne," Kryn grumbled ahead of us.

"As in Kellam Mythorne, the Unseelie King?" I asked, feeling a ball of dread knotting itself in my stomach.

Kryn nodded without taking his eyes off the road. "The same bastard."

He was deigning to speak to me? To actually acknowledge me with something other than a sneer?

"His people," Kryn said. "Not him personally, of course. I'm sure his bony ass is comfortably ensconced in one of the many velvet thrones he has lying around Highmire."

"But I thought these lands belonged to the Seelie Court," I said. "Why would he…?" I trailed off, realizing what this sort of aggression must mean.

"There is unrest like I told you before," Jeondar said. "Mythorne is unhappy with his share."

Kryn sneered. "That's one way to put it."

I felt that much was left unsaid, and I would've asked if I'd known how, but I knew very little of Fae politics. All I knew was that, in the past, the two courts had fought terrible battles, and their peace had been hard won.

As we pressed forward under the thick canopy, everyone kept watch, as if fearing another attack.

My thoughts swirled, recalling what had happened, the way Kalyll had acted. I watched his stiff back as he rode at the front, several yards ahead of Arabis.

Something was wrong with Prince Kalyll Adanorin.

This time, I hadn't imagined that darkness in his eyes. Those had been veins, pulsing with dark blood. I had seen something the day he fought Kryn. I thought I'd imagined it, but today it was plain. He'd stood right in front of me, ready to chop my head off, a completely feral expression on his face.

Though, maybe that didn't necessarily mean something was *wrong* with him. Maybe I was just getting to know his true self. Yet, something told me that wasn't the case. Something was *off* with him. And what if that was precisely the reason for my presence here? What if he was sick? I'd seen worse things ailing people. I'd seen a little girl whose organs shifted while her body remained human. I'd seen vampires wasting away after a single dose of a mage-manufactured drug. I'd seen a demon wounded by a celestial blade, bleeding golden blood. What was to say the Seelie Prince hadn't been bitten by a bug that turned him into an asshole for half the day?

It sounded crazy, but there was an odd pattern.

"I think we're being followed," Jeondar said, interrupting my thoughts.

My heart went into overdrive as I imagined the people who had killed Valeriana's family stalking us.

"Are you sure?" I asked, my voice trembling and betraying my fear.

"It's Valeriana," Jeondar said. "What you said to her worked."

I started to glance back over my shoulder.

"No. Dryads are proud. Let her believe we don't know she's there."

"But how will she keep up with us?"

"Don't worry. The trees will help her."

I didn't know what that meant, or how the trees could help her, but my ignorance was no surprise. Here in Elf-hame, I was more than a fish out of water. I was worse than a dinosaur in the wrong realm *and* time altogether.

About an hour after we encountered Valeriana, Arabis pulled ahead of the prince and increased our pace.

"It's hard to tell the time with all of these leaves up there." Cylea glanced up at the thick canopy. "But it seems Arabis thinks we should hurry."

"We *should* hurry if we want to get to Imbermore before sundown," Silver pointed out.

We switched from a clipped walk to a canter. I worried that Valeriana wouldn't be able to keep up with us, but Jeondar looked unconcerned about it, so I didn't say anything.

Sometime later, we broke out of the trees into wide grasslands, flanked by a large body of water on the right.

I slowed to admire the beauty. Expansive blue skies hanging over azure waters that sparkle with the sun. Patches of colorful wildflowers among grass as tall as our horses' knees. Flocks of golden birds flying overhead, their plumage so beautiful that it glinted brilliantly with the sun and caused me to avert my eyes. What looked like miniature deer grazing placidly, their antlers twined with vines. And in the distance, a few-hours-ride away, tall spires that had to be part of Imbermore.

"Finally," Jeondar said, pausing next to me. "Home is in sight." He trotted away.

I called for him. "What about Valeriana?"

He reined in his horse. "Oh, yes. I forgot." He rode back to the edge of the woods and let his voice project outward. "We know you're there, child. Come out."

We waited for a moment while Silver, Cylea, and Kryn continued ahead, though at a slow pace.

I scanned the trees, finding no sign of the girl. "Are you sure she's there?"

Jeondar nodded. "I'll ride ahead a bit. I have a feeling she'll come out for you."

I opened my mouth to protest, but he turned his horse and quickly joined the others. Dandelion leaned down to eat grass, her body swinging gently as she shifted her weight from one leg to the other.

I cleared my throat. "Come out, Valeriana." I quickly added, "Please."

Nothing.

I glanced the other way to see how far the others had gotten. Not very far. It seemed they still didn't trust me not to ride off into the sunset. When I glanced back toward the trees, Valeriana was standing there, her eyes on the ground and her hands tied into a knot in front of her.

"Hello there," I said, dismounting. "You must be tired after following us for such a long time."

She shook her head but didn't look at me.

"Hmm, Jeondar said the trees would help you travel. I think that is amazing. Where I come from, they don't have people who can travel along the trees like you."

Her rosebud mouth stretched into an almost smile. "Dryads travel *through* the trees." She corrected me, seeming amused by my lack of knowledge.

"Oh, even better. That is really cool."

She frowned. "Cool?"

"Yes, it's what we say when something is impressive, awesome." She nodded.

"So... I take it you decided to come with us?" For the first time, I wondered if I'd assumed incorrectly. Maybe she wasn't coming with us and instead was only making sure we got out of her forest.

Her little face showed the internal battle she was waging. It seemed she was considering leaving her home behind.

"I'm also away from home," I said. "I'm not even in the same realm." I chuckled sadly. "But I know I will return. I know nothing will keep me from going back." I set my jaw with conviction, making myself a promise.

She took a step toward me, but just as she did, a stream of vines came out from her legs and feet and anchored themselves in the ground, halting her. I stared in wonder, understanding the way the forest called to her and her aching desire to stay.

My heart twisted, and a lump formed in my throat for this little brave girl, who likely knew no other home and was terrified by what lay beyond the borders of what had once been her safe haven.

"Are they good folk?" she asked, glancing toward the others who had, at last, paused their horses to wait for us.

I bit my tongue at the answer that rose to my lips. Kidnappers weren't good folk. Good folk didn't do awful things for good reasons, did they? Except as I sat there—thinking that the girl should come with us for her own well-being and safety—I knew I was about to do something awful. I was about to lie.

"They are good folk," I said, hoping my doubts didn't reflect on my face.

Slowly, the vines that had sprung from her legs and feet retreated and she stepped closer.

The lump in my throat grew tighter. Why she had decided to trust me—a total stranger, a human—was beyond me, but I could see it in her eyes. She had made a decision to place her life in my hands. I'd seen that expression before, the same one my little patients held when I assured them I'd make their pain go away and heal their scrapes and broken bones. I could always deliver when it came to those kinds of things, but this was different. I had no idea what lay ahead of us. I had to trust that my gut feeling about Jeondar was correct. He'd said he could find her a home.

Witchlights, this is so hard!

I considered myself a good judge of character, but there were always people who were cunning enough to fool anyone. Kalyll's face flashed before my eyes.

Pushing those thoughts aside, I extended a hand in Valeriana's direction, smiling gently. "Will you ride with me? Dandelion is very gentle." I patted the horse's neck.

The girl seemed uncertain, but then she took a deep breath and straightened to her full height, gathering her courage. "I will."

She took my hand, and I pulled her closer to Dandelion, letting her caress the animal's neck. Her eyes lit up as she threaded her fingers through Dandelion's mane.

"Let me help you up." I went to grab her waist to hoist her up, but before I even blinked, she'd already climbed in front of the saddle with an agility that astounded me. It seemed like her foot had barely touched the stirrup and her hands were scarcely involved in the process.

I climbed after her, feeling clumsy as hell in comparison. Soon, we were trotting to join the others. When we reached them, Valeriana seemed to shrink in the circle of my arms. She didn't look at them but focused on braiding Dandelion's mane instead.

Jeondar smiled knowingly and nodded his approval.

As we started toward Imbermore, I glanced ahead, searching for any sign of Kalyll and Arabis, but they were gone. The sky above would start growing dark soon, which meant we should be making camp soon, the way we had every day since we left Pharowyn.

"Are we stopping?" I asked.

"Not tonight," Jeondar said. "We'll reach the gates in good time for a proper dinner, a warm bath, and comfortable sleep on a feathered mattress."

That sounded wonderful.

"Stop talking dirty to me, Jeondar," Cylea purred.

They laughed, while all I wanted to do was plug Valeriana's ears.

Everyone's mood seemed to grow lighter the closer we got to the city. Even Kryn abandoned his constant frown and seemed more than eager to get there.

The sky was dark, with a waning moon hanging high above by the time we reached the gates. Hundreds of torches illuminated the massive entrance, a mental set of doors that rose thirty feet up in the air and was carved with an intricate design of a slice of ocean with rolling waves above and marine life teeming beneath it. Taking in the whole thing, I saw a giant octopus, coral reefs, undulating algae, a foaming surf, and a vast sky above all of that.

Both Valeriana and I ogled in wonder.

"The gates are closed," Silver said, stating the obvious, though I could read the true message in his comment: that the city gates were normally open to let travelers in, and that if they were now locked, it meant danger was nearby.

"Where are the prince and Arabis?" I asked.

"They must have gotten through before they closed the gates for today," Jeondar said as he jumped off his horse and walked toward a small door to the right side of the gate.

I thought getting in might be an ordeal, but in no time, we were walking through the side door, pulling our horses behind. The guards on duty—tall Fae males dressed in red tunics with sun-shaped emblems at their breasts and wearing leather harnesses around their shoulders and waist—bowed respectfully as we passed. They peered curiously at Valeriana and me, though only for an instant, their deference surprising.

As we mounted our horses again and moved through the city, Valeriana and I wore twin pictures of open-mouth amazement.

I had seen paintings of Fae cities in my realm, but they were only crude representations of reality. Imbermore was unlike anything I'd ever seen or could have imagined. The place was like Venice on steroids. The entire city seemed to be built over water.

We maneuvered the horses through cobblestone roads, but the preferred method of transportation was small boats gliding over perfectly blue water. They glided over the surface as if propelled by magic. The buildings were all constructed from stone that seemed to grow from the depths of... what? An ocean? A lake? A huge river? Whatever it was, the web was intricate with falls, streams, canals, aqueducts, and water features that seem to defy gravity. The place was unreal, and I was awestruck.

But my astonishment didn't end there, not even close.

I hadn't considered where a prince and his retinue would spend the night. If I had, I might have concluded that the Summer Court Palace would be just the place for such a party, but even so, I wouldn't have imagined the grandeur of said palace. The structure was massive, its tall entrance hewn from white stone and adorned with intricate carvings. Steps that rose for three stories led to it. Four tall spires soared into the air, capped with blue roofs that match the color of the water that surrounded it like a giant moat, a moat that didn't seem to have been built to offer security but pleasure, judging by the many colorful boats that meander through the intricate waterways.

By the time we reached an entrance on the side of the palace, I was so turned around that I knew I wouldn't be able to find my way out of the city on my own. My senses were on overload, bouncing from one marvelous thing to another. We crossed the wooden gates into a cluster of beautifully organized stables, where attendants rushed to our side to take our horses.

Valeriana dismounted with ease, making me feel like a clumsy bear despite my attempts to appear graceful. Dandelion's mane was fully braided in an intricate pattern that looked like a trellis. It made the mare look almost regal.

"That's really pretty," I pointed out.

The girl just shrugged as if it were nothing.

As an attendant pulled the mare away, I reached out in concern.

"It's fine, Dani," Jeondar said. "They'll take good care of her. I promise."

I nodded and felt Valeriana inch closer to me, practically hiding behind my leg.

Silver, Cylea, and Kryn tore through a side door without waiting for us to join them.

Jeondar shook his head. "They'll be drunk within the hour," he said. "C'mon, I don't know about you, but I'm starving, and if we don't hurry, they'll leave no food for us."

I was hungry too, and a hard drink would truly take the edge off. I started to follow Jeondar, but Valeriana stayed behind, nailed to the spot. I offered her my hand. She took it and interlaced her fingers with mine. Clutching me tightly, we left the stables.

We followed through the doors the others had used and traversed a narrow hall adorned with equine-related objects like stirrups, intricately carved leather straps, paintings of majestic stallions, and prairies strewn with wild horses.

The palace was as labyrinthine as the city, and in no time, I was twice lost. At some point, the decorations changed dramatically, becoming luxurious, ostentatious even. Everything seemed to be made out of gold: carved, painted, or sculpted by a masterful artist.

At last, we arrived at a large hall with ceilings as high as a cathedral's and just as intricately decorated. A long table that could accommodate upwards of fifty people stretched before us. It was mostly empty except for people gathered at the far end, near a twelve-foot-wide fireplace that glowed with a cozy fire.

The biggest smile I'd ever seen on Jeondar lit up his face. He strode forward with long steps and walked right into the arms of a tall male who had risen from the head of the table to welcome him.

"Father," Jeondar said, embracing the male and thumping his back.

I blinked as I approached, scrutinizing Jeondar's father and quickly finding the resemblance: the same mahogany skin, the same warm and gentle eyes. It was all there, if with a slightly older tinge.

"Son." He thumped Jeondar's back in turn. "I'm so glad you're home." He was dressed in a red velvet tunic and wore a crown inset with rubies as large as golf balls, which had to mean that he was... the King of the Summer Court.

Holy Shit. I never suspected that Jeondar was a prince.

CHAPTER 14

The king pulled away from his son, held him at arm's length, and examined him from head to toe, wearing a proud expression. After he was done confirming Jeondar was in one piece, he switched his attention to us.

"Father," Jeondar jumped in, "this is Daniella Sunder. She's a healer and hails from the human realm. Dani, this is my father King Elladan Lywynn."

The king took a step forward and bowed respectfully. "Welcome to Imbermore, Lady Sunder."

I felt frazzled, unsure of how to greet a king, so I just mimicked him and said, "Thank you, King Lywynn."

"And who do we have here?" He inclined his head to peer behind my leg, where Valeriana was hiding.

"We found her in Mid Crosswood. She's one of the dryad folk. She said her clan was attacked, and she was left without a family."

As Jeondar spoke, the king's face grew somber, the large smile he'd worn since we arrived fading and giving way to worry lines.

"I promised we would find her a home with a different clan," Jeondar added.

The king nodded, then pressed a fist to his chest. "May their souls linger in the earth at the roots of the mother tree."

Valeriana's lower lip wobbled, and I thought she might break out into sobs, so I squeezed her hand gently, offering her my strength, and she managed to hold herself together.

King Lywynn spread his hands toward the table. "Please, join us. You must be hungry."

Silver, Cylea, and Kryn were already there, large platters of food and goblets of wine planted in front of them. They looked comfortable, as if it wasn't the first time they shared a table with the King of the Summer Court. There were other people seated there, which Jeondar politely introduced, but which I quickly forgot, especially when a servant deposited a silver plate heaped with food in front of me.

Valeriana sat by my side, her feet dangling, her small frame dwarfed by the adult-sized wooden chair. She tore into her food as soon as it arrived, making me wonder how long she'd gone without a proper meal. I noticed there was no meat on her plate, only vegetables and fruit, and a dish that was made with tiny eggs cut in half to reveal their bright orange centers. She ate those with relish, making sure to scoop enough sauce with each bite.

I went first for the wine and nearly moaned in pleasure at its fruity taste. The wine we'd been drinking on the road had been good, but this was absolutely exquisite. The food was also marvelous. Pork that melted in my mouth and was perfectly seasoned with figs and thyme. Soft toasted vegetables, some unknown to me, accompanied by the crunch of walnuts and the tang of a rich wine-based sauce. Barley and mushrooms garnished with herbs I didn't recognize, and warm bread rolls with butter melting at their center.

Jeondar sat across from me after having removed his weapons. He looked happy, something that was betrayed by a glint in his eyes, even when he wasn't smiling.

"I've ordered my favorite dessert for you." He winked at Valeriana. "I think you'll love it. You too, Dani."

I nodded in approval. "I've never been known for turning down any kind of dessert."

"Good to hear." I glanced around the table as I speared a piece of meat. "Where are the prince and Arabis?" I asked again.

"They've likely... gone to bed already."

I frowned, thinking of how Kalyll and Arabis always disappeared when the sun went down. Where had they gone? My mind was whirling with wild conjectures when I sensed the conversation taking a serious turn. The somber words drew my attention.

"The gates only remain closed at night," the king was saying, an elbow on the table as he used his forefinger to fiddle with a thumb ring. "It's been many, many years since we've had to do that." It didn't look as if the decision pleased him. "And now this," his dark gaze drifted to Valeriana, "what you said they've done to a dryad clan on our land." He pressed his fist to his mouth, anger simmering in his expression. "We shall send guards to protect those who live in Mid Crosswood." He nodded to himself, the announcement seeming to give him a modicum of peace.

"But your lands go far and wide, my lord," Silver said, "and there aren't enough guards to protect everyone."

"Perhaps there is something *you* can do to help," the king responded with enough bite in his voice that everyone at the table seemed to tense.

"He is, father. He is," Jeondar assured him.

The king's gaze drifted to Kryn, and the whole interaction reminded me that the Winter and Fall Courts—to which Silver and Kryn respectively belonged—aligned with the Unseelie Court, something that King Lywynn seemed to hold against them.

Jeondar threw a pleading look across the table, as if begging his father to see things differently. The king played with his ring again, then gave a slight nod to his son and steered the conversation to lighter topics.

"The Summer Solstice Ball is tomorrow night. It shall be a grand event. My queen has exhausted herself in preparation, just the reason she's already in bed, resting."

One of Jeondar's eyebrows went up at the mention of the queen, which made me realize he hadn't asked about her when we first arrived, and that it must mean said queen was probably not his mother. If I'd been away, and I'd just returned from a long trip, I would surely ask about my mother. It was also possible that, if she was his mother, they'd had a falling out. I figured I would find out sooner or later.

When we were done with our main courses, a pretty Fae girl with curly red hair down to her waist came around, carrying small porcelain plates topped with miniature tarts.

The tarts had a crumbly bottom and were topped with candied strawberries and cream whipped to a point. Valeriana and I wasted no time tearing into them. Jeondar watched closely for our reaction and nodded proudly when we both hummed in appreciation.

"That did not disappoint," I said.

The king and his other guests retired after finishing their dinner, leaving only our group behind. They shared a large decanter of wine between them and guzzled it like parched camels.

Silver hiccupped and swayed on his chair.

"You're such a lightweight," Kryn said.

He and Cylea appeared perfectly sober despite the rate at which they kept tipping entire glasses down their throats.

"I'd better stop." Silver pushed his glass away even as Cylea refilled it.

"Don't be such a bore." Cylea pushed a lock of blue hair behind her pointed ear. "We can sleep as late as we want to tomorrow."

Silver shook his head and glanced toward the door in the corner, the one through which the servants had been coming in and out.

"I have a date with a pretty redhead." He rose to his feet, his chair scraping the stone floor. Taking a deep breath, he shook his head as if to clear it, then headed out, weaving as if he wouldn't pass a breathalyzer test.

"We just got here and he can't keep it in his pants for one night," Cylea complained. "How about a game of Loots?" she asked Kryn.

He nodded. "Just one, then we raid the cellar."

"I'm sitting right here, you know?" Jeondar crossed his arms.

Kryn blew air through his nose. "Like you don't raid my cellar when you come to Thellanora."

Jeondar watched them go, shaking his head and smiling fondly. "They deserve a break, I suppose."

"What about you?" I asked.

"I have to meet with my father to give him a report."

Next to me, Valeriana nodded off for a second. She blinked rapidly and scrubbed at her face, fighting her fatigue.

"Looks like someone needs to go to sleep," I remarked, giving her a sidelong glance.

"I don't," she protested. "I'm perfectly all right."

Jeondar and I exchanged a knowing glance.

He got up from the table. "I'll get someone to show you to your chambers. In the morning, just come back here for breakfast."

Ten minutes later and after walking through several lavish halls and climbing a few sets of stairs, a tiny pixie with translucent wings and blue skin showed us to a chamber, a cloud of gold dust swirling around her. She waved a hand at the door and it opened. She fluttered inside, waving her little hands at a few lamps that bathed the room in warm light.

"The view is lovely from the balcony." She pointed at a set of double doors. "The washroom is that way, and that door leads to a closet with plenty of clothes for you, Abin Manael."

"Call me Dani, please."

She seemed dubious about my request and continued explaining. "If you need anything else, pull this," she pointed at a golden chord that hung at the side of a big canopy bed, "and I'll be here to help you. My name is Larina, by the way." She switched her attention to Valeriana, whose large green eyes scanned the place distrustfully. "I'll show you to *your* chamber. Come with me." She fluttered toward the door, her wings making a small whirring sound.

Valeriana sidled close to me as Larina glanced back with knitted eyebrows.

"She can stay with me." I put a hand on the girl's shoulder, who blinked gratefully at me.

"Very well. Safe dreams." Larina inclined her head and left.

"Why don't we check out the washroom?" I said, but Valeriana only peered longingly at the bed.

"Too tired for a bath?"

She nodded.

"Then how about we find something for you to sleep in?"

I walked toward the closet and threw the double doors open. Lights came alive of their own to reveal an ample space filled with beautiful garments, all perfectly sized for a woman my age. There were evening gowns, tunics, leggings, shoes for all purposes, and what looked like swimwear... or was it lingerie?

It was ridiculous.

I found a flowing tunic that could serve as a nightgown for Valeriana and walked back out into the room to find that she was already curled up in bed, sound asleep. I walked closer and watched her. She was so beautiful and tender. My heart tightened to think of all the pain she'd been through. Pulling the covers from the bottom of the bed, I folded them over her small body. She burrowed into their warmth, sighing, her face relaxing further as sleep took away her worries.

I was as exhausted as Valeriana and wouldn't have minded collapsing on the bed and letting sleep take me, except I sorely wanted a hot bath.

Rubbing the back of my neck, I walked into the bathroom and wasn't disappointed. A large marble tub was the focal point. It sat at the back of the space, a beautiful stained glass window depicting a peacock resting above it.

I sat on a turquoise settee and removed my shoes and clothes. Before I even reached the tub, water of perfect temperature started pouring down a golden faucet. Almost moaning, I sank down and let part of my worries be washed away, while the rest surrendered to my dreams once I crawled into bed next to the tiny dryad.

My eyes bolted open, and I nearly screamed as a hand pressed to my mouth.

"*Shh*, it's me, Cylea."

I blinked repeatedly, willing my heart to slow. It was beating out of control, adrenaline hot in my chest.

"Come with me." Cylea grabbed my arm and practically dragged me out of bed.

I glanced back at Valeriana. She stirred, but remained asleep.

"What is going on?" I asked once we were out in the hall.

"Come, quick!" She took off, urging me on.

I gathered the long tunic I'd worn to sleep and followed.

"It's Arabis," Cylea said. "She's hurt."

I moved faster then, realizing this was a medical emergency.

After several turns down a few long halls, we rushed into a large bedroom with a large bed in the middle. I rolled up my sleeves as I approached the bed and assessed the situation.

Arabis looked tiny on the massive bed, her face as pale as the sheets that cover her.

"What happened?"

Kryn—who sat on the other side of the bed, holding her hand—pulled the covers back to reveal a gaping wound in her middle and a whole lot of blood.

I'd learned to keep my reactions to myself, so my face remained stoic, giving nothing away. The wound was serious, though. It was a miracle she was still alive.

"Save her!" Kryn ordered.

"Clear the room," I said.

"C'mon, Kryn," Cylea tried to usher him out.

"I'm not going anywhere," he growled.

"At least get off the bed then," I said as I used my skills to take Arabis's vitals. Her blood pressure was low, and her heart was beating fast to compensate. I relaxed a little. It wasn't as bad as it looked.

Steadying my initial nerves, my training and experience kicking in, I focused on the wound, which was on the left side of her abdomen area. A piece of flesh was missing, the edges around it ragged. There were other puncture marks around it that immediately alerted me to the type of wound. These were bites from a large animal. I'd seen enough children bitten by dogs not to know what I was looking at.

I laser-focused my skill to evaluate the damage. I did my best to construct an image of her injury, the tissue around it, her vital organs. It was hard not having a visual aid. At the hospital, I would be using ultrasound to assess the exact nature of the damage. It would be fast, effective, and error-free. Still, the practice had dulled my natural skill. It took longer than it should have to assess the torn muscle tissue, but I was glad to find no injury to her stomach and kidney, which had been missed by a hair's breadth. Still, she had lost a lot of blood, which meant it had been a while since she'd been attacked.

"Her vital organs are intact," I said, trying to offer comfort to her friends. "She's lost a lot of blood, though, so I will lend her some of my energy."

As I spoke the words, I sent healing power into Arabis. She gave an audible sigh of relief, and the pinch expression on her face eased. A second sigh of relief came from Kryn.

With that done, I stretched my hands forward, held a few inches from the wound, and started repairing the damage, slowly knitting sinew together until the hole closed and a thin layer of pink skin was left in its place.

When I was done, I cracked my neck and pulled away from the bed. "All done," I announced. "She'll be fine. She needs to drink a lot of fluids."

Kryn rushed to Arabis's side and snatched her hand, looking relieved.

"What happened to her?" I asked Cylea.

"We... don't know," she responded, and something told me she wasn't telling the truth.

"That was an animal attack."

"I thought so."

"Where is the prince?" He had been with Arabis.

Cylea shrugged. "I hope he's all right. He... didn't come back with her."

The Seelie Prince was missing?! If that was the case, why didn't she look concerned?

"He knows how to take care of himself," she said when she noticed my surprise. "I wouldn't worry about him." She patted my shoulder and walked toward the bed.

Kryn took his green gaze away from Arabis for a moment to look at me.

"Thank you," he said. He was sincere and his attitude toward me was, for once, kind of nice.

"I'm glad she's all right," I said. "I'll go back to my room. If you need me again, just come get me."

CHAPTER 15

Despite how tired I was, I woke up early the next morning. It was barely the break of dawn, but my mind was already reeling, thinking about Arabis, the prince, Valeriana... everyone except myself.

It was a common problem: relegating my needs in favor of everyone else's.

The girl had crept closer to me in her sleep and was still out like a light. I slowly got out of bed, making sure not to disturb her, and went into the closet. I changed out of the long garment and donned the most practical clothes I could find: a red velvet tunic with embroidered edges, a pair of tan leggings, and knee-high brown leather boots. It was way fancier than I would've liked—especially when I tied a carved belt around my waist—but the Fae didn't favor jeans and T-shirts, so I had no other choice. I ran stiff fingers through my hair and went to put my hair up, but my ponytail holder broke. *Great!* I'd have to improvise something later.

I left the room, closed the door quietly behind me, then made my way back to the large dining room in search of something strong to drink. I foolishly wished for coffee, though I knew tea was my closest option.

A lock of hair fell in front of my face. I pushed it back. The palace was quiet and seemed empty, and I took my time going downstairs, walking slowly, lost in my own thoughts. When I arrived, food was already laid out on one end of the large table, sun spilling over it through a tall set of doors that led to what appeared to be a balcony. I thought I was the first one there until I noticed someone standing past the doors.

The set of the wide shoulders and the glint of raven blue hair were unmistakable. Prince Kalyll was standing with his hands on the railing, looking down on the city.

The harsh words he said to me yesterday echoed inside my mind, and I took a step back, determined to leave and come back later, except, just as I was about to turn away, he glanced over his shoulder and spotted me.

The brilliant sun bathed his features, making his intense blue eyes shine. Stubble lined his jaw, something I hadn't seen before. There were also large circles under his eyes and the undeniable tinge of bone-deep fatigue shaping his expression. He had always seemed so perfectly put together that seeing him like this made him feel more real and less like a male from myth and adventure.

He turned away from the brilliant morning and walked inside, his heavy boots tapping on the stone floor as he approached me.

He stopped a few feet away, his gaze roving over my face, seeming to take in my unbound hair as it flowed over my shoulders. A shiver ran down my spine as he scrutinized me, and I hated my reaction. It was incomprehensible and completely out of place.

Kalyll inclined his head. "I hope you slept well, Ms. Sunder."

I clenched my teeth together and raised my chin, anger building in my chest. "We're back to good manners, are we? Don't waste your breath."

I turned to leave, but he grabbed my elbow and stopped me. That stupid lock of hair fell in front of my face again.

"I wish to apologize for my behavior yesterday," he said. "For the impolite things I said to you."

Blinking up at him through the lock of hair, I resisted the urge to blow it out of the way. His hand abandoned my elbow, and he gently pushed the strand behind my ear. A shiver tiptoed down my spine. Somehow, I found the strength to pull away from him, breaking contact and despising the way my attention focused on the warm sensation his touch left behind.

He apologized, Dani. Focus on that.

So... his apology had sounded sincere enough, but I didn't want to deal with that either. Something was way off, and I wanted answers, but he wasn't going to tell me anything until we left Imbermore. I was tired of his reticence and half-explanation, so I just nodded.

"Sure thing," I said, turning away again. "Apology accepted."

"Please, don't go," he said, and there was so much yearning in his voice that my feet came to a halt of their own accord.

Slowly, I faced him and took him in for a second time. On closer inspection, I could sense his fatigue and exhaustion went deeper than only the physical. He was also emotionally drained, weighed down by his responsibility, perhaps. Or maybe by the haze of secrecy that seemed to surround everything about him.

"Eat breakfast with me?" He gestured toward the table and pulled a chair out.

I sat and started to pick up some food, but he brushed my hand away from the tongs I'd been about to grab. I tucked my hand under the table, rubbing the fingers he'd grazed.

"Allow me." He picked up my plate and went around, placing different things in it—an egg nestled in a silver holder, roasted meat, fresh fruit, pastries, more than I could eat in one sitting. When he was done, he deposited it in front of me.

Fancy Daniella Sunder being served by a prince. Yet another ridiculous thing.

He picked up a cup, filled it, placed it atop a small saucer, then handed it over.

"And a surprise," he said, then sat across from me and gathered a similar breakfast for himself.

I stared into the dark drink. "Is this... coffee?"

"It is." He poured a cup for himself. "One of the many things I enjoy from your realm."

That got my attention.

"I've spent some time there due to diplomatic endeavors," he said when he noticed my surprise. "And I found quite a bit to my liking, despite how different everything is. I hope that you can say the same thing about Elf-hame once you leave."

I made a sound in the back of my throat as I considered. "I like the wine so far... and Dandelion."

He smiled, his sculpted mouth stretching gently. It was a genuine enough smile, though it did nothing to erase the sadness in his eyes.

"Are you all right?" I asked, unable to help myself.

"I am. Thank you for inquiring."

"You're lying." The words jumped out of me even as I tried to hold them in.

His cobalt blue eyes locked with mine from across the table. I expected him to deny it, but he appeared resigned.

"What is wrong with you, *Kalyll*?" I used his name for the first time, which, judging by the raised eyebrow he gave me, he noticed all too well.

"Many things are wrong with me," he said.

"Are you... are you ill?" I couldn't shake the feeling that his behavior was caused by forces outside of his control. It was stupid. He was probably just a temperamental asshole prince, who could get away with treating people however he wanted whenever his mood soured.

"Ill?" he echoed, seeming amused for some reason. "No, I'm not ill. But enough about me," he waved a hand in the air, "tell me more about you." His attitude changed on a dime, going from reflective to casual.

I blinked at him, recognizing his behavior for what it was: a performance.

"That won't work with me," I said.

He took a sip of his coffee. "What do you mean?"

"You can't brush me off with platitudes. I don't do *shallow*."

"I see." One of his perfect eyebrows arched up. "Others will start coming down for breakfast soon, so why don't we finish eating and then take a walk? The gardens behind the summer palace are something to behold."

I nodded, feeling oddly nervous. After that, I was barely able to nibble on a pastry, though I had no trouble downing two cups of coffee.

Before anyone else made it to the table, Kalyll led me out of the dining room and down a hall that cut across a large kitchen. As we passed, the busy staff stopped what they were doing and bowed deeply to the Seelie Prince. I caught a glimpse of tons of food in different stages of preparation, and a large number of Fae of different species; such I'd never seen. There were people with wings, horns, tails, hooves, scales, and skin tones that would put a painter's palette to shame. I would've loved to stop and talk to all of them, but the prince gave me no time for more than a few nods and smiles.

As we reached the gardens, crossing under a stone arch, all thoughts of what we left behind flew right out of my mind. I sucked in a breath, awe washing over me.

"I told you the gardens were beautiful," Kalyll said, gesturing toward a stone path lined with emerald green grass, colorful plants, and trees draped in cascading purple flowers.

We walked in silence for some time as I admired a waterfall splashing into a pool of water strewn with water lilies. Next to it, there was a bush replete with blooming red roses. Kalyll cut one of them and offered it to me.

I took it with a shaking hand, unsure of what to say.

When we reached a secluded spot that faced the waterfall, the prince found a tree with swooping branches and we sat on a bench under its shade, a carpet of soft clover under our feet. I pushed a stubborn strand of hair away from my face and tucked it behind my ear. Gurgling sounds surrounded us, creating a private space, safe from prying eyes and ears.

"Where to begin?" Kalyll ran his thumb over his lower lip, thinking.

"I don't know," I said, staring at the rose. "Sometimes the beginning is a good place. Sometimes it's not."

"In this instance, I'm afraid it's the latter."

I opened my mouth to say something but didn't know what, so I waited. I was afraid that if I pushed him, he would clam up and tell me nothing.

"You must understand that you cannot repeat what I'm about to tell you to anyone. It would endanger many things, the most important of them, my people."

I nodded.

"Can I trust you?" His gaze seemed to reach deep inside me as he demanded an answer.

A part of me, the part that was still angry about being uprooted from my life, wanted to learn all his secrets just to use them against him, to turn his existence upside down, and then laugh in his face, gleefully enjoying my revenge. But that part of me was infinitesimal. It was the tiny devil on my shoulders that I never listened to because I always did what was right, because, like my youngest sister said, I was a goody-two-shoes. So when I answered him, it was with the conviction that I would never betray his confidence.

"You can trust me," I said.

He smiled gently. "I think I already knew that."

Taking a deep breath, he angled his body in my direction, causing his thigh to brush mine. His warmth seeped through my leggings, and I couldn't find it in me to shift positions to create some distance between us.

"You are not entirely wrong, Ms. Sunder. You asked me if I am ill, and perhaps that's not far from the truth. Something *is* wrong with me. Or perhaps wrong is the incorrect word and I should say... different. Recently, there have been... changes. None of it is good, especially the timing. These changes, they were always meant to happen, except I didn't know it." A muscle jumped in his jaw, and he glanced away from the water to look at me.

For some reason, my heart raced. I disguised my nervousness by tucking that stubborn lock of hair behind my ear, then wrung my hands together, fearing what he would say, sensing how significant this revelation would be, how critical to his job as a prince, how entangled with the reasons for my presence here, how central to the quest ahead of us, how... how... *everything*.

He went on. "You are a very perceptive woman, and I can tell that your mind has already been hard at work on this riddle. Undoubt-edly, you've noticed my absences during the night, and my change in temper before that." He looked up through the branches and leaves above us as if to check the time based on the sun's trajectory, the way Arabis always did. "At noon, I won't be quite myself anymore, and tonight, I will be unable to attend the Summer Solstice Ball."

Hanging from his every word, I pressed a hand to my chest and felt my heart racing as if it rested on my very fingers.

Kalyll ran a hand over his brow, then rubbed circles on his temple. He was quiet for a long time, and I sensed how difficult it was for him to keep going, to actually confide in me the closer he got to the truth. Without thinking, I pressed a hand to his thigh. He tensed under my touch, eyes flicking in my direction. Through his trousers, I felt hard muscle, latent strength that had been honed to lethal perfection.

"Why?" I asked. "Why will you be different?"

He stared at the ground. "Because... I'm cursed. Because my blood is cursed."

CHAPTER 16

*C*ursed? *His blood is cursed?*

What could he ever mean by that?

"I don't understand," I said.

"Sometimes I don't understand it myself." He chuckled sadly. "What you see now it's who I am. I have full control of my emotions, my temper—not to say I can't lose it sometimes." An apologetic shrug. "But after the sun reaches its peak, something else takes over, and I can only sit back and watch. Then at night... that something else does a lot more than control my temper. It changes me completely, turns me into a mindless monster that I'm completely and utterly incapable of stopping."

I remember the darkness swirling around his eyes, the bulging black veins as he spat biting words at me and almost killed Valeriana.

"That is why Arabis is always with you," I said. "Her power can stop you."

"Not always." His fists tightened until his knuckles turned white. "I hurt her last night. I almost killed her."

I gasped.

"I know you healed her, and I thank you greatly for it."

All I could do was shake my head to indicate it was nothing.

"You see, she and I stayed beyond the walls to ensure everyone's safety here in the palace. For half the night, I roamed the woods." His eyes grew dark and distant. "Then the beast got it in its head to enter the city. Arabis tried to stop me, and for the first time, I didn't listen to her. I attacked my friend and almost killed her. It took all of her strength to issue one final command. She was already wounded and the extra effort... it could have been her undoing." He met my eyes, his expression pleading. "If the beast doesn't listen to her anymore, what am I to do?" The last few words were a whisper full of dread and hopelessness.

I didn't know what to say, not that the lump in my throat would've allowed any words to come out.

"What will stop me tonight?" he asked. "The entire city will be in celebration, and without Arabis, the walls are not enough to keep me out." He rose to his feet in one fluid motion, anger rolling off of him. When he glanced at me, I expected to see those dark veins around his eyes, but his skin was clear.

I tried to think logically. "The walls are thick and high, and there are guards."

He answered with lethal calm. "The walls and guards don't stand a chance."

"There must be something else you can do."

"Kryn has an idea." His expression waivered between hopeful and defeated.

"That's... good."

We were quiet for a moment. He walked to the edge of the pool and stood with his back to me. He took several deep breaths, and when he came back and sat, his face was clear, his demeanor serene. As my mind whirled with questions, I felt his attention on me. He was assessing me, judging my reaction.

At last, he said, "You don't seem very shocked about what I've just revealed—not like Arabis and the others were."

"Maybe it's because I don't understand all the implications."

He shook his head. "No, that's not it. I'm sure you grasp the precariousness of my situation and what it means for a Seelie Prince to be... thus encumbered. I think maybe it's because you are very perceptive and empathetic."

What he was saying sounded absurd. He barely knew me, and the few interactions we'd had weren't enough to give him that kind of insight into who I was.

"I can tell you think I'm talking nonsense." He seemed amused by that. "But I will keep my own counsel."

"You're entitled to do that, I suppose."

He grunted deep in his throat, and the sound seemed to bury itself under my skin in a way that was entirely too much like a physical touch.

Eager to dismiss the sensation, I blurted out, "I assume that this... curse is the reason I'm here."

"It is."

"You think I can somehow break it, then?"

"No."

I frowned, confused. "Then what?"

"I'm not sure."

My confusion deepened. "What gave you the idea that I can do anything about it? Why kidnap me?"

"The Envoy told me you would help."

"The Envoy? Who the hell is that?" It was my turn to stand and be angry. I even left the rose on the bench.

"She's a powerful seer. As the future king, I was required to visit her after my last birthday. She was supposed to tell me I would be a good leader for my people. Instead, she foretold something quite different."

"What exactly?"

"I'm not at liberty to share all the details at the moment."

"Why not?" I demanded.

"What the Envoy tells the prince is not to be shared with anyone else."

"And I supposed it was this Envoy's bright idea to send us on horseback."

He shrugged, giving nothing away.

"What kind of *bull* is that? And I'm sure you've spent enough time in my realm to know what part of *bull* I've left unsaid," I snapped, losing the bit of calm that remained in me. The prince was so well-spoken that I felt cross talking like this, but whatever. He could bite me if he didn't like it.

Instead of offended, he appeared amused, judging by the smile he seemed to be fighting.

"My distress amuses you? Is that it?"

He put on a serious expression. "No. Not in the least."

"Then why do you look like the cat that gobbled up the canary?"

"For no reason."

"*Bullshit.*" I let him have the whole damn word.

"Ms. Sunder, forgive me. I don't wish to upset you."

"Stop calling me Ms. Sunder. It makes me think you're talking about my mother."

"It is the only thing you've allowed me to call you."

"I know, but I..." *Dammit.* My anger had gotten the best of me. Now what? I threw my hands up in the air. "You can call me whatever you want. I don't care."

He rose from the bench and stood directly in front of me. "Then I shall call you Daniella." He pronounced every syllable as if savoring them. "It's a beautiful name."

Damn all the witchlights if his raspy voice and the way he was looking at me as he said my full name didn't send a thrill through me. What was happening? Why did he have this effect on me despite the fact he'd undone my life in one swift stroke?

He took a step closer, his hypnotic eyes capturing mine. "You are—"

But I never learned what he was about to say because Silver came jogging down the path. "There you are!"

Kalyll stepped away from me with a jerk and arranged his expression into something bland. "Is something the matter?"

Silver stopped. He'd been running, but he didn't even look a little winded. "Your presence is required." He looked straight at me.

"My presence?"

Even Kalyll looked surprised at that.

"It's the girl," Silver said. "She woke up and didn't find you in bed. She came down to the dining room looking for you, and I don't know what happened, but she..." He shook his head at a loss. "She's holed up under a chair, holding a knife and hissing at everyone."

"Oh, God." I had completely forgotten about Valeriana.

Feeling guilty, I ran up the path the way we'd come, Kalyll and Silver right on my heels. I rushed through the kitchen and made it back to the dining room. I heard the commotion just as I crossed the threshold.

"Would someone hurry up and do something?" an annoyed female voice said. "I'd like to eat my breakfast in peace."

I ran in to find Jeondar and Cylea with their backs to the fireplace. They were facing an upholstered chair that sat against the wall, while the king, Kryn, and a woman I hadn't seen before sat at the table.

"It's all right, girl," Cylea was saying. "No one's going to hurt you."

"I want Dani," Valeriana demanded.

Without a greeting, I ran to Cylea's side, followed her gaze, and saw Valeriana's face peeking from behind the chair, a knife glinting in her hand.

"I'm right here," I said. "It's fine. Everything's fine."

Valeriana hesitated for a moment, then dropped the knife with a clatter, crawled out, and wrapped her arms around my waist. I smoothed her hair and whispered soothing words. She was trembling, and as I tried to peel her away from me, she only held on tighter, her large green eyes nailed to the person sitting next to the king.

From the small but intricate crown the female wore around her head, I could only assume she was the queen. She was a haughty-looking Fae with glimmering blue skin and long black hair adorned with sparkling sapphires. Her pointed ears were twice as long as anyone I'd met so far and ended in too-sharp points. She wore heavy, dark blue makeup around her eyes and had long lashes that appeared fake, but I had a feeling were not. Two lines of glittery powder ran from the top of her head down to her eyebrows. They continued under her eyes and almost reached her jaw. She was beautiful. There was no denying that, but there was a certain edge about her that immediately put me on my guard.

And I wasn't the only one who felt that way. Clearly, Valeriana did, too. Though she'd gone a bit overboard with her reaction. Maybe she was too wild to live among this kind of people.

I glanced toward Jeondar. "I will take her back to our room."

The king rose from his seat at the head of the table. "Before you leave, allow me to introduce Queen Belasha of the Winter Court."

The Winter Court? Interesting.

The blue-skinned female twisted her azure-painted mouth and scrutinized me with a raised eyebrow. I didn't like the way she was looking at me, not one bit, but I remembered my manners for civility's sake.

"It's a pleasure to meet you, Your Majesty."

"Likewise." She speared a piece of melon and stuffed it in her mouth, quickly looking bored and as if she'd forgotten I was there.

Jeondar appeared embarrassed. Clearly, this woman was not his mother. The king, however, only smiled, a male besotted by beauty and blinded by love. His smile only grew wider when he noticed Kalyll standing behind him.

"Prince Adanorin," he exclaimed, respectfully pressing a fist to his chest and bowing.

They exchanged pleasantries while I wondered if it would be impolite to sneak out. The king pulled Kalyll to the table, offering him the seat to his right. He ended up sitting next to Kryn, who leaned in to whisper something in his ear as I tiptoed out of the room, Valeriana practically running ahead of me.

Too late, I remembered I'd left the rose Kalyll gave me behind.

CHAPTER 17

O nce in our chamber, I led Valeriana to the bed and sat her on
top of it. "Are you all right?"

She frowned, looking uncertain.

"There was no reason to get scared."

"Yes, there was."

"Oh?"

"That female..." She trailed off and hugged thin arms around her
torso.

"You mean the queen?"

A quick nod.

I sat next to the girl, my legs dangling off the tall canopy bed. "She
looked kind of mean, didn't she?"

"She looked like *her*."

I turned my head to face the girl. "Her?"

"The female... the female that killed my father."

I felt a twitch in my chest and wrapped an arm around Valeriana's
back, pulling her close to me. "I'm sorry. That must have been really
scary for you."

"She's bad."

I understood she meant the queen because pointing out that the
female who killed her father was bad would've been redundant.

"Just because they look alike doesn't mean the queen is like that other female," I said carefully, hoping my words wouldn't upset her further.

"You saw her. She has hatred in her eyes, just like the other one did."

I didn't think I could argue with that. I could see why Valeriana would think this, though hatred was probably the wrong word. Self-importance, arrogance, narcissism might have fit better, but the girl was too young to know the difference.

"Well," I said, "you don't have to worry about her. You can stay here."

"But you left."

"I did.

I dealt with children enough to know that they could get clingy and that, if allowed, it wouldn't be good for either of us.

"I was hungry," I said, "and you were asleep. I'm certain you're safe here, even if I have to go somewhere." I was firm to make sure she understood I wouldn't stay cooped up in here, even if it was her choice to do so.

She didn't seem pleased with that, but didn't argue further. I sat for a long moment, thinking I should check on Arabis at some point, then jumped off the bed and pulled the thick, golden cord the pixie had indicated. Within minutes, there was a tiny knock at the door.

"Good morning, Larina." I smiled as the pixie fluttered into the room, traces of golden dust trailing behind her.

"All the sunshine to you." She inclined her head. "How may I help you?"

"I'm sorry to bother you as there is plenty of food downstairs, but do you think you could get something for Valeriana to eat?"

"Of course, I will be back swiftly." She was gone before I could even ask the girl what she would like to eat and before I could think to say thank you.

I turned to Valeriana. "While we wait, how about a bath?"

I was afraid she would refuse, as children are known to hate baths, but she nodded eagerly and rushed into the bathroom. When I got there, I found her naked, her dress discarded on the marble floor, and her wooden crown resting on top of it. The tub was already at work, filling itself with water that I knew would keep its perfect temperature until the end of the bath.

The girl climbed in and placed her fingers under the running stream, wiggling them, enjoying the feel of that precious liquid. I knelt by the tub and grabbed a bar of jasmine-scented soap.

"I can wash your hair." I held up the soap.

She nodded, and I scooped water into a lightweight wooden, seashell-shaped container.

Valeriana closed her eyes as I rubbed her scalp and worked the soap to build suds in her bushy green hair. When we were done, I went into the closet and fetched clean clothes for her. I chose a similar dress to the one she'd been wearing since I knew children appreciated familiarity. There hadn't been children's clothes in the closet last night, but they had appeared somehow. The dress was light green and had a fitted top with a skirt made of overlapping pieces of sheer fabric. It came down to her knees and complimented her skin tone perfectly.

When we walked out of the bathroom, we found a full breakfast set on the console table by the door, which Valeriana treated exactly the way she'd treated dinner last night: ravenously. She seemed content enough, and that set me at ease for the moment.

A knock came at the door, and I opened it thinking it was Larina, except Prince Kalyll, himself, stood on the other side. I stared up at him in surprise. He had changed and was wearing all black. His shoulder-length hair was pulled into a ponytail, and the scruff that had covered his jaw was gone. He looked devastatingly handsome, yet my fingers seemed to tingle with regret as if they longed to experience the now-gone roughness across the length of his jaw.

I tore my gaze from his face, suddenly concerned about the way my body seemed to respond to him.

As if you will ever touch the Seelie Prince like that. The male wasn't only out of my league... he was out of my species, my way of life, my entire realm. *Get a grip.*

"Is something the matter?" I asked, without looking back up.

"I would like to ask for your help with something."

"Of course, give me a moment." I turned to Valeriana. "I need to go, but I'll be back."

"When?"

I glanced over my shoulder back at the prince. He shrugged and shook his head to indicate he had no idea. It wasn't wise to leave Valeriana unattended for an indefinite amount of time—not after this morning.

"Um, would you be comfortable if Larina keeps your company?"

"I like pixies," she said. "One of my best friends is a pixie. They're good folk."

"Good." I pulled the cord again, and Larina appeared behind the prince. She hovered there, her head inclined respectfully.

"Larina," I said, "I know you must have a thousand duties, but do you think you could stay with Valeriana while I go with the prince?"

"I'm here to fulfill your wishes, and if my services aid Prince Adanorin in any way, I am honored."

Kalyll bowed slightly, the embodiment of charm. "I am grateful, Abin Manael."

Larina's cheeks turned violet, and I figured that was how a blue-skin person looked when they blushed. The pixie fluttered into the room, and as I stepped into the hall and closed the door behind me, I sensed I was leaving Valeriana in good hands.

The prince led me to a large study where Cylea, Kryn, Silver, and Jeondar were seated comfortably around a low table, while Arabis reclined on a chair, feet up on an ottoman, and a hand pressed to her stomach. The space had an open, airy feel thanks to a city-facing balcony similar to the one found in the dining room. The sound of rushing water came in through it, as well as a fresh breeze that smelled of distant rain and sweet flowers.

Arabis put her hands up in the air. "Welcome to the Sub Rosa Circle, Daniella Sunder."

CHAPTER 18

The Sub Rosa Circle?

Sub Rosa as in secret? It had to be. I'd read many old texts in my quest to improve my healing skills. It was something I started doing in high school, something I quite enjoyed, and it was in those texts where I'd encountered the term. In my realm and this one, the rose had an ancient history as a symbol of secrecy and undercover things, which was exactly what this quest appeared to be.

Arabis smirked, and it was obvious that the name was a joke they used amongst themselves. I quickly assessed her from a distance. She was much recovered, a feat of her rapid Fae healing abilities.

"Kalyll said he let you into our little secret." Cylea patted the seat next to her, and I sat without a word, assaulted by an odd feeling of belonging, as if by stepping into this room I had crossed an invisible line, and I was finally inside the circle with them—not just standing at the fringes.

A minute ago, there had been no going back home because I didn't know the way and I didn't want to die. Now, as six pairs of eyes regarded me as one of their own, my reasons for staying did a one-eighty. Everyone's demeanor was different, even Kryn's, if only slightly. It was as if the trust Kalyll had offered me by telling me the truth had extended to them. I'd always had something like that with my family, but never with friends. In fact, I had few of those, and I certainly wouldn't have trusted any of them with a secret like Kalyll's.

Did their smiles mean I wasn't only inside their Sub Rosa Circle but also their friendship circle? The thought of it made me strangely emotional. It was at that moment that I understood the depth of their friendship for the first time. If they could trust me by proxy, it meant they trusted each other blindly, maybe even with their lives.

There was only one problem: I only knew part of the truth. There was more. I knew there was, which meant Kalyll's trust extended only so far. So even though I was inside the circle, I was still far from the center. Either way, I was deep enough that I wouldn't be able to jump out if I tried. But even as scary as it all felt, the promise of belonging, of friendship, was alluring.

Funny how I never realized I was missing something.

Kryn, sitting to my left, leaned forward, picked up a crystal decanter, poured an amber-colored drink, and offered it to me.

I blinked in surprise.

He inclined his head. "This comes from your realm—one of Kalyll's finds. I guess it's not all bad over there."

I took the drink and looked into his emerald eyes. They weren't exactly friendly. Yet, there was a level of acceptance in them, even if it seemed reluctant. His gaze flicked toward Kalyll as if asking *happy now?* The prince's only sign of acknowledgment was a slight crinkling of his eyes.

After a sip of my drink, which turned out to be the smoothest Scotch I'd ever tasted, Kalyll sat on the arm of the sofa across from me, where Jeondar and Silver were also sipping from glasses similar to mine.

"Glenfiddich single malt. 1937 rare collection," Kalyll said.

"So this is why it's too expensive for the likes of me to afford a fine drink," I said, "what with hoity-toity Fae princes paying whatever price from their endless coffers and taking it across the veil."

Kryn chuckled, almost despite himself.

"Hoity-toity?" Silver echoed.

"It means supercilious," Kryn explained.

I gave the redhead a raised eyebrow.

He shrugged. "I've spent some time in your realm."

That came to me as a surprise.

Kalyll sat quietly, enduring the talk about him with barely a roll of his eyes. He seemed used to being the butt of the joke and took no offense.

"Dani—can I call you Dani now?" Silver went on without waiting to see if I agreed. "Dani seems to agree with you about Kalyll, Kryn."

"Well, it's not hard to see that his coffers are deep and, indeed, keep his ass spoiled," Kryn responded, unwilling to admit he and I had anything in common.

"There has to be a benefit to offset all the nuisances I must endure," Kalyll said, making a flourish with his hand and acting all prince-like.

I smirked. I'd never heard him make a joke, and I found myself wondering how different he must be from the prince I knew so far.

"Yeah," Cylea said. "Example number one... you." She stared pointedly at Kryn.

"Thank you." Kalyll looked to the heavens. "Someone recognizes my plight."

"*Pshaw*, you would be lost without me." Kryn batted a hand at the prince.

"This banter is very charming," Arabis said, "but we don't have long before noon, and if Dani is able to help, it may take time. So let's get down to business. Shall we?"

Kalyll began explaining immediately, turning his full attention to me. "Remember how I explained earlier that the city walls won't stop me from coming in tonight?"

I nodded.

"So instead of keeping me out, we will attempt to keep me in."

"Like locked up in a cell somewhere?"

"Correct."

"But if the thick walls and guards can't stop you, how can a cell?"

"I will be tied up with Qrorium chains."

"Qrorium?" I echoed. "I assume that's some special material."

Jeondar pushed to the edge of the sofa. "Yes, it's a rare metal, very strong. My father has a set of chains that was once used to restrain a dragon."

"And it will be enough to hold Kalyll?"

"Yes?" Cylea said, but it sounded like a question.

Wait a minute? They were worried that Kalyll would be able to break the type of chains that could hold down a dragon? To think of that level of strength contained in Kalyll was mind-boggling. I shivered.

"As you can see, we are not confident," Kalyll said. "And this is where you come in."

I leaned forward.

"Kryn had an idea," the prince went on. "He thought you might be able to concoct a brew that will keep me subdued."

"Mind you," Kryn jumped in, "we've tried all sorts of things already. Nothing has worked. Stillstem, which can knock giants on their asses for an entire day, kept him down for a matter of minutes."

My mind already whirling with possibilities, I jumped to my feet and started pacing in front of one of the bookshelves. No one said anything, but I could feel their eyes on me.

Stillstem was a heavy anesthetic, too strong for humans. I was aware of clinical trials in my realm that had failed even when stillstem was used in infinitesimal doses. If it hadn't kept Kalyll asleep for long, what else could?

He had mentioned not being able to control his emotions.

I turned back to the group. "Did you try marsh flower?"

At the hospital, I used marsh flower to calm anxious patients. It didn't always knock people out, but it relaxed the nervous system and had a calming effect on strong emotions.

"We did," Arabis said. "It might've had a small effect."

"Was it administered in its pure form?" I asked, already suspecting the answer.

"It was."

"That's what I thought." It seemed no one here had figured out that combining marsh flower with stinging nettle compounded its effects. "And did he drink the stillstem?"

Arabis nodded. "Yes, we gave it to him in tea form."

"I think there's something I can try, but I need a few things. Is there an apothecary we can go to or a place like Yalgrun's Wares in Pharowyn?"

"Imbermore has it all." Cylea jumped to her feet. "I can take you."

"This is not a dress shopping trip, Cylea." Kryn gave her a pointed look.

She rolled her eyes. "I know that."

"Do you?" Arabis stood, a hand on her middle as she winced.

Kryn made as if to also stand, looking at Arabis in concern for an instant. Then, as if remembering he wasn't supposed to care, he leaned back, crossed his legs, and examined his fingernails.

Arabis started toward the door. "I'll go."

"No, you won't. Doctor's orders," I said emphatically. "Cylea and I can take care of it."

"I'll come with you," Silver offered.

I glanced up at Kalyll.

"I would like to accompany you, but I have matters to discuss with King Elladan," he said, and I felt a twinge of regret at not having him show me around the beautiful city I'd only glimpsed last night.

"And Kryn and I need to do the same," Jeondar said.

Cylea practically skipped toward the door, the blue tunic she wore fluttering behind her. Its fabric was see-through, revealing the exact shape of her breasts and almost giving a preview of her nipples. She looked beautiful and lighthearted, ready to conquer the world with a radiant smile.

Arabis hobbled forward. Kryn offered her his arm, but she dismissed him.

"I'm not that crippled *or* desperate," she said, standing straighter and leaving the room.

Kalyll hung back, and as I followed after the others, he caught my gaze.

"May I have a word, Daniella?" he said.

Kryn closed the door to the study on his way out, leaving Kalyll and me alone in the room.

"I... want to thank you," he said, closing the distance between us and standing only a couple of feet away. "I know you don't have much of a choice, but your willingness means a lot to me."

"It's what I do," I said. "Concocting a remedy for you suits me."

"Don't disparage it. It means a lot to me."

That stubborn lock of hair slid out of place again, and I swatted it away with irritation.

Kalyll reached a hand behind his head and unbound his hair in one quick motion.

"May I?" He held up a strip of leather, then walked behind me.

Light fingers gathered my hair, sending shivers as they brushed the tender skin of my neck. I bit my lower lip to stop my body from trembling. I heard him inhale as if he were taking in my scent. *Oh, God!*

"There." He came back around. "Better?"

All I could do was give him a weak nod.

He held my gaze. Reluctantly, as if he were fighting the urge, his eyes slid down to my lips.

Cylea knocked on the door. "C'mon, the morning hours are wasting away."

Both Kalyll and I jumped.

He bowed slightly and awkwardly. "Thank you again." He walked to the door and opened it. "I'll be waiting for your return."

CHAPTER 19

B efore leaving, I ran back to the room to check on Valeriana. As I approached the door, I heard her giggling and leaned in my ear to listen. She and Larina were playing, and from the sounds of it, they were having a lot of fun.

"You will never get me," Valeriana was saying. Scampering steps echoed inside the room.

"Come back here, you treacherous toad. I will turn your hair into lettuce leaves if you don't give me back my crown. I am your queen, you rascal."

Valeriana giggled again, and I couldn't help but smile. I backed away from the door. They were doing just fine without me. I would have to do something to thank Larina.

I walked back and found Cylea and Silver waiting for me.

"Hurry, human," Silver said.

"Don't get your panties in a wad. I'm coming," I said.

"Panties in a wad?" He raised a platinum eyebrow.

"It means *don't get upset over nothing*."

He nodded appreciatively. "You'll have to teach me more of your sayings."

"Please, don't." Cylea shook her head.

Ten minutes later, we were exiting the palace.

"We should go to Ren's Runes," Silver suggested.

"We're not going there," Cylea said adamantly. "You only want to go there because The Veiled Face is nearby. We're going to The Sage Crystal."

"I feared you would say that." He ran a hand through his cropped platinum hair and veered in a different direction. "I'll be seeing you later."

"You're a bastard, you know that?" Cylea called out. "Gah, he's insufferable. You can never count on him."

He waved without looking back, his gait all swagger, which many of the ladies walking down the street seemed to appreciate.

"What's The Veiled Face?" I asked, though I could very well guess the answer.

"A whorehouse," she answered plainly.

We walked in silence for a few blocks, and I took the opportunity to appreciate my surroundings, practically gaping at every structure we passed: ornate clock towers with canals running under their arched porticos; majestic fountains with jets of water shooting over statues of nymphs, sirens, satyrs, and all manner of fae creatures; gardens hanging with myriads of flowers that turned the air sickly sweet with their scent; small floating houses traversing the canals in every direction.

"What do you think of Imbermore?" Cylea asked in her husky voice.

"It's unlike anything I've ever seen."

"That's probably the same thing I would say if I visited your realm."

"That's true."

"I've never seen a car. Kalyll and Kryn have told me about them, and they certainly sound interesting."

"Rush hour would certainly make your jaw drop." Though probably not in a good way.

After a few blocks, we entered a commercial area with many stores adorned with carved wooden signs.

"Just another block." Cylea pointed ahead.

With the novelty of the city wearing off a bit, my thoughts turned in a different direction. "So... how do you know Kalyll?"

"We all grew up together. My father is a duke, friends with the Spring Court king. Growing up, I spent many summers in Elyndell."

"So you are all royalty?"

She nodded. "Kryn's father is an earl and part of the Fall Court Council. And Silver's mother is a baroness. She is lady-in-waiting to the Winter Queen. Not a job I envy. His father died in battle, so Silver is all she's got."

"So, how long have you known each other?"

"If you want to know our ages, just ask, Dani."

Shit! She saw right through me. I smiled apologetically.

Cylea laughed. "Kalyll is one-hundred and twenty-six."

I gulped because the male was a hundred years older than me and that made my head spin. Also, because Cylea mentioned the prince's age and no one else's. Why would she do that? Her raised eyebrow and crooked grin gave me the answer. She could tell I liked the prince.

Damn, my back-stabbing, traitorous body.

"Um, the Qrorium chains," I quickly changed the subject, "you didn't sound very sure about them."

Her expression grew pensive. "When Kalyll shifts... he's very strong."

"Shifts? What do you mean?"

"Oh, he didn't mention that part?"

"No. Well, he did say he changes, but I thought he was referring to his temperament. He called himself a beast, but I didn't think..."

"It's not only his temperament." She didn't elaborate. In fact, she tried to deflect by pointing to a dress shop. "Oh, what a lovely gown. I wish we had time to go inside."

"What does he shift into?" I asked, determined to get my answers.

Her blue eyes narrowed. "You should let him tell you."

"Why not you?"

"He's very sensitive about this whole thing."

"Don't you think I should know?"

She moved her hands up and down as if weighing something invisible. "There is lots to know, and it's all very sensitive information."

"And you all don't trust me," I added what she left unsaid.

"I don't mean—"

"Yes, you do. And it's fine. I totally understand." I tried to act like I didn't care, but for some stupid reason, it hurt my feelings to be left out, to learn that there was another circle within the circle.

She threw her hands up in the air. "It's not like you don't know already."

"Huh?"

"You saw him, Dani."

"What are you talking about?"

"That wolf that almost ate you. That was him."

My mouth hung open as shock tingled its way down my spine and the image of that ferocious, massive creature flashed before my eyes.

"He told us that he chased you into the barrens. He remembers everything he does when he's like that, even if he can't stop himself. I think that's one of the reasons it's so hard for him."

I struggled to get the image of those huge teeth and strange talons out of my head and process what she was saying.

"Every morning, he's so mad at himself. Not like today, though. He was *destroyed* after what he did to Arabis."

I'd seen it firsthand when I ran into him in the dining room. He had seemed lost.

"I really hope that whatever you concoct helps him," Cylea said. "He's so dangerous, unstoppable. If he gets loose here..." She gestured with her hands and shook her head. "I don't even want to think of the casualties, of how it will affect him. We've been on the road ever since this started, and all along Arabis had been able to control him, but..." She trailed off, her expression pinching in worry.

"I can't guarantee that it will," I said, finally finding my voice and feeling the true bulk of the responsibility that had landed on my shoulders. "It could take many tries to find the right ingredients, the right doses. Maybe we need a different plan, a better one."

"There is no other plan, Dani. He said that the beast *wants* to get into the city and cause chaos, even if he goes beyond the walls and rides as far away as he can on Stormheart, he would make it back in half the time, and he would get in. We were counting on Arabis keeping him in check, but..."

"Witchlights!" I'd known the situation was bad, but having the image of that wolf in my mind drove it all home as nothing else could.

Cylea stopped in front of a heavy, arched door. The sign above it read The Sage Crystal and depicted a bearded, long-robed man holding a staff with a glowing green gem at its tip. In essence, a sage holding a green crystal. Very clever.

She paused as she grabbed the doorknob and glanced back at me. "This had better work, Dani. No one can find out about him. No one. Do you understand?"

I did understand. If his people found out he was an out-of-control monster, it would undermine his rule. No question about that, except... there was more. I knew there was more. Some other secret they hadn't shared with me. Either way, I had no other choice but to help.

"I will do my best, Cylea, but I can't guarantee anything. You have to understand that. I just learned about all of this today. I don't doubt I can eventually come up with something to help him. That's how much confidence I have in my skills, but you better pray I have a lucky break and I get it on my first try. Otherwise, you'd better hope those chains hold."

She blinked several times, as if reassessing me. "Confidence looks good on you, Dani. You should wear it more often." She turned, opened the door, and entered The Sage Crystal.

CHAPTER 20

The Sage Crystal made Yalgrun's Wares look like a vending machine compared to a superstore. The place was ten times as big, but it wasn't the size that mattered. Not in this instance. It was the variety of ingredients and artifacts that made the difference.

"This place is amazing!" My gaze followed the length of a floor-to-ceiling cabinet with hundreds of tiny drawers labeled in perfect scroll. "I could spend days here."

"We don't have days. We have an hour, so we better go to Lady Thaciana directly."

Cylea hurried along toward the back of the store, passing tables laden with wrapped herbs, dried mushrooms of rare species, dropper bottles filled with dozens of precious essences, tinctures, powders, rolled-up scrolls labeled with spell names, tiny mirrors, bones, mortar and pestle sets crafted from many different materials, candles, figurines, the works!

I'm in heaven! It certainly smelled like it. The combination of herbal scents was nearly intoxicating to someone like me.

Several attendants watched us go, their admiring gazes reluctantly switching from Cylea to me. They scanned me with distrust, surely unaccustomed to seeing humans this far from any trading post. Something in me wanted to shrink at their scrutiny, but I kept my chin up and smiled politely. If I was the first human they'd ever met, I considered it my job to give them a good impression of my kind.

"All the sunshine to you, Abin Manael," Cylea greeted a female, who sported something I'd never seen on a Fae: wrinkles. If she were human, I would have calculated her age somewhere above eighty, but she wasn't, so I didn't dare try to put a number to it.

Lady Thaciana was sitting behind a wide counter, a shelf with hundreds of bottles behind her. She had lush gray hair that fell in loose curls to her shoulders. She wore a forest green dress with delicate lace around the collar and the end of the long sleeves. A brown sash adorned with silver buttons circled her small waist.

"All the sunshine to you, child," she said in a gravelly voice like a smoker's. Her green eyes and full attention quickly shifted to me.

A cat meowed, and for the first time, I noticed a feline perched across her shoulders, partially hidden by her gray hair. The cat's hair matched hers almost to perfection, but not only that, his eye color also matched his owner's.

Cylea cleared her throat. "Lady Thaciana, this is Daniella Sunder. She's a friend of mine and a very talented healer. She's in search of some ingredients and implements, and I told her this was the best place in Imbermore to acquire what she needs."

"I thank you for such a generous endorsement." Lady Thaciana gave a slight bow.

The cat jumped off her shoulders and onto the counter. It examined Cylea, then me. After another meow, it jumped to the floor and disappeared from view.

Lady Thaciana reached under the counter and procured a piece of parchment and a piece of graphite. "You may write what you need here, and I will procure it for you."

"Thank you." I took the graphite and scribbled the ingredients first, then paused, unsure whether or not they knew what a syringe was and if they had one.

Then I decided that someone who owned a place like this must have many years of experience in the trade and would endeavor to make themselves familiar with all healing techniques available to them. The Fae knew about our realm just as well as we knew about theirs, and the treaty we had in place allowed for all kinds of "cross-training."

I finished my list and pushed it in Lady Thaciana's direction. She picked it up with a bony, wrinkled hand and quickly perused its contents. She picked up the piece of graphite, jotted something on the list, then turned to one of the attendants, a dwarf barely taller than the counter whom I hadn't noticed before.

"Dedron, fill this order, please," she said.

He quickly disappeared through the back door, reading the list through round spectacles and stroking a long beard.

Lady Thaciana turned to Cylea. "I hear the prince is at the palace."

"He is." Cylea nodded.

"He will be the talk of the ball, then."

Cylea only offered a smile. The prince would be chained and drugged. He would be conspicuous in his absence, which would certainly be a reason to gossip about him.

"I still remember the first time he came to Imbermore," Lady Thaciana said. "He was only a boy."

"How long ago was that?" Cylea asked.

She thought for a moment. "I guess about a hundred and ten years or so."

The reminder of Kalyll's age made my stomach twist.

"Even then, all the young females lined up to see him," the lady added.

"It sounds like not much has changed." Cylea chuckled.

"He is a handsome fellow. I've met him twice. Made me wish I was younger." She let out a croaky laugh.

"It doesn't hurt that he'll be the king one day." Cylea's comment sounded jaded, which made me think she'd probably found a good number of queen wannabes among Kalyll's admirers. Apparently, there were gold diggers everywhere.

"For me, that is the only drawback," Lady Thaciana said. "Being queen... what a nuisance."

She was about to say something else when Dedron came back carrying what looked like a shoebox. He placed the box in front of Lady Thaciana with a slight bow. She halfway lifted the lid, gave a quick look, then pushed the box toward me. I reached for it and was about to open it when Cylea gave me a nearly imperceptible shake of the head, as if it was considered rude to ensure nothing was missing. The Fae were weird.

I gave the box a tap. "Um, thank you."

Lady Thaciana wrote something on a piece of paper and handed it to Cylea, who read it, then reached into her pocket and procured two gold coins.

Witchlights! Two gold coins?! I've never spent more than ten silvers at Yalgrun's, which was about two hundred dollars. Two gold coins were—I quickly did some mental math, translating from coppers to silvers to golds—over two thousand dollars. *Holy shit!* That syringe cost a pretty penny.

Cylea bowed. "It was a pleasure seeing you, Lady Thaciana. Until we meet again."

On our way back to the palace, I held the box close to my chest. "This better work for two gold coins."

"The gold is of no consequence, Dani. If it works, the king's crown would be a worthy price."

Way to make the heavy weight on my shoulders triple.

CHAPTER 21

At the brutal pace Cylea set, we made it back to the palace in no time. Kryn was waiting for us, pacing down the length of a long rug in the foyer of the side entrance through which we'd left.

"Finally," he said in greeting, then led us through many labyrinthine corridors and down a set of winding stone steps that ended in what looked like a forgotten section of the palace. It was a windowless space that revealed itself when a few sconces came to life on their own, as if they sensed our presence.

The area was filled with unused furniture, covered in sheets. Past the cramped, relic-strewn front, there were three doors. Kryn opened the one to the left. The hinges squeaked and the bottom scraped the stone floor. More sconces came on beyond the door to reveal a cavernous space that felt like some sort of subterranean cave. The sound of trickling water came from the back.

My eyes adapted slowly to the dimly lit area, and following the sound of water, I found a pool of water that disappeared into a dark tunnel.

Kryn turned to me. "Can you work here?"

I glanced around. "I need a table, water, and a flame. The rest should be in here." I held up the box.

"Water?" He pointed toward the pool in the back.

"Is it clean?"

"Yes. Suitable for drinking even."

"Then it should do."

"Good. There should be a table out here." Kryn left the room.

I followed Cylea's gaze and noticed a pile of chains coiled on the ground. "Those held a dragon once," she said absently, her blue eyes scanning the large space. "They're made from the rarest, most expensive metal known to us, and now they lay here forgotten."

Kryn came back carrying a mid-size table as if it weighed nothing. He set it down in a corner near the door. "Here is your table. I'll come back with the flame." He disappeared again.

I placed the box on the table and finally opened it. I took everything out, one thing at a time, and was relieved to find everything there. In fact, there seemed to be something extra. At the bottom of the box, I found the list I'd made for Lady Thaciana. I read what she'd added under the items I jotted down.

Hemlock.

Poison? She gave me poison? Why?

Hemlock would affect the nervous system the same way stillstem did, except it was deadly, even in small amounts. I glanced over at the ingredients, which were clearly labeled, placed the hemlock back inside the box, and replaced the lid. My thoughts whirled. Lady Thaciana had deduced that I was trying to make some sort of sedative, and she thought hemlock would help. And it might, in the right dosage, except I couldn't risk it. If I killed the Seelie Prince... I didn't even want to think about it.

"Everything in order?" Cylea asked over my shoulder.

I startled. "Uh, yes, it is. Even the syringe." I pointed at the all-glass and metal instrument. It looked like the old-fashioned kind, but it would do the job. Same as the flasks, tongs, mortar and pestle, dropper, leather-bound journal, and graphite the lady had provided.

"What is that for?" She watched the pointy needle distrustfully.

"It's called a syringe. It will allow me to administer the stillstem intravenously. That way, it should have a stronger and faster effect."

She went pale, instantly becoming one of those people who are terrified of needles. "Better Kalyll than me. How long will it take to get things ready?"

"Not long once Kryn gets here."

She nodded. "They'd better hurry. King Elladan can be long-winded."

Wasting no time, I got to work on the marsh flower, working it to the right consistency in the mortar and pestle. The yellow flowers were super fresh, as if they'd been recently picked.

"Can you get some water in this?" I gave Cylea one of the narrow-neck flasks.

Kryn came back shortly, accompanied by Arabis, who greeted me with a smile.

"Feeling much better." She patted her stomach. "You're a hell of a healer."

"I'm glad to hear it."

Kryn placed two flat stones and a sizable oil lamp on the table. "Take your pick," he said.

I frowned at the stones.

He picked them up. "I didn't know if you literally needed a flame or just heat." He knocked the two rocks together, and they began to glow. He set them back down on the table. I placed a hand over them and felt the heat slowly build. Magical heating rocks.

"Won't they burn through the table?" I asked.

"No. Only the top part will be hot. The bottom remains cool."

"How hot do they get?"

"As hot as you want. Just knock them together again to increase the temperature. Make sure to hold them from the bottom, though."

"This would be great for a hot stone massage."

"A what?"

"Never mind." I went back to work, heating the water over the stones. It boiled in no time as I held the flask with the tongs over their heated surface.

Neat!

I measured the resulting flower powder carefully, using only my senses. As part of my healing skill, I'd always been able to measure with precision down to a milligram. If only my skill also included knowing the right dosage for each patient, but for that, I needed to use book-acquired knowledge alongside the person's weight, height, and age. Though with the Fae, it was different. They were strong and sometimes their special abilities interfered with things. Add to that Kalyll's ailment, or whatever it was, and things got even more complicated.

Once the mixture was done, I infused it with a hint of my power. Cylea watched as glowing light flowed from my fingers into the flask, changing its yellow contents to a shimmering red.

"What does that do?" she asked as the last of my magic infused the compound.

"It will allow the marsh flower to bind to cell receptors and do its job more easily."

Kryn narrowed his eyes and grunted, but said nothing. He'd been standing next to the table, arms crossed, as he watched. He'd been nice enough as he fetched everything, but clearly, he still hadn't warmed up to me.

"This is finished." I set aside the flask with the red liquid and picked up the bottle of stillstem. This one was already in liquid form. Unlike the marsh flower, it didn't need to be fresh. I set it aside since we wouldn't need it until later.

"That's it?" Cylea asked. "What about this?" She peered inside the box. "Did you forget an ingredient?"

I shook my head. "No. Lady Thaciana added something extra."

Cylea frowned. "What is it?"

"A poison."

"Why would she do that?"

"I think she inferred what I would be concocting and added something she thought might be helpful. But I don't feel comfortable giving it to the prince. It could turn... deadly."

Cylea considered for a moment and seemed about to say something, but closed her mouth instead.

"Where in the devil are they?" Kryn turned away from the table and stomped out of the room.

"We don't have long," Cylea said. "He should be in chains before his mood changes." She started pacing, making me nervous. He would also need to drink the marsh flower elixir before that happened. I doubted he would take it voluntarily once he got pissy.

Thankfully, a moment later, steps echoed outside the door and the prince strode in, followed by Jeondar and Kryn.

Kalyll's eyes immediately found mine. I felt a thrill as he looked at me, and once more, I was angry at my double-crossing body, which seemed to respond to him the way moths respond to the fire.

Oh Dani, this isn't good. Stockholm syndrome anyone?

"Where is Silver?" Kalyll asked, glancing around and looking angry.

"Don't worry about him." Cylea rolled her eyes. "The whore went to Gleelock Alley."

"We don't need him," Kryn said.

"I'm here. I'm here." Silver rushed into the room. "Don't get your panties in a wad." He winked at me, as if thanking me for increasing his repertoire of crass things to say.

The prince huffed.

"What happened?" Cylea asked.

Jeondar waved a hand. "The queen was in attendance. Let's just say she got on our nerves."

It seemed Queen Belasha didn't talk the same politics as Kalyll.

"Let's do this then." Kryn closed the heavy wooden door, then walked to the chains, followed by Kalyll and the others.

Between Kryn, Jeondar, and Silver, they picked up a heavy metal ring that had three chains sprouting from it. Each chain was attached to a huge spike embedded in the rocky ground. The ring had a hinge on one side and loops on the other. Grunting, the three males placed the ring around Kalyll's waist, then snapped it close, securing it through the loops with a lock the size of my fists.

"You might want to sit," Kryn suggested.

Kalyll shook his head and planted his feet squarely. "Let's go, slowly."

The others let go of the ring, and Kalyll nearly sank to his knees with its weight. Quickly, they attached smaller chains to his wrists and ankles, weighing him down further. Still, Kalyll remained on his feet, though he was visibly trembling with the effort.

Witchlights! How strong was he?

His cobalt eyes met mine and he nodded.

I took the flask with the marsh flower and walked to him.

He glanced at his restrained hands, then licked his lips. "I think I will need your assistance."

My stomach buzzing with nerves, I pressed the flask to his chiseled lips.

"It will be bitter," I said as I tipped it.

He dropped the shimmering liquid, never breaking eye contact. His throat worked up and down as he swallowed. When he was done, I pulled the flask away. He closed his eyes, and when they sprang open, they were dark, those dark veins moving under his skin.

I gasped and jumped back as he lunged, teeth bared.

My heart dropped. The marsh flower hadn't worked.

CHAPTER 22

"**S**tand back, beast," Arabis ordered.

I jumped back as the command reverberated through the space, making the water in the pool ripple. My back smashed into Jeondar just as the chains went taut, holding a wild-looking Kalyll back by mere inches. He sneered at Arabis, ignoring her command and growling in my face. Wine-laced breath tickled my nose. No doubt, the conversation with King Elladan had been carried out over drinks.

"Your trashy little potion didn't work, *witch,*" Kalyll spat, his already deep voice a few octaves lower.

Jeondar placed his hands on my waist and took a step back to put some distance between us and the prince. Kalyll took notice of Jeondar's hands on me and pulled against the chains, his chest rumbling. Surprisingly, the chains no longer seemed to weigh him down as they had just seconds ago. He appeared unbothered by them as if, as soon as his mood changed, his strength had grown exponentially.

"Is that all you've got?" he asked me, then laughed cruelly. "You're worthless."

I knew it wasn't Kalyll speaking, but the word still bothered me.

"Fuck!" Kryn cursed. "What now? When he shifts, those chains may not be enough."

"They won't be, you idiot," Kalyll assured him.

Kryn's green eyes flashed with irritation. He glanced back toward the table where the syringe sat. "What about that?"

"Just try it, and I'll bite your face off," Kalyll threatened, looking straight at me. "I..." He shook his head, taking a step back. "There is..." Another shake of his head as he squeezed his eyes shut and seemed to fight against some internal force.

When his eyes opened again, they were clear. His legs trembled, and he collapsed to his knees, chest pumping as he breathed.

"Did it... work?" Arabis asked incredulously.

Kalyll glanced up, looking confused. Kryn seemed to reevaluate me, then slowly approached the prince.

"Stay away," Arabis warned him.

Kryn ignored her. "Hey, is that you?"

The prince nodded, then peered up at me, his expression etched with gratitude. "It's... working." He managed a smile, a sad one.

I walked to the table and retrieved the journal and graphite stick. Approaching slowly, I asked him, "Is it safe to get close? I would like to take your vitals."

Kalyll gave me a single nod.

Of course, he could be lying, pretending to be all right, but the bewildered expression on his face, the utter relief at not being controlled by whatever lived inside him, told me otherwise. I kneeled next to him as the others remained back, staring in awe.

"How do you feel?" I asked in a quiet voice.

"Strange. I was able to push the beast back. It's still there, though."

I glanced down at his bound wrist. "May I?"

He gave me a slow blink in assent.

I placed two fingers on his warm wrist and felt his pulse. It was strong and fast. I jotted down the number. Next, I checked his temperature by pressing a hand across his forehead. Those hypnotic eyes remained on my face the entire time, while I did my best to focus on my work.

"What time is it?" I asked the others, writing down his elevated temperature. "A clock would be useful in here."

"It's only a few minutes past noon," Cylea said. "I'll go find a clock." She left, closing the door behind her.

"Why don't you scoot back?" I suggested. "Lean your back against the wall. The weight of the chain might be easier to bear that way."

"Let me help you." Kryn came closer.

Kalyll's head jerked in his friend's direction, his eyes seeming to flicker as if that darkness was trying to push its way to the forefront. My lungs froze, and I didn't dare move. Kryn put his hands up and stepped away.

The prince took a deep breath and the darkness receded. He bowed his head, eyes closed, as he took several more deep breaths. When he glanced up again, there was a ring of dark blue around his bottomless pupil.

"I don't need help." Kalyll stood with great effort, walked to the wall, then sat, reclining his back on the rough stone.

I glanced over my shoulder at the others and found that they were looking at me strangely. Kryn wore a deep frown, and I sensed he didn't like one bit that Kalyll seemed comfortable with me, but not him.

Careful not to make any sudden movements, I kneeled by Kalyll's side again and examined the ring around his waist.

"I'm worried all that pressure might hurt your hips," I said.

"I'll be fine. If it does, I'll heal. If it doesn't heal, I have you." His tone was slow and intimate, as if he didn't want the others to hear what he was saying, except with their Fae hearing, they were capturing every word, no doubt.

"You said you can still feel... the beast?" I asked tentatively, afraid that acknowledging its presence would bring the darkness forth again.

He nodded.

"And just now," I gestured back with my chin to where Kryn stood, "it took over because... it felt threatened by Kryn? Or some other reason?"

Kalyll thought for a moment, then shrugged without giving me an answer.

"I want to understand how we can help you keep control, and what things we should avoid."

Still, Kalyll provided no answer.

"Is the beast preventing you from responding?"

At this, he shook his head.

"Okay, not very helpful."

"Sorry, it's... improper."

I frowned and opened my mouth to say something, but Kalyll cut me off.

"Please, don't ask." He glanced down the length of his body. "How long will the elixir last?"

"I can't really say. It's the first time you've taken it, so I'll take notes to keep track." I held up my journal. "Next time, we'll know more. I can already tell that a higher dose would be safe next time. I will make another batch, and when you start to feel the effects wearing out, you can drink it. Sound good?"

"Sounds good."

I started to stand, but his hand snatched mine, keeping me in place.

"Yes?" I asked.

He stared.

"Do you... have a question?"

He shook his head and let me go. I walked back to the table and quickly made a second batch, this time using one and a half the amount of marsh flower I'd used before. Cylea came back with a pocket watch, which she handed over.

"Here. It's Kalyll's. I remembered he had it. He got it from your realm," she said.

The piece was made out of polished silver with a delicate rose etched on the lid. I opened it and marked the time. It was 12:26 PM, per the Roman numerals that adorned the face of the classic piece.

"Thank you." I slipped it in a pocket of my tunic so I could have it handy, then returned to Kalyll's side.

"How do you feel now? The same?"

He nodded.

I sat cross-legged next to him and took his vitals every few minutes, jotting down the results and the time. His pulse had slowed down a little, but it was still above normal.

"I never thought this would be possible," Kalyll said after we'd been sitting quietly for almost an hour. "Your magic is special." That gratitude from before returned to his features.

I shrugged, feeling a blush bloom on my cheeks.

"We tried a lot of different things. Nothing worked."

"I got lucky."

"I don't think luck has anything to do with it." He swallowed thickly and squeezed his eyes shut for a moment.

"Are you okay?"

He took a deep breath. "Fine."

"Let me know when you think you should take the second dose."

"I will. What about the stillstem?"

"We will save that for later. Combined with the marsh flower, I hope it will be enough to prevent you from shifting."

His face lit up. "I pray you're right."

"Me too. But don't get your hopes too high."

"It's hard not to. This is the first time I've been myself after midday in a while."

"There's something I'm worried about," I said with the intention of being as honest as possible.

"What is that?"

"You might become resistant to these compounds."

His expression fell.

"But I'll keep trying different things if that happens," I said quickly, not wanting him to worry.

"Thank you, Daniella. How could I ever repay you? I took you from your home and I—"

"Let's not go over that again. What's done, is done, and we have to make the best of it."

A muscle twitched in his jaw as he clenched his teeth. I sensed he wanted to say something to disparage his honor for plucking me from my life, but I couldn't find it in me to blame him anymore—not after seeing what he was going through and understanding his desperation.

"This is boring," Silver whispered, though his voice echoed through the cavernous space.

"You're insufferable," Cylea hissed.

Kalyll smiled. "I don't think you all need to stay down here. In fact, it might raise suspicion if everyone is missing. Best to show your faces, get ready for the ball. We all missed the noon meal already. I'm sure King Elladan was wondering where we were. Silver, why don't you and Cylea go."

Cylea walked closer cautiously. She stopped a good distance away, evaluated Kalyll, then came closer and closer. The prince didn't react the way he had with Kryn.

Her clear eyes scanned Kalyll with obvious sadness. "I'll go, then bring back some food for you and Dani."

"Great idea. She must be hungry. I should have thought of that."

"I'm fine. It's no big deal," I said.

"It is a big deal," the prince contradicted me. "In every way possible, we should all endeavor to make Ms. Sunder comfortable and safe. Is that understood?" This was an unequivocal command, which everyone answered with, "Yes, My Prince," and a fist on their chest.

Their seal surprised me, especially because I didn't feel I deserved such special treatment, no matter the circumstances that had brought me here. But I didn't argue. I sensed going against Kalyll on this particular point would take me nowhere.

Silver sauntered through the door after Cylea, already talking about what he would eat for lunch.

"If he wasn't so good in a fight," Kryn said, "I would suggest we leave him behind. I doubt he would mind, especially if he can spend his evenings at The Veiled Face or one of those other places in Gleelock Alley."

"*Pshaw*, don't act like you wouldn't do the same," Jeondar put in.

Kryn gave him a dirty look, then turned his attention to Arabis. After a few beats, he made his way toward her, walking casually and looking at anything but her eyes.

"Um, how do you feel?" He pointed at her stomach.

"Much better, thank you for asking," Arabis responded, also avoiding eye contact.

I threw a questioning look toward the prince. He rolled his eyes upward as if to say he was tired of Kryn's and Arabis's song and dance. So there *was* something there as I'd sensed. I couldn't help the curiosity that rose inside me. From the way Kryn groveled, it was clear he'd done something to piss her off. I didn't know Arabis well, but something told me she wasn't simply being difficult. Whatever Kryn had done deserved the bulk of her animosity.

"You're very methodical," Kalyll said as, sometime later, I jotted down another set of vitals.

"It's important to get things right."

He glanced at the food basket on the floor, which Cylea had brought moments ago. "You barely ate anything."

"*You* barely ate anything."

"It's difficult with these." He glanced at his shackles.

I had offered to feed him, but his pride hadn't allowed it. Instead, he opted for taking bites from a bread roll, shakily lifting it to his mouth and biting big chunks to make the most of each movement.

"You're just one of those stubborn patients," I said, a smile tugging at the corner of my mouth.

"Am I?"

"Yes, next thing you'll throw a tantrum and say you need a TV in your room."

He chuckled. "You're not used to dealing with old curmudgeons like me, are you?"

"Curmudgeons," I repeated, laughing at the word.

He opened his mouth to say something, then shut it again, his teeth clicking together, his body tensing all over. His eyes flicked toward the table where the elixir sat, his silent way of telling me he needed it. Now!

I jumped to my feet, retrieved the flask, and ran back. Without ceremony, I placed a hand behind his head, pulled his hair to tip his chin back, and fed him the elixir. I sighed with relief when he didn't fight me and swallowed every last drop.

Setting the flask on the floor, I took his pulse. It was elevated again, even faster than it had been after the first dose. Jeondar, Kryn, and Arabis stood nearby, ready to intervene if necessary, but Kalyll remained in place, even if his fists were trembling with white-knuckled strength and his teeth were grinding audibly.

One of his hands flew open and snatched my wrist. He pulled me toward him until my nose was inches from his, and his dark eyes were staring right into mine.

"Let her go," Arabis ordered, her voice feeling like something tangible, like a brush over my skin.

Kalyll squeezed me harder until I gasped in pain.

"Please, Kalyll, let go. You're hurting her." Arabis again, though this time her skill was laced with something much different. Instead of authoritarian, she sounded pleading.

The prince still ignored her.

"You are a clever witch," Kalyll rumbled in that deep voice that seemed to come from the heart of a mountain. "A pretty one, too." He licked his lips.

"What the hell?" Kryn said behind me.

Kalyll reached behind me and untied the leather strip he'd used to bind my hair.

"Ah, much better this way." He leaned closer, his mouth mere inches from mine, his breath smelling of marsh flowers rather than wine this time.

I breathed rapidly as my heart pounded, sending bursts of adrenaline through my veins. He could kill me, snap my neck in an instant, but it wasn't the fear of death that sent heat coursing through my body.

He inhaled sharply, taking in my scent, then sighed as if it pleased him.

"Let me go," I managed in a weak whisper.

"No," he said, savoring the word and whispering it against my ear.

"My wrist hurts. You'll break it. Please, Kalyll."

As I said his name, he threw his head back and growled, the column of his neck working up and down. His arm trembled as he slowly released his grip, one finger at a time, and finally let me go.

I scooted back out of reach, cradling my wrist and wincing at the pain. I immediately allowed healing magic to flow into me, and the ache ebbed until it was completely gone.

When Kalyll opened his eyes, he was in control again. Embarrassment colored his cheeks when he looked at me.

"Are you all right? Please tell me you're all right."

"I'm fine. See?" I lifted my wrist and showed him. "I healed it right away."

"Stay away from me. Don't come near."

"I have to. I need to keep an eye on you."

"He's right," Kryn said. "He's too unpredictable. He could kill you before you have time to even blink. He's lethal all on his own, but with the beast in control..."

I decided not to argue. Instead, I walked back to the table and prepared the water to make another dose of the elixir. Though I would have to see how the new dose affected Kalyll before I could measure the marsh flower. I checked the pocket watch. It was two—about five hours left before Kalyll's shift.

"Are you hurt?" Arabis appeared at my side.

"No, I'm fine."

"He... he listened to you," she said.

I shook my head. "The elixir kicked in. It seems to take a few seconds to take effect."

Turning away from the table, I approached the prince. His head was thrown back against the wall, and he was taking deep breaths that made his wide chest expand until his tunic looked as if it might rip open.

My journal and flask were laying close to him on the ground. I needed to reach them, but I waited until his breathing slowed. Then his head slumped to one side, and he looked at me from under heavy lids.

"I'm sorry. I tried to stop..." He trailed off.

Carefully, very slowly, I reached for the journal and flask and pulled them back quickly. His lips pressed into a thin line, and he blew air through his nose, looking angry at himself. As we watched him in silence, his eyes drooped close and, after a long moment, his breathing became steady.

"Is he... asleep?" Jeondar asked.

Arabis frowned. "It appears so."

"I gave him a heavier dose and laced it with more of my power." After setting my things on the table, I tiptoed closer to Kalyll, then kneeled and took his vitals. For the first time, everything was normal, no accelerated pulse, no slight fever. "The last dose lasted approximately four hours. My guess is this one will last until seven. Before it's time for the shift, I'd like to administer the stillstem."

"How long will he be asleep?" Kryn asked.

"I don't know. I only have preliminary data. I can't go by that."

"This is good though," Arabis said. "Very good."

I held my judgment. I liked to see consistent results before becoming too optimistic.

CHAPTER 23

We sat quietly once more. Arabis had a book that she'd found amongst the furniture outside the door, which she was reading under one of the sconces. Kryn had taken to pacing in front of the water, seeming lost in thought, while Jeondar reclined against the wall with unsettling stillness.

Almost an hour into Kalyll's snap, Jeondar made his way to the door. "I'll get Silver and Cylea. It's time we show our faces upstairs. I'm sure my father is wondering where I am. We'll have to take turns appearing at the ball tonight, even you." He glanced at me.

"Me? No, I can't leave. I have to watch him."

"My father will want to see you, make sure you're enjoying yourself. You can make a quick appearance and then come back. Like Kalyll said, it would seem suspicious if you're not there."

I nodded, but I wasn't happy about it. I didn't like abandoning my patients.

Silver and Cylea returned sometime later, and Kryn and Arabis left, though they looked as unwilling as I felt.

"Incredible," Silver shook his head. "Never thought that beast could be subdued."

Cylea approached me. "Are you all right? Jeondar told me what happened."

"I'm fine. Just a bit of pain, nothing I couldn't heal myself." I flexed my wrist to show her she had no reason to worry about me. I wasn't the patient. Kalyll was.

Twenty minutes in, Silver's constant sighs of boredom turned out to be more annoying than Kryn's pacing. Honestly, it wasn't as if they were doing anything worthwhile.

"Here, read this." Cylea chucked Arabis's book at Silver. The book flew past him, defying his Fae reflexes, and splashed into the water.

Kalyll woke up at the sound and was immediately on his feet, crouching in an attack stance, darkened eyes roving over the space.

I threw a dirty glance in Silver and Cylea's direction. She shrugged and mouthed, "Sorry."

Palms up, I spoke to Kalyll. "It's all right. Everything is all right. Why don't you sit back down?"

He looked at me, chest heaving, hands fisted in front of him.

I smiled. "A book fell in the water. That's all."

He frowned, as if processing my words.

"It's a shame," I went on, trying to distract him with senseless talk. "I hate it when books get damaged. I even hate it when people dog-ear the pages. It's a crime. I want to yell at them. I mean... haven't they heard of bookmarks?"

His eyes cleared. He staggered backward, his back hitting the wall. Cylea exchanged a glance with Silver, then gave me a surprised once-over. They were acting as if this was all me and not the marsh flower elixir. Maybe because they could only think of Arabis controlling him with her voice, but they were so wrong.

Kalyll slid down the wall and sat on the ground. "I was asleep?"

"You were."

"Something you haven't done in weeks," Cylea said.

"Is that true?" I asked.

Kalyll nodded. "The beast doesn't rest, and I've been busy. No time to waste my few waking hours in bed."

"Is it safe if I come close to take your vitals once more?" I asked.

"How long has it been since I took that last dose?"

"About one and a half hours, so judging by how long the first one lasted, I think everything will be safe until seven, but you know better."

"I feel... I think it's safe as well."

"Good."

I kneeled by his side and got to work, telling myself that it was unprofessional to enjoy the feel of his skin against my fingers and the way his eyes examined my face and seemed to linger on my lips, though surely, I was imagining that.

"I am embarrassed," he said, in a whisper so low that I doubted Silver and Cylea could hear, especially since they were arguing in not-so-hushed tones about the book.

"You shouldn't be," I said as I wrapped my hand around the front of his elbow to take his blood pressure. "You were deep in sleep and the sudden splash startled you."

He shook his head. "No, not about that, but about hurting you and... the things I said to you."

Pausing, my hand still around his arm, my eyes locked with his as I glanced up. "Please, don't worry. I know it's not you."

"Is it not?"

I frowned, confused.

"Is it not the darkest side of me?"

Honestly, I had no idea. I didn't know the nature of what he called a curse on his blood. Was it a different entity living inside of him? Was it something else?

"I don't know," I said. "Maybe we can talk a bit more tomorrow. There's so much you haven't told me about how this began. If I'm to help you further, I need to understand everything."

He grunted, letting me know he didn't like that idea. Instead, he said, "Do something for me."

"What?"

"Stay away as much as you can."

"Okay."

"And... know that were I in full control of myself, I would never be so forward."

"Forward?"

He glanced at my loose hair to remind me of the way he'd un-bound it. He had asked for my permission when he first tied it—kind of—but he'd roughly removed it with an entitled, possessive air. There was a difference.

"Of course you wouldn't. You're the Seelie Prince." I tried to make it sound like a joke, but the comment seemed to carry an underlying message: *You're the Seelie Prince, and I'm no one.*

"I am but a male, and you are—" He stopped as if biting his tongue. "You should prepare another elixir, don't you think?"

He was right. The evening was fast approaching, and I had to ensure he didn't get out of this room.

"I'll take it now," Kalyll said as soon as I finish making the third dose of the marsh flower elixir. "The last time we waited a bit too long," Kalyll added. "Let's be safe and let me drink it now."

I made the next dose slightly stronger, though not too much. He had slept soundly, but his vitals had been normal. I figured he could probably withstand double the last dose, but I was about to inject him with stillstem, so I didn't want to take any risks. I checked the time on the pocket watch. It was past four.

While I worked, Jeondar returned and seemed relieved to find everything the same.

"Everything all right up there?" Kalyll asked, rolling his eyes toward the ceiling.

"Yes. My father asked about you. Arabis told him you were resting, that you've been working too hard lately."

The prince grunted, then turned to me. "Ready?"

I nodded, while I nervously went over more mental calculations. The second dose had lasted a bit over two hours so far. Extrapolating from how long the first dose kept him calm, I could safely assume that he had another twenty minutes left and that the third dose would give him three more hours. A fourth dose along with the stillstem, and things should hold until dawn.

"Here you go." I tried to bring the flask to Kalyll's mouth, but he took it from me—not letting me help him this time.

I tried not to feel disappointed as he pressed it to his lips with a shaking hand that struggled against the weight of the manacle. When the flask was empty, he handed it back, his mouth working against the bitter taste of the marsh flowers. His hand dropped heavily to his lap and he stared at it, annoyed.

"I wish we'd had time to work up a dose to make these chains unnecessary."

"Me too."

"The stillstem now?" he asked.

I shook my head. "I'll wait for a bit."

"Once I'm asleep, you should take a break. You've been here long enough."

"I'd rather not. I always stick by my patients when we try new things."

"You have to show your face at the ball," Jeondar said. "At least for an hour."

"Honestly, attending a party while I have a patient in a... delicate state is not the best idea."

Kalyll chuckled. "I'm not in a *delicate* state. I assure you."

"Maybe not, but it is a delicate situation, nonetheless."

The prince's mouth twisted to one side. He couldn't argue with that. Still, he had another point to make.

"It will be bad enough that I won't be there. Your presence at the ball will... help avoid additional questions and speculation of any kind."

"Yes," Jeondar agreed. "It's already bad enough we have to be in and out. And bad enough, we're leaving Imbermore tomorrow."

"We are?" I'd thought we would stay longer, especially if we figured out a way to keep Kalyll under control.

"We need to get to Mount Ruin as soon as possible," Kalyll said. "I can't perform my duties if I'm a raging beast or a benumbed corpse half the time, and the solution to all of this lies there. The journey is long, and the sooner we leave, the better."

"Makes sense," I said. "But still, I'm sure no one will miss me at the ball. I'm staying here."

Jeondar huffed. "You don't know my father. He'll want to see you, talk to you, make sure you're enjoying your stay. Naturally, he is very curious about your presence here. Then there is Valeriana. Larina has done a good job entertaining her, but she sent a message that the girl's starting to get restless. You should probably see her."

Valeriana. I'd completely forgotten about her. A new worry flooded me. If we were leaving tomorrow, how would I be able to ensure her safe delivery to someone who could take care of her? I needed to talk to Jeondar about it, though this didn't feel like the time.

"Fine," I gave in. "But only for an hour, then I'm coming right back."

"Good," Kalyll said groggily from his spot on the ground. His eyelids were drooping, and he seemed to be fighting the renewed effects of the elixir, though he promptly lost that battle.

"I hate to see him like that," Cylea said.

"Me too." Jeondar shook his head. "At least he's getting some much-needed rest now."

I waited until a quarter before 7 PM to load the syringe with the pure essence of stillstem. I flicked the barrel to force the air up, then pushed the plunger until a clear drop appeared at the needle point. Next, I imbued the liquid with my power until it shimmered silver, and walked to the prince's side. I didn't want to startle him, so I spoke his name gently.

"Kalyll, wake up. It's time for the shot."

He didn't stir.

I took his hand in mine and squeezed, enjoying its warmth and strength.

Still nothing.

I squeezed harder and shook him a bit. His eyes opened a crack.

"Hey, it's Dani."

"Daniella," he corrected in a lazy voice.

"It's time for your shot. I didn't want to startle you."

"Go ahead," he mumbled, stretching his right arm in my direction and blinking slowly, fighting to stay awake.

I rolled up his sleeve to reveal a muscular arm. His biceps was thick and his skin perfectly golden. Several veins were visible over the surface of all that strong sinew, so it was easy to find one at the crook of his elbow.

He flinched slightly when I inserted the needle. "It will feel a little cold," I said as I pushed the plunger.

I watched him closely and realized he was fast asleep once more. His expression was peaceful. He was achingly handsome, and I felt as if I could keep on looking at him for hours, admiring the perfect symmetry of his face, the fringe of his darkest blue eyelashes, and the curve of his lower lip.

Get a grip, Dani.

I swiftly removed the needle, rolled down his sleeve, and walked back to the table, telling myself what dangerous ground I was treading. Developing a crush on the Seelie Prince would be a monumental mistake, a recipe for getting a broken heart without the benefit of an affair. No dates. No romantic foreplay. No sex. Only a heart shredded into a million little pieces.

After retrieving my journal, I went back and sat next to Kalyll. I took his vitals several times, keeping a professional attitude, never once staring at his lips or letting myself enjoy the feel of him as I touched him.

"How is he?" Jeondar asked.

"His pulse is slow but still within acceptable levels."

"Perhaps you should go now. See Valeriana, get changed, and make an appearance. Make sure to talk to my father, and if he asks where we are, say you just saw us dancing with someone."

"Even Kalyll?"

"No. He would be hard to miss if he was actually there. I'll tell my father Kalyll is indisposed."

Jeondar took my journal, placed it on the table, and walked me to the door. I planted my feet as he tried to lead me outside and glanced over my shoulder.

"He'll be fine. Arabis and I will take good care of him, and if he wakes up or even stirs, I'll come to fetch you."

I nodded and left, quickly finding the way to my room. When I got there, there was only silence on the other side of the door. I knocked lightly, then walked in.

Valeriana was sitting on the bed, cross-legged, some sort of board game between her and the pixie. The girl's green eyes flashed in my direction, then back to the pieces on the board. Her rosebud mouth was set in a pout and her green eyebrows were knit together in a frown. She was mad at me.

"Hello," I said, trying to sound chipper.

Larina greeted me with a bow. "Hello, Lady Sunder."

"I'm sorry I've been gone for so long," I said. "I was really busy. The prince had several things for me to do."

"It is no trouble, lady," Larina said. "Valeriana and I had great fun today, didn't we?"

Valeriana shrugged, looking indifferent.

"Well, Larina," I said, "I appreciate your efforts, even if Valeriana doesn't."

The girl perked up at this. "Who said I don't?"

"Oh, I just thought you looked bored."

"I'm not bored. I'm angry."

Good. She was talking and relating how she felt. So many kids didn't know how to do that. I'd met my share of children who had never been encouraged to express how they felt, though I figured it was too much to expect from parents who didn't know how to do it either.

"I understand," I said. "You have good reason to be angry. We took you from your home, then left you in this room without explaining why."

Valeriana picked up one of the pieces from the board and rolled it between her fingers. "It wasn't so bad. Larina is very fun to be around."

Larina smiled, and I did too.

"I'm glad to hear that, and I hope neither one of you will mind sharing a bit more time together. There is a ball tonight, and I have to be there."

I thought Valeriana might get angry again, but instead, she jumped off the bed and ran into the closet.

"You need to wear this." She came back, carrying a gown that was nearly three times her size. "Larina dressed me like a princess earlier, and we pretended to go to the ball, though she said children aren't allowed." She pouted. "We were talking and thought you would look beautiful in this."

"It is absolutely gorgeous." I gaped at the magnificent dress. "You two have excellent taste."

"Larina is an expert at the balls," Valeriana said. "She can arrange your hair and do the paint on your face. She also has this little bottle with something that smells like freshdew roses."

"It does sound like Larina is quite the expert, and I am in desperate need of one. I know nothing about Fae fashion."

Valeriana jumped up and down. "She taught me a little. I can help."

"Then, by all means." I spread my arms out, putting myself at their mercy.

For the next twenty minutes, Larina worked on my makeup and an intricate hairstyle that involved her fluttering around my head, pulling strands of hair this way and that until she was satisfied.

"Amazing work, Larina." I admired the intricate layers she'd created.

"One last touch." She applied a bit of pixie dust here and there, giving my hair more body and a little shine.

"Is she like a hair witch?" Valeriana asked.

"I guess," I said, because I didn't know if hair witches were real or if being called one might offend Larina.

Without me hardly noticing, the pixie procured a necklace, which she quickly hung around my neck.

"Oh, who does this belong to?" I fingered the heavy piece, which consisted of seven large ice-blue jewels and many smaller white ones surrounding them. "Am I allowed to wear this?" The necklace appeared expensive, and the last thing I needed was to get accused of thievery.

"It belongs to me," Larina said. "It was a gift from Prince Jeondar's mother."

"Oh, no, no. I can't wear this." I started to unclasp the back.

Larina's face fell. My hands stopped at the sight of her downcast expression.

"What if somebody recognizes it and...?" *they throw me in a dungeon for the rest of my life.*

"Oh, no one will, if that's what you're worried about." Larina flew down to the makeup table and sat on a silver powder canister. "She received it as a gift from a foreign dignitary and had no occasion to wear it before she..." Her little eyes wavered as she fell silent. It seemed to me that the pixie had been very fond of the former queen.

"It's hardly appropriate for me, Larina. I'm no queen. It doesn't feel right to wear it."

"*I* can't wear it, and someone should. Valeriana told me what you did for her. She's one of the minor folk like me, and not many bother with us."

Minor folk? I had a vague understanding of what that meant. Fae like pixies, dryads, pookas, brownies, and others were treated the way minorities were sometimes treated in our realm, except perhaps worse. Some of them were slaves for the entire expanse of their long-lived lives. Was that the case with Larina? Was that what would become of Valeriana if she wasn't placed somewhere with her kind?

"Thank you, Larina. I feel honored. I will wear your necklace with pride." I couldn't find it in me to turn her down.

Her face lit up, and that was all I needed to make the decision feel right.

With my hair and makeup done, I walked into the bathroom and changed into the gown. When I came out, Valeriana clapped her hands and jumped in excitement.

"We were right. You look beautiful."

The dress expanded around me, ballooning from my middle to the floor. The bodice was strapless, the color of Kalyll's hair. It pushed my boobs up and narrowed sharply toward my waist. From there, pleats of tulle rained down, layered perfectly to create volume, their color gradually changing from midnight blue to snow white.

A pair of slippers was waiting for me in front of the bed.

Larina pointed at them. "Those are the best I could find. They are simple, but comfortable. Besides, no one will see them under the dress."

"They're perfect," I said as I slipped the flaps on and wiggled my toes inside of them. They were absolutely comfy, and I much preferred them to any shoes that would pinch my toes. I was used to scrubs and sneakers, so they were right up my alley.

As I walked by the mirror on my way out, I had to do a double take. I was unrecognizable. Mom and Toni would have a fit. They loved dressing up, whereas my youngest sister preferred jeans and a hoodie. Foolishly, I wished I had my phone to take a selfie, except that wasn't the only thing I found myself wishing for.

I would have liked for Prince Kalyll to see me as I was: my mahogany hair swept up elaborately, my waist accentuated by the gorgeous gown, and my breasts looking luscious in the tight bodice, sparkling slightly with pixie dust.

"Dance a lot," Valeriana said. "You have to tell me all about it."

"I will, and thank you, you two."

They waved and smiled as I walked out the door and made my way downstairs, chiding myself for being so stupid.

CHAPTER 24

M usic guided me to a ballroom the size of two basketball courts. The place was swarming with people under the glow of fairy lights that seemed to float against a dark sky. The entire tableau was an assault on the senses.

The melodious notes were enchanting. The palette of colors in the outfits of both males and females, a riot to my eyes. Different scents filled my nose as I turned this way and that: honey, lavender, roasted meat, fresh rain, and many more I couldn't name but seemed to beckon me.

The sound of trickling water drew me right to a floor-to-ceiling waterfall glowing red with what looked like tiny living creatures. The cascade flowed into a pool where iridescent fish of different colors swam lazily among undulating plants.

As I walked further into the room, the floor turned soft, and I glanced down to find a bed of tiny purple flowers, which changed to yellow, then blue as I kept going—a veritable living carpet. Many marble statues stood around, each more expertly carved than the next.

A handsome satyr wearing an embroidered skirt with a scarlet sash across his bare chest captured my attention. His hooved legs were covered in brown fur, and small horns grew out of the sides of his forehead. His dark hair was swept back at the sides, forming what looked like tucked-in wings and ending in points at the back. Two patches of white hair started at his temples and were also swept back, looking like smaller wings on top of the bigger ones. His eyebrows rose upward in sharp points, and he had a small beard that also had a pointy end.

He stopped and bowed respectfully. His eyes were unusual with horizontal pupils and nearly no white around their golden irises. Aside from their strangeness, the admiration in them was undeniably familiar. He seemed to approve of what he saw.

"I have never seen you before," he said in a lilting accent and sounding as if he disapproved of his inability to know absolutely everyone. "My name is Lyanner Phiran at your service." He bowed, putting one perfectly polished hoof in front of the other and one hand on his chest, while the other one made a flourish.

I blinked at his gallantry. I had never been greeted in such a manner, and I couldn't argue that it was flattering. And his name... it sounded familiar.

"I am Daniella Sunder," I offered in return.

"What is a human doing in Imbermore? It's not unusual to see one of your kind in Elyndell, but here, so far north, it's nearly a novelty."

I had no idea how to answer his question. Luckily, at that moment, Cylea appeared accompanied by Silver, which meant Kryn and Arabis must be with Kalyll now.

"Drakeansoul!" she exclaimed and laid two kisses on him, one on either cheek, her sapphire gown sparkling like the ocean under a brilliant sun.

Drakeansoul? I thought for a moment, then remembered. This was the dragon trainer Cylea had so excitedly talked about.

"Darling, so good to see you," Lyanner said, turning to face her. I noticed his silver hoop earrings and matching eyeshadow for the first time. The male had flair. There was no doubt about it.

Silver and Lyanner greeted each other with a slight bow and a fist on their chests, formal and distant.

"I heard your troop was here," the satyr said. "And Adanorin." He looked around as if he expected to see Kalyll walking behind his friends.

"Kalyll is indisposed," Cylea said. "We've traveled long and hard, and he's had little rest. Royal duties."

It wasn't all a lie.

"I see you've met Dani." Cylea smiled in my direction.

"You mean you know this bespelling creature?"

"Yes, she's traveling with us."

The end of one of Lyanner's pointed eyebrows rose even higher. "Is that so?"

"Yes, she's an extremely talented healer. Kalyll owes her family a favor, so he's escorting her to Fylahexter as he makes his circuit of royal visits."

Fylahexter? That was the human settlement Jeondar had told me about. It seemed like a fair excuse for my presence here.

"Interesting." He eyed me, his frown smoothing.

Cylea was a smooth liar. I wasn't sure if she'd come up with this explanation earlier or on the spot, but either way, she almost had me believing that was exactly what I was doing in Elf-Hame.

"And what kind of favor could that be?" Lyanner pursed his lips.

"You'll have to ask Kalyll about that. Not sure if he'll tell you, though. There are secrets that not even the great Drakeansoul knows."

Silver smirked, and Lyanner blew air through his nose as if to say there weren't too many of those kinds of secrets.

At that moment, Jeondar cut through the crowd and exchanged formal greetings with the satyr. The former peered at the latter with narrowed eyes for a moment, then shifted his attention to me, offering me his arm.

"Come with me, Lady Sunder. My father is inquiring about you."

I looped my arm through Jeondar's.

Lyanner's interest in me seemed to redouble.

"A pleasure, Drakeansoul." Jeondar nodded once, then dragged me away.

Once we were a fair distance away, I asked, "Everything all right with... you know?"

"Yes."

"Good."

I leaned closer and whispered, "You don't seem to like Lyanner."

"I like him well enough, but he's too meddlesome for his own good. It's best to remain mum around him."

"Yes, I got that impression."

"He's good at what he does. The few tame dragons that can be found in Elf-Hame were trained by him, and other rich and powerful people have made Lyanner rich and powerful in his own right. But I believe dragon training isn't his only source of wealth. I think he deals in secrets too, which, depending on their magnitude, can be sold for more profit than the biggest of dragons."

I shivered at that. If someone like Lyanner learned about Kalyll's ailment, I could only imagine what they would do. The secret I knew was of major magnitude for sure, but it was only the tip of the iceberg. There was more they hadn't told me, something spies would sink their teeth into like a juicy steak. Another shiver ran through me.

This topple-a-kingdom kind of intrigue wasn't for me.

As I walked with Jeondar toward a raised dais where the king and queen sat, I did my best not to gawk at everyone we passed. This realm was overwhelming, and it would take some time to get used to it.

We were almost to the dais when Queen Belasha noticed us coming. Immediately, her eyes flew to the necklace at my throat, and the way her mouth turned upside down made me realize that wearing the jewelry had been a mistake, after all. I wanted to disentangle myself from Jeondar and melt back into the crowd, but he led me toward the king and queen, who had started descending to meet us at the bottom of the stairs.

"Lady Sunder," King Elladan greeted me. "You look lovely in that gown."

I bowed respectfully. "Thank you. It appears your palace has magical closets with gowns that fit their guests perfectly."

He chuckled and gave me a knowing smile.

"And jewelry as well," the queen said. "That is a lovely necklace. Of Ye'narian make, if I'm not mistaken."

Jeondar glanced down and frowned at the necklace.

Self-consciously, I placed a hand on my chest, fingers brushing the necklace. Crap. "Um, I don't know. I was—"

A terrible roar broke through the din of the party. My blood turned to ice at the timely interruption, though I would've rather explained where the necklace had come from. Instead, I whirled to face the crowd as it erupted into chaos.

People stampeded out of the giant ballroom, some finding the exits quickly, and others tripping on the trains of long gowns and on each other.

"What is happening?" King Elladan demanded. "Guards!"

The guards who had been standing by the dais were already moving, heading toward the commotion. Jeondar and I exchanged a heavy glance. His eyes seemed to say, "*It's him.*"

This was bad. Really bad.

How had Kalyll woken up from all those heavy elixirs? And more importantly, how had he broken the Qrorium chains?

The ballroom had gone from paradise to bedlam in under a second. A royal fight was taking place at the opposite end of the long room, and from the looks of it, it involved luminous bursts of magic, splintering wood, clashing metal, horrified screams, and those terrible, terrible blood-curdling growls.

Jeondar turned to face the king and queen.

"You two, get out of here," he ordered.

"I'm not going anywhere." The king unclasped the brooch at his neck, and the cloak he wore slipped to the ground. "Whoever dares disturb our peace will pay for it dearly."

"Father," Jeondar protested as fire crackled on the king's fingers and he marched toward the fray. Jeondar jumped ahead of the king, the same fire magic appearing in his hands. "My queen, you and Lady Sunder go to a safe room," he called over his shoulder.

I glanced toward Belasha, who seemed to have no intentions of going anywhere. Instead, her gaze was intent on the chaos, and her neck flexed in every direction as she tried to get a better view.

"We should do as Jeondar said," I suggested, but she looked at me as if I were an annoyingly distracting gnat.

Jeondar and the king hadn't gotten far when there was a collective scream and something large came slashing and barreling through the retreating crowd, sending them flying outward like hollow bowling pins. A couple fell limp and bloodied, their eyes staring emptily. *Oh, God.*

The blood froze in my veins as the huge beast I'd seen that day in North Crosswood came face-to-face with Jeondar and the king.

Kalyll towered over them, a wolf-looking creature three times the size of any normal canine, ribbons of darkness trailing behind him.

Belasha gasped. "Elladan!" Panic over her husband suffused her voice and she sprang toward the king.

"Wait!" I tried to grab her arm, but she had Fae speed and slipped away easily.

"You will pay for this." The king threw his hands forward, directing a stream of fire straight at the beast's huge, roaring maw.

Jeondar did the same, and I pressed a hand to my mouth, my heart skipping a beat as a mass of fire enveloped Kalyll.

When the flames dissipated, the beast stood untouched, but one thousand percent more pissed off. Roaring, he reared up on hind legs, then swiped one of his strange taloned hands, paws, whatever they were, at the king.

"No!" Jeondar cried out as his father went flying and crashed against the wall.

Guards suddenly appear behind the beast, some with their swords drawn, others with magic at their fingertips.

The beast leaped past Jeondar even as the latter blasted fire at Kalyll's underbelly as he soared overhead. One leap and the beast stood in front of the queen. His eyes flashed blue with unmistakable fury. It seemed that, all along, Belasha had been his target. The beast seemed apt at holding a grudge, and maybe this had something to do with their disagreement earlier today.

Rather than look intimidated, Belasha stood her ground and flung a hand toward one of the marble statues. There was the sound of rock groaning, and the massive sculpture of a sphinx—half woman, half lion—came to life. It jumped from its pedestal, making the floor quake.

As Kalyll was distracted by the animated chuck of rock, I grabbed the queen's elbow and tried to pull her back. "We should get out of here."

"Don't touch me," she spat, shaking me off.

The sphinx lumbered toward the beast. The guards stood back. Kalyll stared impassively at its foe. Then, as if he were doing nothing more than brushing lint off his shoulder, he rammed into the sphinx with a mighty crash and broke it into a million pieces.

Belasha gasped and took a step back. If she had known that not even Qrorium had been able to stop him, she might have run to safety with me. Now, instead, she was the focal target of a very angry, vindictive creature.

"Belasha, run," the king's hoarse voice called from behind the beast.

But it was too late to run. The beast attacked.

Without thinking, I ran in front of the queen and planted my feet firmly.

"Stop," I said, my tone calm as resignation washed over me.

I expected to die, expected my bones to be crushed under the pressure of the beast's mighty jaws. Instead, I found myself face-to-face with a pair of large, luminescent blue eyes.

My chest vibrated as the creature roared in anger, his terrible force restrained by... by what? Why wasn't it attacking? Why wasn't it making a meal out of me as the queen found her chance to escape?

I stared into the depths of those unfathomable eyes. Something lived there that I recognized. It wasn't anything I could truly see, but something I felt in my soul, like recognizing a familiar tune or catching a scent that unleashed a thousand sought-after memories.

Kalyll was in there, and he was fighting *not* to harm me.

"Go," I whispered.

The beast shook his head, the thick mane swaying from side to side, that darkness that possessed Kalyll also fighting.

"Please, go," I begged.

For a moment, the beast shook on the spot, caught in a battle of wills. His head jerked to one side as ragged breaths tore out of him, sounding like half growls. His huge, razor-sharp teeth gleamed with saliva, and large drops of it splattered to the flower-covered floor.

Fear ran liquid in my veins as I prayed for Kalyll to prevail. Then, at last, the beast gave a frustrated growl, ran toward an open balcony, took a great leap, and disappeared into the night.

Legs wobbling, I lowered myself to my knees, unable to keep standing. My insides felt strange, watery somehow, as if the fear had dissolved them or replaced them.

"A healer," Jeondar shouted, his voice sounding as if it was traveling through a long tunnel. I raised my eyes in his direction. He was kneeling next to his father, applying pressure to his chest. Someone, a slender Fae with hair like spun gold, rushed in to help.

Belasha took a moment to ask me how I was doing, glancing down at me with a frown and an expression that suggested her mind was swimming with thousands of questions.

"Are you all right?" she asked again.

I nodded. She turned away and rushed to her husband's side. I remained where I was, eyes nailed to the balcony, the image of that large beast soaring through the air imprinted in my mind. The drop from here was over five stories. Would Kalyll be okay?

I shook my head at the stupid question. He had just fought a marble statue and won.

"Hurry," Belasha urged. "He's going to bleed to death."

As if under a spell, I rose to my feet and made my way toward the king. There were no thoughts in my mind. The fear had stripped it bare, and something other than conscious thought drove me there.

It wasn't until I saw the gaping wound in the king's chest that everything snapped back into place, and my training and instincts took over.

CHAPTER 25

I dropped to my knees in front of the king.

"The queen is right. You need to hurry, or he will die," I said, itching to jump in, but knowing that I would be out of place to intervene.

The Fae healer's eyes snapped up in anger. His expression was like an open letter that expressed his blatant disgust for my kind. It was the same look I'd seen in that female who didn't help me when I was first kidnapped. His magic *was* healing the wound, but for all his haughtiness, if this was the best he could do, he had no business attending to the King of the Summer Court.

He kept working, making no significant progress.

Jeondar glanced from the male to me, and so did the queen. He seemed conflicted for a moment, then made up his mind.

"Let her do it," Jeondar said, pushing the Fae healer away to give me room.

"I will not be held responsible *when* the king dies," the offended healer snapped.

But I ignored him, and without hesitation, got to work saving the king. Thankfully, and as difficult as it was without a visual aid, I'd had enough time to make a full assessment of his wounds and knew that the first order of business was to heal the descending aorta to immediately stop the bleeding.

The Fae healer seemed to have no knowledge of anatomy and had been trying to heal the entire wound rather than focus on what mattered most.

My hands glowed with a familiar light as I focused on mending that essential artery. It was a matter of seconds before it was sealed and the worst of the bleeding contained. After that, I worked on repairing the punctured right lung and lacerated liver. Those took longer to set right. I wished for equipment to suction the mess and give me a better view. This was the way that Stale doctors and Skew healers worked in my realm, but I had no such advantage here. Instead, I needed to rely solely on my skill. I didn't have much practice healing this sort of wound without visual aid. This way it was slower than having other hands assist in keeping things mess-free, but I had what it took.

The entire time I kept a watch on the king's vitals, the bulk of my skill wrapped around his body to assess the severity of his condition and ensure his well-being.

"By Erilena," the queen whispered as King Elladan's wound sealed and his breathing grew steadier once his lung sealed.

My head grew woozy with the effort, and I braced a hand against the floor, continuing to let my healing energy flow into the king. I pulled back just as I became faint. Jeondar was there, bracing me up, and regarding me in awe.

"He needs more—" I started, but Jeondar cut me off.

"Golred can do the rest." He nodded toward the astonished-looking Fae healer, who blinked and sheepishly let his healing energy flow into the king.

I took several deep breaths to regain my strength and watched with relief as Jeondar's father opened his eyes and looked around.

Belasha threw her arms around her husband. Quietly weeping, she thanked a deity I was unfamiliar with.

"You saved him," Jeondar said, his amber eyes brimming with gratitude and relief. "How can I ever repay you?"

I shook my head. "I swore an oath. It's my duty."

"What do you need?" he asked.

"Just a little rest and water, lots of water."

The king tried to sit up, even as he fought against the results of the debilitating blood loss.

"Don't." I placed a hand on his arm. "You need rest, too."

"That was a *shadowdrifter,*" he spat. "How did it get in *my* city?"

Shadowdrifter? What was he talking about?

Jeondar tensed at the mention, but quickly jumped to his feet and issued instructions to some of the guards. "Help the king and queen to their chambers and guard their door. Golred, go with them and ensure my father's progress."

"Yes, Your Highness," the guards and the healer responded in unison as they rushed to follow their orders.

"Go out there and protect the palace," Jeondar instructed the remaining guards. "Also, inform Captain Nataar and direct her to send guards to defend the denizens against that beast. Tell her I will join her shortly in the Strategy Room."

A series of thumps followed as fists pounded on chests, then they were off. With that done, Jeondar turned to me and helped me to my feet.

"Can you walk?"

I nodded.

We hurried out of there.

"Kryn and Arabis," I said, struggling to keep up and fighting a dizzy spell.

"I know." There was deep concern in his voice. They had been with Kalyll. What if...?

God, let them be okay.

The many halls we traversed were empty, eerily quiet, as if everyone had found a hiding place and was silently praying for their lives.

When we got there, broken furniture greeted us in the front room. The door that led to the pool was off its hinges, claw marks etched on the heavy wood.

"Kryn," Jeondar called. "Arabis." His steps were slow, a sign of the fear he felt about what he would encounter beyond the threshold.

We walked in. The space was empty, the Qrorium chains broken. Jeondar's gaze roved over the floor and walls. He was looking for blood, I realized. Thankfully, there was none. He frowned and glanced toward the pool.

"They've probably gone after Kalyll," I said, praying that was true.

Slowly, he turned toward the chains. The ring that had been around Kalyll's waist was twisted and broken in half.

"He is stronger than I thought," he said in a whisper that barely carried through the space.

I shook my head. "I don't understand. Both the first and second doses kept him calm for hours. The last one should've..."

"What?"

"Oh," I pressed a hand to my forehead. "It was the stillstem. I should have thought of it. It interacted with the marsh flower and must have canceled out its effects. It blocked the cell transporters. Shit, shit! This is all my fault."

"No. You're not to blame for this. Only one person is."

I searched his face, wondering what he meant. I was about to ask, but I swayed on my feet, and he reached out to steady me.

"I'm fine." I took a deep breath as the world around me settled.

Jeondar picked up a clean flask from the table and filled it up in the pool. "Drink this. It's perfectly clean. All the water in Imbermore is potable."

At that moment, I wouldn't have cared if the water were swimming with tadpoles. I drank it all, then kneeled by the pool to get more.

Something broke the surface of the water.

I yelped, kicked back, and fell on my butt. I stared at the two-headed monster, but quickly realized it was no monster at all. It was Kryn and Arabis.

"What in the name of Esthar?" Jeondar blinked at the soaking wet pair.

They swam to the shore and got out. Their hair was plastered to their skulls, and their clothes dripped puddles under their feet. I stood, confused. Had they been down there holding their breath all this while?

"We hid in a small under-chamber that holds a pocket of air," Arabis said when she noticed my confusion.

Kryn's gaze went from the chains to Jeondar, then to me. "How bad is it?"

"Bad."

"Fuck."

"Where is he?" Arabis stepped forward, wearing a beseeching expression.

"We don't know," Jeondar said. "He burst into the party. Everyone saw him."

Kryn's fists tightened at his sides. "Fuck. Fuck."

"He almost killed my father. If it wasn't for Dani, he would be dead."

Kryn opened his mouth, but Arabis beat him to it. "Fuck. Fuck. Fuck."

"He was going straight for Belasha. He was holding a grudge for this afternoon. She would also be dead if not for her." Jeondar looked at me curiously, as did the others.

"How did you stop him?" Jeondar asked.

"Um... I begged him to go."

Everyone looked as if I was drunk, high, *and* crazy.

Kryn looked skeptical. "He has never listened to anyone, except for Arabis, and even her very substantial power doesn't work anymore. Why would he listen to *you*?"

"I don't know," I snapped, growing angry at the way he made the simple word "you" sound like an insult. "But he did. I told him to leave, and he jumped off the balcony."

"That makes no sense," Kryn argued.

"Whether it makes sense or not," Jeondar cut in, "it is what happened, and sitting here arguing about it isn't helpful. We have to find him. Let's go." He didn't wait to see if anyone followed. He just marched out the door, unapologetically wearing the authority of a prince.

When we reached the top of the steps, he turned to me. "Get back to your room and rest."

I wanted to argue, but he left me no chance. He moved with that extra speed the Fae possessed, and before I could even form the words, all three of them were gone.

Once in my room, I was relieved to find Valeriana asleep, relieved to lay my weary head down on the soft pillow. My mind turned and turned with a million questions, but a particular one kept repeating itself.

What is a shadowdrifter?

The mere mention of the word had made Jeondar tense. There was so much they weren't telling me, and it wasn't fair—especially not after tonight. Their cagey behavior made me angry, but as I thought of Kalyll out there and all those people in the city... Hurting Arabis had upset him so much. How would he feel about the people he'd killed tonight? And what if he was killing more innocent folk right now? The weight of his guilt might undo him.

I tossed and turned while Valeriana slept with abandon. At some point, she scooted closer and threw an arm around me. Her warmth and quiet breathing gave me comfort, and I found myself drifting off.

A sound woke me. My eyes sprang open. The room was illuminated by the gentle light of dawn. It was coming from the balcony. I lay very still and listened. There was a groan. Someone was out there.

I pulled away from Valeriana, careful not to wake her up, and tiptoed toward the double doors. Through the sheer curtains, I saw a figure. I held my breath, heart hammering. I leaned closer for a better look.

Kalyll!

I pushed past the curtains, opened the door, and stepped outside. The scent of fresh water floated in the air. A light wind stirred my hair. He was in human form, hunched over as he held the railing and panted. I didn't dare move any closer or say a word. He stayed like that for several minutes while I wrung my hands together. His hair was disheveled, but his clothes were clean, unaltered. How had he gotten all the way up here?

"Is the king dead?" he asked in a deep voice that drove itself into my very bones.

"He's not. He's healed."

He let out a trembling breath, and at last, straightened and turned to face me. His eyes were dark, haunted. He seemed slightly wild still, not quite in control.

"I killed four people," he said. "*Killed* them."

My heart ached for him, for the guilt that brought such anguish to his face.

"I've killed before, in battle, but this was different. This was... vile."

"Kalyll, I'm so sorry," I said. "It's all my fault."

"Your fault?" He frowned abruptly. "How could it be your fault? You stopped me from killing the queen. And it was your voice in my head that kept me from killing any more people."

"I made a mistake. The elixir, I—"

There was a flash of movement, and suddenly I was against the wall, Kalyll's hands on my shoulders, his face mere inches from mine.

"It's *not* your fault." His breath brushed my lips.

There was still a measure of darkness in his eyes, and a sharp slant to his features that made him look untamed. His gaze fell to my lips. He hissed in a breath through clenched teeth. He was fighting against his desire to kiss me. It was obvious. I knew well that he wasn't in full control, knew that I should make this easy for him, but I didn't want to. So instead of pushing him away, I licked my lips and lifted my chin slightly.

I leaned forward, ready to kiss him. His beautiful mouth parted and one of his arms snaked around my waist, pulling me to him.

"Dani!" Valeriana's panicked voice came from the room.

Kalyll blinked. His eyes clearing, he took a step back, appearing both relieved and disappointed that our lips hadn't touched, while I only felt the latter.

Damn kid.

"I'm out here," I called, then to Kalyll I expressed my disappointment. "Too bad." I smiled.

He returned my smile, then took my hand and deposited a chaste kiss on my knuckles. "I will see you soon."

As he still held my hand, he turned to dark mist and was gone.

What the hell?!

I rushed to the edge of the balcony and scanned all around. No sign of him.

Shadowdrifter. The name made more sense now.

The word echoed in my head. The king had said it as if it were a terrible, dreaded name, as something a respectable person—especially a Seelie Prince would never be. The name made no sense for the very solid beast that had interrupted the party, but it made total sense for the prince and the vanishing act I'd just witnessed. Then I remembered, I'd seen him do that before... in the forest, the day we found Valeriana.

The kid poked her head into the balcony. "What are you doing?"

"Um, just admiring this beautiful dawn." I gestured toward the blue and pink sky. "But let's call for some breakfast, why don't we?" I ushered her back inside. "We'll need it. Today will be a long day."

CHAPTER 26

L arina was fluttering around the room, using her magic to deposit our empty breakfast dishes atop a tray. Per Jeondar's instructions, she'd also started packing a few necessities for our trip, which included some of the comfortable clothes from the closet.

I was getting ready in front of the mirror and picked up the leather strip Kalyll had given me to hold back my hair. I fingered its supple texture, remembering the desire in his eyes, feeling that uncalled-for want surge at the thought.

Shaking my head, I gathered my hair in a tall ponytail. Through the mirror, I could see Valeriana sitting on the bed, fiddling with the pieces of the board game she'd been playing with Larina yesterday. We would be leaving her behind today, and I couldn't help but wonder if she would be upset about my departure.

When I was happy with my hair, I picked up Larina's necklace and walked in her direction as she used her magic to pack a perfectly folded tunic into a leather bag.

"Thank you for letting me borrow your beautiful necklace," I said, offering it back.

She flew up to flutter at eye level, a trail of pixie dust in her wake. "You are welcome, Lady Sunder, but I..." She hesitated, looking troubled.

Was something the matter? Had I damaged the necklace? I examined it quickly and saw nothing wrong with it.

"I'd like you to have it," she blurted out.

"What? No. It's very generous of you, but I can't accept it."

"I could never wear it, and it's perfect for you."

The pixie barely knew me. Why would she offer me something so valuable? Maybe it was a cultural thing, and her kind was liberal with gifts, but where I came from, this wasn't done.

"I appreciate the thought, Larina, but I cannot accept it," I said more firmly this time.

Larina's cheeks lit up bright purple. "I am so sorry." She reached out a hand, released a little pixie dust, and the necklace disappeared from my fingers.

I felt a bit flustered and tried to explain. "Um... we humans avoid giving each other such special gifts unless it's a birthday or anniversary of some kind." I didn't want to say it was flat-out weird for someone you'd only met to offer you such an extravagant present, so that was the best I could come up with.

Larina waved her little hands in the air. "I understand completely, My Lady. I need human etiquette lessons."

Valeriana watched the entire exchange from the bed, looking puzzled, but she didn't say anything.

"I'll go downstairs to find Prince Jeondar to discuss... some arrangements," I told the girl. "Larina will stay with you for a bit."

They both nodded, and I made my way out. I had picked a pair of black leggings and a green embroidered tunic that went perfectly with my olive skin. I'd even used a bit of the makeup Larina had left behind last night. Large butterflies flapped their wings in my stomach at the thought of seeing Kalyll. I had so many questions for him.

I thought I might find him in the large dining room, but the servant there told me they were all at the stables. Somehow, I remembered the way there, and indeed, found everyone gathered in the courtyard. Jeondar was issuing instructions for the attendants, all relating to getting the horses ready and packing for our journey, while the others stood in a circle off to the side. It was so early that the sun was yet to provide enough illumination, and a few sconces still offered their magical glow.

"Good morning," I said.

They all turned to face me and inclined their heads in greeting. I approached, feeling self-conscious about the way they were looking at me. There was respect and appreciation in their expressions, and even Kryn seemed to have removed the stick he carried up his butt.

I wondered if this was Kalyll's doing, especially since I felt guilty about my mistake with the elixir.

The Seelie Prince broke the circle and stepped forward to greet me with a bow. "All the sunshine to you, Daniella." He'd tamed his hair, tying it away from his face and adding a few small braids here and there. He'd also shaved, and his eyes were a lighter shade of blue that I hadn't seen before. The circles around his eyes were still there but were not as prominent. He appeared slightly younger, I decided, and marveled at what a little rest could do for someone's appearance.

With some difficulty, I shifted my attention to Jeondar. "How is your father?"

"He is well. All thanks to you."

"I'm glad to hear it." I paused, doing my best not to squirm under everyone's scrutiny. "Um, I was wondering about Valeriana's situation. Did you have the chance to make any arrangements?"

Jeondar nodded. "I did. I took care of it as soon as we arrived. In fact, there will be someone here to pick her up before we leave."

"Oh, I'm so relieved."

"You've been so good to that girl," Cylea said. "I have no patience with children. I think I may be allergic to them."

Silver huffed. "Give it another hundred years and you'll want an entire brood."

"You're describing a nightmare." She walked off, shaking her head. "I need to finish packing."

"Me too." Silver followed after Cylea.

"And me." Kryn was next.

Kalyll walked into the stables without saying a word, leaving me with Arabis.

She placed a hand on my shoulder. "Are you feeling all right this morning? I heard it took a lot out of you to heal the king."

"I'm fine. Thank you for asking. I'm used to working with a team of people who take care of extraneous things. In a way, I think that has made me soft." I laughed.

"I would call you anything but soft," she said. "You're making all of us reevaluate our impression of humans."

"Good to hear."

She glanced towards the stables. "He's troubled. The people he killed last night, it will haunt him for a long time, but it could've been much worse, and we owe it to you that it wasn't."

I shook my head because I knew better. "I feel responsible, Arabis. I messed up."

She took my hand in hers and squeezed. "Get that notion out of your head. Dozens, if not more, would be dead if not for you. I don't know how or why, but you have influence over him."

"That's ridiculous."

She raised an eyebrow. "He huddled under a bridge the entire night and fought the beast's desire to come back to the palace and slay the queen. Only the sound of your voice in his head kept him from doing it."

"Maybe the elixir had something to do with it," I reasoned. "Maybe it made him more receptive."

"Maybe, but I don't think that's the reason." She patted my shoulder and walked off. "By the way, he wants to talk to you."

As I turned toward the stables, my heart started beating faster.

It had been a very long time since any male had this effect on me. I hadn't felt this compelled by another person since my first year in college, when I dated a handsome bear shifter named Jonathan.

Since then, I'd dated Stale men and Skew males alike, and they had all failed to excite me to the same level. Even when there was some chemistry between us, for reasons that escaped me, they didn't stick around for long, and I couldn't say I was disappointed to see them go. I missed them sometimes, but it was more out of a desire not to be alone and to feel loved and special. I didn't need a man to make me feel whole, but it was nice to have someone to share things with, to rely on when things got rough.

But why, oh why, had this particular male reignited my long-lost desire? A prince, of all people? Someone unattainable because our lives were so different, and because there were too many barriers to break through. As the future king, he was likely expected to marry for political reasons.

Ugh, I shook my head. What the hell was this stupid train of thought? What did marriage have to do with any of it?

Passion needed no vows.

Who was to say we couldn't simply enjoy whatever this was? Because he felt it too. I knew he did.

Biting my lower lip, I walked into the stables. Kalyll was in front of Stormheart's stall, running his large hand down the length of the animal's neck. When he sensed me standing there, he threw a quick glance at the attendants, who immediately got the hint and made their way out into the courtyard, leaving us alone.

I walked closer and stopped a few feet away from him. "Arabis said you wanted to talk to me."

"Yes. I wanted to tell you that I will send for additional supplies from The Sage Crystal. We can at least keep using the marsh flower elixir."

This wasn't what I was expecting, but I did my best to hide my disappointment. "We certainly can."

"Perhaps you can provide a list."

"Of course."

He nodded, then glanced at the hay-strewn cobbles under his feet. I thought he would avoid talking about the spark that was between us, but I was glad to discover he wasn't that type of male.

"The curse," he started, "it heightens my emotions, makes them more intense and hard to control."

Shit. It sounds as if this conversation would be along the lines of "*it's not you, it's the beast.*"

"I understand," I said, determined to save him the trouble as well as to save both of us the embarrassment. "No need to explain." I started to turn away, but he stopped me with a hand around my elbow.

"I don't believe you do." His voice was an octave lower as he whispered. "The beast doesn't make me feel anything I don't already feel. What is it about you, Daniella Sunder?" He cupped my face in one hand, his thumb caressing my cheek and sending a delicious blush up my neck. "It's not just me who feels this way, is it?"

I shook my head. "It's not."

He leaned closer, his nose nearly touching mine. "Good, because I mean to make you mine."

His mouth crashed into mine, his lips insistent as they moved against mine. A delicious thrill drove down the length of my body, straight to my core. He wrapped a large hand around the back of my neck and hooked another around my waist, pulling me to him.

His kiss was full of passion and hunger, and I matched it with my own desire, stroke for stroke. What his lips did to me was un-matched, and it made me realize all other kisses before this one had been a poor practice. The way my body responded to his was unlike anything I'd experienced in the past.

When he had thoroughly explored the corners of my mouth and the shape of my lower and upper lips, his tongue slipped inside and tasted me once, then again. Slowly, velvet soft.

Kalyll pulled away, inhaling sharply.

His eyes were entirely black, faint dark veins pulsing around them. "I need... to stop," he said haltingly. "I feel—"

"Don't you dare," I replied recklessly.

That was definitely the right thing to say because he whirled me, pushed me inside a vacant stall, and pressed my back against the wall. He kissed me again, the hand at my neck tangling in my hair. My nipples pebbled as desire electrified me. Arousal ran slick in my panties, and my core ached for the attention it hadn't received in quite some time.

Kalyll moaned and pressed the length of his body flush against mine. I nearly came at the feel of his erection against my stomach. It was considerable in size and very firm. I wanted to reach down and stroke him, but some instinct of self-preservation stopped me. I sensed that this wildness in him wasn't something to trifle with.

My hands explored his chest, ridges upon ridges of perfect muscle. My right hand climbed to his neck, and I ran my fingers along the edge of his sharp jaw. His shoulder-length hair brushed the back of my hand, feeling like silk.

His lips abandoned mine and trailed kisses to my collarbone, then up to my earlobe. "I want to fuck you," he said, his language sending a thrill of surprise and excitement through me.

"Such foul language from a prince," I managed between ragged breaths.

"I will have you," he promised me, "but not here." He pulled away with some difficulty, and I nearly whimpered in protest.

The darkness around his eyes receded. "I can feel the beast at the fringes," he said. "Though I shouldn't, not at this hour. What is this you do to me?"

I shook my head at a loss. "Have you... been with someone since it started?"

"I have."

His admission was plain, a fact, something that had happened before I even met him, and yet a pang of jealousy hit me. I pushed the irrational feeling away.

"And you didn't feel the beast then."

"I did not, but at the risk of saying too much, it's never felt this good."

Oh, he was a charmer, all right.

"It is the truth," he assured me when he noticed my skeptic frown. Suddenly, his head turned to one side. "They're coming back." He gestured toward the stall's exit. "After you."

I would be lying if I didn't say that, at that moment, I wanted the entire Fae realm to disappear so Kalyll and I could have a roll in the hay. Literally. Still, Logical Dani knew it was better this way. She was waving a huge red flag, warning me that whatever this was, it couldn't end well for me.

A roll in the hay with someone who makes you feel this way will ruin you forever, that level-headed, party pooper said. *You'll keep your panties on and your hands to yourself if you know what's good for you.*

I couldn't really argue with this logic. It had a lot of merits, but no matter how loudly Logical Dani laid out her case, she also knew the meaning of the word *inevitable*.

CHAPTER 27

"I don't want to stay here," Valeriana begged, clinging to my leg.

I looked up at Jeondar, scrunching up my face in question. This was what I'd been afraid of. I didn't want her to have to be forced to stay. I wanted her to *want* to stay.

We were in the large dining room, where we'd all congregated to say our goodbyes. Everyone in our group was there, and also the king and queen.

Jeondar glanced around, looking at a loss. "They're supposed to..."

A servant rushed through the door, accompanied by a tall woman, who was nearly Kalyll's height. She was dressed in the same fashion as Valeriana and had green skin, though her hair and eyes were brown.

"Prince Jeondar," the servant said. "Rosetta of Chel Grove is here to see you."

"Thank Esthar," Jeondar said under his breath, then walked ahead to greet the newcomer.

Witchlights! In the nick of time.

Rosetta of Chel Grove inclined her head. "My apologies for my tardiness. I headed this way as soon as I received your message."

At the sound of the female's singsong accent, Valeriana let go of my leg and turned to face her. She blinked her huge green eyes, and something in her face seemed to change, something almost imperceptible that, for the first time since I'd met her, made her look fully at ease.

"Not a problem," Jeondar said. "The important thing is that you're here."

"Where is the child?" Rosetta asked.

"Here." I stepped away from Valeriana, who remained mostly hidden by me.

Rosetta's face lit up with a smile, and so did Valeriana's.

"I have come to take you home," Rosetta said.

The child hugged herself, and it was clear to me that she was trying not to cry with relief.

My heart warmed up for her. I leaned down to talk to her. "It was great meeting you, Valeriana of Mid Crosswood. I will never forget you."

"And... I will never forget you. Maybe we'll meet again."

"Maybe."

"This is very auspicious," the king said. "Rosetta and Valeriana, you're welcome to stay here as long as you want until you're ready to depart to your home."

"Thank you, King Elladan. A couple of days of rest will suffice, and I hope I may be granted an audience to talk about what happened to Valeriana's clan, and the threats now looming over my clan."

The king's face darkened at the possibility of more bad news. Kalyll also seemed to tense. He seemed frustrated, as if he wished he could do something here and now, but his quest was more important. In order to be able to serve his people, he needed to be in control of his full capacities. His eyes met mine from across the room, and I offered him a reassuring smile.

I'll do everything I can to help you was the message I tried to convey.

He nodded as if he understood, as if he trusted me.

I just prayed I wouldn't let him down.

An hour later, we were outside the walls of Imbermore, headed north.

The Sunder Mountains loomed ahead, looking closer than ever. Still, I didn't let that fool me. I'd gotten better at estimating distances, and my guess was that traveling only in the morning would take at least twenty days to reach them.

Kalyll rode ahead, setting the pace. I hung back for the first hour, but no matter how hard I tried, I couldn't take my eyes off his straight back, couldn't stop craving the feel of his muscles at my fingertips—not to mention his lips on mine.

When the craving for his company got the best of me, I rode forward and joined him.

"Hey," I said, as eloquent as a rock.

"Hey back." He winked, which was charming as hell.

There was an awkward silence until I got my raging hormones in order.

"How long will it take us to get to Mount Ruin?" I asked.

"Around twelve days, I hope. We need to arrive on the first day of the new moon."

"Why the new moon?"

He shrugged, avoiding the question. More secrets.

I sighed. "Well, at least that's less time than I thought."

"I'm being hopeful. I'm counting on Stormheart carrying my limp, useless body without complaining after I take the elixir. You may have to tie me to his back to prevent me from falling on my face, though." He seemed amused at the thought.

"I see."

Once more, we rode in silence for a few minutes. As I tried to spark some conversation, I mulled over how little I knew about him. After

I broke up with Jonathan—once that amazing chemistry between us fizzled out and I realized we had nothing in common—I started dating males of substance, guys I could have interesting conversations with to make up for the lackluster sex. At some point, I'd decided that it was impossible to have both body and mind chemistry, that I had to content myself with one or the other—not that I ever found another Jonathan. Not until now.

"So... what does the prince do with his time?" I asked, unsure of whether or not I wanted him to be the full package. Because if he was, what then?

"Lounge around and eat cheese and grapes," he said.

"Oh."

He laughed. "Hardly. Honestly, it's not an easy life. Some would say *'oh, poor little rich prince, his life is so miserable with all that gold and comfort,'* but they haven't been in my shoes. My younger brother... now, he could tell you all about the cheese and grapes."

"I imagine that being the heir to the throne kept you away from enjoying the same pleasures?"

"Exactly. I had to learn about, well, everything."

"Everything?" I asked with a raised eyebrow.

He shrugged. "It felt that way. History, philosophy, diplomacy, geography, mathematics, religion, strategy, sociology, politics, the list goes on and should be multiplied by two."

I frowned, not getting his meaning.

"I had to also learn those things in relation to your realm," he explained.

"Ouch. And were you the scholarly type?"

"I had no choice but to be. It was either try to enjoy it or be entirely miserable. Thankfully, there was also battle training, which was where I released all my frustrations."

I nodded thoughtfully. "Yeah, I suppose I've had it easy compared to you."

Frowning, I started to fear that once he found out more about me, *he* would be the one wondering if I possessed any *substance*. If he launched into some philosophical discussion, I would be lost.

"It's not so bad now that my core education is complete," he said. "There's always more to learn, of course, but these days, my woes are entirely different, as you well know."

"Besides us, are there others who know about your ailment?"

He shrugged.

"Your parents don't know?"

At this question, a muscle ticked in his jaw. "My father doesn't know, and he should never know."

For a moment, a dark cloud seemed to settle over his brow. If even the mere thought of his father learning of his condition soured his mood so drastically, I didn't want to imagine how he would feel if he actually found out. But what about his mother? What was he leaving unsaid?

I wanted to ask what would happen if we didn't find a way to cure him. Would his grape-eating brother have to become king? Would that spell disaster for the Seelie Court? Probably, if his brother was as inept as Kalyll made him sound. But I knew I couldn't ask any of this. It was too personal, not to mention a subject that seemed to put him in a bad mood.

Kalyll took a deep breath, glanced at the faraway mountains for a long moment, and when he turned to look at me again, his expression was tranquil, genuinely, which I admired. He seemed very good at compartmentalizing his feelings, even with all the terrible things he was dealing with. The emotions relating to the deaths he'd caused last night would have been enough to bring a lesser male to his knees, but not Prince Kalyll Adanorin.

"I want you to know that I sent a message to your sister," he said.

"What?"

"Toni will soon know where you are and with whom. I didn't want your family to worry about you, and I know that peace of mind will be yours as well."

"Thank you."

"Please, don't thank me when I created the problem in the first place."

My family would have a million questions, but at least they would know I was okay and would stop wondering if I'd ended up dead in a ditch or trapped in a maniac's basement.

"There's something else you should know," Kalyll added, his cobalt eyes connecting with mine and looking as serious as a heart attack.

"What is that?"

"I haven't been able to stop thinking about this morning."

My breath caught as his deep voice racked over me, doing things to my body that other males hadn't made me feel even with their touch. God, it wasn't fair—not if I couldn't make him feel the same way. This male knew how to seduce, for sure. Maybe seduction had been one of the subjects he'd learned to become an effective king.

Was I a match for him? I had to try to be.

I held his gaze and slowly licked my lips. "I already forgot about it," I said, sounding regretful. "Perhaps I need a reminder."

Kalyll squirmed on top of his saddle, which let me know I *did* have the same effect on him. My stomach fluttered at the thought because he wasn't just any male. He was a Fae prince with not only the body and face of a god, but from what I'd learned so far, also a brilliant mind and the heart of a lion.

"It would be my pleasure to offer you one," he said. "I have—"

Kryn rode forward to join us. He looked between Kalyll and me with something like displeasure, as if it bothered him that we were talking.

"Something the matter?" Kalyll asked.

"Jeondar says we're being followed."

"Is that so?" Kalyll grunted, irritated. "I feared someone might get that idea."

"Cylea's vote is on Lyanner Phiran. He says he was being nosy at the ball, asking all kinds of questions. It wouldn't be the first time he sticks his nose where it doesn't belong."

"Let's work on throwing them off our trail. Let's head for the trees."

Kryn nodded and rode back, but not before shooting me a dirty look. Great. We were back to square one. I thought he and I had made some progress, but that was too optimistic of me.

For the next couple of hours, we weaved through different paths in North Crosswood. It was far more interesting than riding in the open, but it would, no doubt, add time to our travels.

"Won't they be able to track us, anyway?" I asked Kalyll.

"Not with Cylea's help."

"Oh yeah?"

"She will disguise our passage."

"How?"

"Why don't you take a look?"

"I shall."

Even though I was enjoying riding next to Kalyll and learning more about him, I turned Dandelion around and found Cylea at the back of the group. She was riding her horse backward with as much agility as Kryn had displayed when he did the same. She wore a bored expression as she weaved her fingers and pointed them at the ground, a flower, or a branch.

"What are you doing?" I asked, eyes scanning the path we were leaving behind.

She didn't answer, only continued to—

A patch of weeds our horses had trampled reformed itself and went back to looking intact. A bed of moss that had the imprint of a horseshoe fluffed itself back up. A broken branch became whole again—everything happened all at once and with the least bit of effort.

"Wow, you can... heal plants," I said.

"You can too, I saw it." Cylea looked bored, almost contemptuous of her gift.

"Not the way you're doing it. Plants are difficult for me, and I couldn't heal so many at once."

"Who cares when the likes of Jeondar could set this entire forest on fire in one fell swoop?"

Clearly, she was bitter about her skill, but she shouldn't be. "It's easier to destroy."

"Than what? Mend the broken stem of a useless weed?" She blew air through her nose.

"I'm sure the others appreciate you keeping our passage secret."

She shrugged and continued waving her fingers at the plants.

"Kryn doesn't have any powers," I said. At least, I hadn't seen any. Another shrug. There really seemed to be no way to turn her opinion around.

After about thirty minutes of making the path we were weaving through look untouched, Cylea and I joined the others.

I noticed Arabis tipping her head back, trying to peer through the trees. Since I knew what she was doing, I pulled out Kalyll's watch from my pocket.

"A little over thirty minutes before noon," I told her.

"That's what I thought. We should find somewhere to stop so he can take the elixir.

We did just that at a small clearing carpeted with dry leaves. I set to work immediately, preparing the elixir. Kryn had let me keep the heating rocks, which made things a lot easier. In a matter of minutes, I had my brew ready, the same dose I'd used the last time. I hadn't had the chance to monitor its effects—I would do that today—but I felt confident it would be safe.

"That's stupid," Jeondar was saying when I approached. "I brought a stretcher. One of the packhorses can pull you."

"I'd rather stay on Stormheart," Kalyll argued.

"You'll fall and crack your head open."

"I'm sure I can manage to stay up on my horse."

"So what? We tie you to it?"

"That won't be necessary."

Jeondar looked at me as if looking for help.

"Um, it will be easier for me to monitor you if you're on the stretcher," I said, which was true.

"What a nuisance!" Kalyll grumbled but got off his horse all the same.

"I'm glad he listens to somebody," Jeondar mumbled as he turned around and left to prepare the stretcher.

Kalyll kicked at the ground with the tip of a black boot. "I'm useless."

"So what difference does it make if you're on a horse or a stretcher?" I asked.

He gave me a narrow-eyed look. "Maybe on the horse I can keep my dignity, at least."

"I see."

"You see what?"

I waved a hand. "Oh, nothing."

"It's definitely something." He took a step closer and looked down at me, an eyebrow raised.

"Oh, just wondering if anything else about you is as fragile as your dignity," I teased.

He chuckled deep in his throat. "I can't wait to show you the parts of me that are anything but fragile."

My face heated as I realized what he was talking about. I fought through my surprise and searched for a clever line of my own to throw him off balance too.

"I shall welcome them with nothing but *tenderness*," I said in a near purr.

He bared his teeth, letting out a little growl. "Ms. Sunder, you better watch the things you say to me, or I will not hold myself responsible."

I opened my mouth to say something, but Arabis walked up to interrupt our banter. She looked at the flask in my hands and said, "You better hurry up and take that."

I felt another blush coming, though this one was for a different reason. I'd been too busy flirting instead of doing my job.

"Here." I pushed the elixir in front of Kalyll, who immediately gulped it down.

"Just as nasty as the last time," he said, wiping his mouth with the back of his index finger.

"Good." Arabis gave me another disapproving glance.

Huh? I thought she liked me, but maybe I'd been wrong. Maybe she was jealous since she'd lost her prince-sitting job. For all I knew, she had a thing for Kalyll, even if they were distant cousins, and she was jealous about more than just losing her job. Maybe she didn't like the Fae prince showing any interest in a lowly human.

"I'd better lie down," Kalyll said, blinking rapidly and swaying slightly on his feet.

"Yes. You'd better." I draped his arm over my back and helped him walk toward the stretcher. Jeondar had it ready, its poles attached to a harness that was strapped around the horse. The stretcher sat at an angle and seemed sturdily built for a male of Kalyll's size and weight.

Only moments after he lay down, Kalyll was out, breathing deeply and looking at peace.

Jeondar wrapped several straps around him, securing him in place. Once that was done, we set out once more. Every so often, we stopped so I could check Kalyll's vitals. It all seemed as expected, but still, as we weaved further up into North Crosswood, my eyes remained on the prince, watching for the slightest change.

CHAPTER 28

K alyll required only two doses to stay asleep until the sun started
going down. He woke up groggily just as we finished setting
up camp at the mouth of a ravine, whose rocky sides rose fifty feet
above us.

Cylea had guided us here since she was familiar with the area. It
was close to the Spring Court, her home. We laid everything out in
front of a small cave, which was the main topic of conversation at
the moment.

"Kalyll will stay in the cave, which we can guard," Jeondar was
saying. "If he comes out, whoever is on watch can raise the alarm.
We can then—"

"Hope we don't get eaten?" Cylea put in. "This is very, very stupid."

"What else do you suggest we do?" Jeondar asked.

"I don't know. Run far away?"

"Maybe you should," Kalyll said from his spot on a boulder, where
he sat holding his head as if it weighed a thousand pounds.

They all looked at me as if I had the answer. "Um, I'll inject him
with a low dose of hemlock. It shouldn't interact with the marsh
flower, but I make no guarantees."

Kryn threw his hands up in the air as if to say, "*What good are
you?*"

"This is not Daniella's fault." Kalyll made an effort to sit up straight. "She's here against her will and doing the best she can to help us."

Kryn huffed, but said nothing else.

"Maybe, as Cylea suggests, it would be best if you leave me here," Kalyll said. "You can find a safe place to rest."

"It would make no difference, and you know it," Jeondar put in. "If you wake up, you'll find us, and then what? We still have to defend ourselves against you."

"And if he doesn't wake up," I said. "He'll have to catch up with us and we will be delayed."

Everyone looked resigned to staying, since the alternatives weren't any better.

"We have a new Susurro, anyway." Kryn looked me up and down with contempt. "She can keep us safe."

"That's enough, Kryn." Kalyll stood, and even though he was unsteady on his feet, he managed to look commanding. "I don't want to hear you trying to antagonize Daniella anymore. Is that clear?"

Kryn offered no answer. He just turned to his horse and started removing its saddle.

The prince turned to me. "Let's get this over with."

He staggered toward the cave, ducked at the low entrance, and disappeared inside.

I turned toward Dandelion, retrieved the medicine from the saddlebag, and got to work. I avoided looking at anyone, but I felt their eyes on me, judging, even Arabis who had been the first one to make me feel welcome. Why were they suddenly acting this way? What had changed?

When I was done, Jeondar came over holding a lit torch. "Ready?"

I nodded, and as we walked toward the cave, I asked, "Why is everyone mad at me?"

"Mad?" He frowned, then hurried to add, "They're not mad, just worried."

"Worried that I'll kill their prince?"

He shrugged and gave me nothing else. As we entered the cave, he held the torch up, allowing the warm light to break through the darkness. The cave was small, no bigger than the guest bathroom in my condo, definitely tight for three people. But at least it had a tall enough ceiling to allow us to stand.

Kalyll was sitting on the ground, elbows resting on bent knees, face buried in his large hands. Something ached inside of me at the sight.

"Hey." I kneeled next to him, holding the syringe in one hand and the flask with the elixir in the other.

"Hey back." He lifted his head and gave me a smile that didn't reach his eyes. Without another word, he downed the elixir, then allowed me to inject him with the hemlock.

I watched him carefully, my heart pounding as his slowed down. I knew he was strong and so was the beast, but hemlock was a poison. What if he didn't wake up tomorrow? I pushed my worries aside and tried to focus on the facts. A heavy dose of marsh flower that would've killed most people had no more effect on him than a sleeping pill, not to mention I'd been cautious with the hemlock—maybe too cautious and in a few hours we would be running for our lives.

His eyes locked with mine until they closed, then he drifted off to sleep. Jeondar went out for a moment and returned with blankets to make the prince comfortable. We laid him flat on the ground, put a rolled blanket under his head, and covered him with another.

"Go eat something," Jeondar said. "I'll stay and watch him for a few hours."

I walked to the mouth of the cave and paused. "I'll come by every so often to check his vitals and see how he's responding to the hemlock."

I didn't want to leave. I wanted to sit next to Kalyll and hold his hand, but I couldn't do that in front of Jeondar. As I made my way out, I tried to tell myself I was only worried about my patient. Nothing more. It was what I would do for anyone.

Yeah, sure. Keep telling yourself that and maybe you'll believe it.

Outside the cave, a fire was going already, and the smell of roasted meat permeated the air. These Fae certainly worked fast, which was a good thing because I was hungry. I ate quietly, sitting on a rock and looking up from my food every few minutes. The animosity that had started... when?—*After you and Kalyll kissed,* my Logical Dani said inside my head—was there every time I glanced at the others.

If they knew Kalyll and I had kissed, why would they care? Few answers insinuated themselves, but I chose to ignore them, preferring to focus on more important things, such as the well-being of my patient. So when I finished my dinner, I walked back into the cave and checked on Kalyll.

"Has he stirred?" I asked Jeondar as I offered him a wooden plate with food.

"Thank you." He took the plate. "And no, he hasn't stirred one bit."

"Good."

"Indeed."

I made quick work of checking Kalyll's pulse, temperature, and blood pressure, jotted everything down in my journal, and walked back outside.

I glanced around, looking for the tent they'd always erected for me, but now that they didn't need to keep me prisoner, no one had bothered to put it together. Or maybe there was another reason. Either way, it didn't matter. There were enough blankets on the packhorses to make myself a cozy spot somewhere. I found the perfect place next to a boulder. I could face the fire while the boulder watched my back. The thought of sleeping completely in the open didn't sit well with me, so the rock would be a perfect nighttime companion, even if I couldn't wrap my arms around it. It aroused me as much as most males, anyhow.

It took several minutes of tossing and turning to make myself comfortable, but I finally fell asleep with the thought that I would wake up in an hour to check on Kalyll. At the hospital, there were rooms for interns, doctors, and healers. They were small but private, with twin beds and night tables. I'd slept countless hours there when I had a patient in a delicate condition, someone who needed constant evaluation or bursts of healing energy. I always set an alarm on my watch to make sure I woke up at regular intervals, but I was sure the lack of an annoying *beep-beep* wouldn't be a problem. My biological clock was well attuned to the demands of my job, and I only failed to wake up on my own when I was extremely tired.

Sure enough, my eyes sprang open almost on the dot an hour later. Silver and Cylea were sitting by the fire, talking quietly, while Jeondar and Arabis lay sleeping at the edge of the camp. I made a face. That meant Kryn was inside the cave, watching Kalyll.

Joy, my favorite person.

But I had a job to do, and no asshole had ever stopped me from doing the right thing.

Just inside the cave, Kryn was reclining against the wall in sight of both Kalyll and the outside. He offered me no greeting, even as I whispered a casual *hello*. I squeezed by him, keeping my chin high, doing my best not to let his arrogance and hostility intimidate me.

As I kneeled next to Kalyll, I was relieved by the tranquil expression on his face. His vitals were slow, but nothing to give me concern. I resisted the temptation to smooth his hair back and instead did quick work of things and stood to leave.

Kryn was looking at me from under an angry frown.

Before I could stop myself, I blurted out, "Do you have a problem with me?"

He crossed his arms, folded a knee, and placed a foot on the wall. "Should I?"

"Did I do or say something to offend you?"

"Did you?"

I huffed and mumbled under my breath, low enough that I knew not even his Fae hearing would pick it up. "I don't have time to deal with assholes."

I marched past him without another word and went back to sleep, facing the boulder to avoid Silver's and Cylea's constant sidelong glances.

I checked on Kalyll every hour without fail. Around midnight, his vitals had gone up, so I injected him with another dose of hemlock. I feared he would wake up when I pricked him, but he remained asleep, his eyes revolving behind closed lids, as he stayed lost in some, hopefully pleasant, dream.

During my rounds, I saw everyone in the cave as they took turns watching their prince. No one was as rude as Kryn, but they weren't too nice either. Only Arabis had anything decent to say.

"I'm glad you found something to keep him calm. Good job."

I thanked her and tried to go back to sleep, but it was close to dawn, and I felt wired up, a consequence of being on high alert, never quite going into a deep sleep. Still, I lay on the ground facing the boulder and missing the warmth of home and my family.

When the first light of dawn insinuated itself, Arabis walked out of the tent and disappeared through a line of bushes, probably to do her business. I sat up, wondering if Kalyll was awake. I feared he would be experiencing nausea from the hemlock, so I went to check on him and found that he was indeed awake.

"Good morning," I said.

A huge smile spread across his face. "Good morning indeed. You did it!" He rose and stretched, his head nearly touching the top of the cave's ceiling. "I feel amazing. I haven't had a night of sleep like that in several weeks."

"Any nausea?"

"No. I'm actually starving."

"That is a good sign. No ill effects from the hemlock."

"I wish I'd had your counsel all along. It would have saved me a lot of trouble."

"Glad I could help." I turned to leave, but he snatched my hand and pulled me to him.

He looked down at me, frowning. "Something the matter?"

Only that your friends are being a bunch of assholes.

"No," I answered instead because I was about to whine to him about it. He'd already asked them to be nice, and the request fell on deaf ears. What else could he do? Force them?

He placed a finger under my chin. "Are you sure?"

"Yeah. I'm just a bit... homesick. That's all."

"I'm sorry. This will be over soon. I promise."

His eyes held mine, and the way he was looking at me did weird things to my chest. There was such tenderness in his expression, such care. Best of all, it felt genuine. And maybe it was because everyone else was being a jerk, but his gentleness touched me.

Slowly, he lowered his lips to mine and kissed me. He pulled away for a moment to look at me again and completely disarmed the protective wall I'd started building around me last night.

He kissed me again, pulling me against his hard body. When I was flushed against him, he made a sound of pleasure in the back of his throat and deepened his kiss. Immediately, I was putty in his hands, and he was the same. When my tongue slipped into his mouth, I felt him shudder slightly, as if he wasn't a grown male accustomed to the rigors of politics and battle, but a young boy who had never experienced a woman's touch. But surely, I must've been imagining things, even if at that moment, it felt as if I could make him eat out of the palm of my hand if I wanted to.

He whirled me around, pressed my back against the wall, and hiked my leg up around his waist, fitting perfectly between my legs. His hardness was exquisite against my core, and I nearly melted in his arms.

"Did you put something in that elixir?" he asked in a rough whisper. "Something to make me crazy about you?"

As hard as it was to clear my head and push on his chest, I managed to put a few inches between us. "I would never! Is that what you think?"

He chuckled. "Of course not. I was just trying to illustrate a point. I believe you're intoxicating all on your own." He dived for my neck to kiss and fondle it with expert lips.

I closed my eyes as a wave of desire crashed into me.

"I fucking knew it!" Kryn's voice growled from the entrance of the cave.

CHAPTER 29

Kalyll pulled away from me faster than I'd ever seen him move, even when he turned to mist or whatever it was he did.

"What the fuck, Kalyll?" Kryn demanded. "What do you think you're doing?"

It took Kalyll a moment to recover and don a nonchalant expression. "This is none of your concern."

"Is it not?" he asked, missing only a hand on his hips to look like some sort of mother.

What the hell was going on here? Why was Kryn acting like a jilted boyfriend? *Oh, God!* Was that it? No wonder everyone was treating me like a pariah.

"Since when do you care?" Kalyll seemed puzzled.

O-kay. From the sounds of it, they had an open relationship, and suddenly Kryn had decided to object to that.

"Since now," Kryn spat.

Kalyll shook his head. "Don't be stupid."

I hooked a thumb toward the exit. "I think I should..."

"No." Kryn blocked me. "You should stay and listen to—"

"You're blowing this out of proportion," Kalyll interrupted.

"Am I? I'm worried, Kalyll."

The prince put on an incredulous expression. "Worried? About a *human*?"

The word felt like a slap in the face. I lived in a world where Stales and Skews got along, for the most part, but I was well aware of the way the different species sometimes discriminated against each other, and the Fae were notorious for thinking we humans were *less*.

I glanced at Kalyll, nostrils flaring.

"Daniella..." He reached out a hand.

"Excuse me." I walked past Kryn, slamming my shoulder into his arm to push him out of the way.

"Wait," Kalyll called, but I was already out of the cave, marching past the trees in search of a place to hide.

I wiped my mouth, hoping to erase the feel of his kiss, the taint of my humiliation. I fought the urge to cry. I would not shed a tear. I would not let this bunch of conceited Fae hurt my feelings. The moment I forgot I was their prisoner was the moment I forgot my place here.

"Daniella." Kalyll was fast behind me.

I looked right and left, trying to find somewhere to hide, but I wasn't the one who should feel ashamed. I hadn't done anything wrong, so I turned around and squared my shoulders just as he pushed a branch out of the way and caught up with me.

He froze and fought to meet my gaze. "I'm sorry. I didn't mean anything by it."

"By what?" I asked, glad that my voice sounded as firm and cold as I wanted it to.

Kalyll stared at the ground for a moment, looking frustrated, then took a deep breath and pressed a fist to his chest. "My comment might have given you the impression that I think myself more than you, but I assure you that is not the case."

"I bet you think those diplomacy lessons paid off." I paused and looked him up and down, trying to make him feel like a piece of garbage. "Well, tell your teachers they failed you. Or maybe it's the other way around."

"I deserve that." He lowered his head, looking properly chastised.

"By any chance, was acting in the repertoire of things you had to learn?"

"I have not been insincere," he assured me.

"Maybe you should qualify that statement to clarify which particular behavior you're referring to."

He said nothing, probably realizing that he'd dug a big enough hole already.

"Let me remind you of something, Prince Adanorin," I said. "You're the one who brought me here. You're the one who needs me, so maybe you and your friends should show some respect to this lowly human?"

"It's not like that. I swear."

"Then how is it?"

"It's complicated."

"Fuck you, Kalyll."

I skirted around him and headed back toward the camp, a brick wall erecting itself between us.

"Wait." He moved to grab my arm, but I shot him a warning glare.

"Leave me alone. From now on, the best you can do is hurry this up so I can get the hell out of here."

He bowed and clicked his heels like a good soldier.

I wanted nothing to do with whatever his drama with Kryn was, and much less with his prejudice toward my kind. All I wanted was to go back home.

I packed my mare in record time and stood off to the side as the others finished gathering their things. Insane ideas assaulted me as I waited. I thought of refusing to make the marsh flower and hemlock elixirs, thought of throwing away the ingredients so they couldn't force me to make them, but that was stupid. It would only make things harder for me, and would delay my return home, so I refrained.

Everyone's looks of contempt continued. Though at some point, Kalyll pulled everyone aside and after that, they went from flat-out glaring at me to ignoring my presence. Only Jeondar remained the same, probably because he felt he owed me a debt after saving his father.

When we got on our way, I steered Dandelion to the left of the group, leaving a wide breadth between us. Every so often, Kalyll cast glances over his shoulder, which I pointedly avoided.

After riding in the front with the prince for a long while, Arabis made her way to me, looking contrite. Had Kalyll asked her to make me feel better? Maybe he had started to fear I would not help him.

"Are you Kalyll's ambassador meant to intercede on his behalf?" I asked.

It would be like a diplomatic prince to use such tactics, I figured.

Arabis smiled. "He did ask me to see how you are."

"What? Did he forget who he's dealing with? We plebeians have no understanding of diplomacy, you see?"

"He just wanted me to make sure you're all right?"

"I'm all right. So go on."

"You're not all right. You're upset."

I took a deep breath to calm down. Normally, I wasn't an angry person. Anger was a useless emotion, for the most part. It only served to ruin your day and cloud your judgment. But even though I'd been trying to brush it all aside, I was still furious.

Furious at myself for falling for Kalyll's act, for finding pleasure in the idea that someone like *him* seemed enthralled by me. Livid that somehow I also seemed to buy into the idea of how great the Fae were when they were exactly or worse than everyone else.

"Upset?" I asked. "What would give you that impression? I'm peachy."

"Sarcasm doesn't suit you, Dani."

"I suppose you're right. That's more Kryn's specialty, I suppose."

"Kalyll is not a bad person."

"He doesn't need defending, Arabis. He has all the power, while I have none." I turned away, blinking rapidly to stave off the tears.

"He is deeply sorry. You may never know how much."

I said nothing, afraid I wouldn't be able to stop myself from crying. To my relief, Arabis rode away and let me be.

When we broke through the trees, I was dismayed to find that The Sunder Mountains didn't appear much closer. Two more weeks. I had to endure two more weeks. I could do it, and after that, I would demand an expedited trip back.

CHAPTER 30

On the fifteenth day after leaving Imbermore, I was tiredly riding away from the group as it had become my habit when we reached a narrow mountain pass that would take us to the other side of the range. We had finally reached the mountains, but I could hardly feel excited about it. The last two weeks had been torturous, enduring everyone's animosity and trying to avoid Kalyll's entreating glances while I served as his nurse.

Though we'd gained some altitude as we traveled, the pass cut between two very steep mountains and would save us a lot of time, for which I could only be grateful.

I kept checking the pocket watch, apprehensive about noontime. I dreaded administering the elixir each day and—

A sound like the hiss of a snake cut through the air.

"Take cover," Silver shouted, urging his horse toward a tall outcrop.

My heart went into overdrive. There was another *hiss*, and an arrow embedded itself in the ground, right next to Dandelion's front legs.

"Shit!"

Panicked, I guided the mare toward Silver and his horse, wishing there was somewhere else to hide, but beggars couldn't be choosers. There were more outcrops, which the others were hurrying to, but this was the closest one. When I was nearly there, I hopped off the mare's back and pulled on her reins until she was fully hidden. She snorted nervously, her eyes wide. I *shushed* her.

"It's going to be all right, Dee."

Silver unsheathed his sword and rushed back out. "Watch my horse."

Asshole! What was I? His groom? Except I would hate for anything to happen to the animal. Silver could get an arrow up his ass, for all I cared.

Heart booming in my ears, I grabbed both horses' reins in one hand to keep them from fleeing, crouched, and peeked around the outcrop. Arrows were raining from the sides of both mountains. They bounced off rocks or embedded themselves into the ground one after the other. How many people were up there? Were they thieves?

An arrow zipped in front of my nose. I yelped and reared back. Praying, I sat tight for a moment. Metallic sounds started reverberating all around, bouncing off the rocks that walled us in. Curiosity got the best of me, and I looked around the boulder again. Kalyll was out in the open, his sword knocking arrows directly from the air.

But of course!

An arrow flew straight toward his head. I held my breath, but I shouldn't have worried because he moved like the wind and cut it in half. In the next instant, he ran up the side of the mountain, headed straight toward the source of the arrow he'd just avoided.

Kryn followed right after, watching his back, deflecting the projectiles coming from behind. Working in tandem and leaping like a couple of professional mountain climbers with goat complexes, they made it to the spot where one of the attackers was hiding. Finding himself assailed, the male jumped out, abandoning his bow and arrow for a sword. He slashed at Kalyll, but the prince easily leaned to one side, avoiding injury and lopping his foe's head off with one swift hit.

I gasped as the head flew through the air, hit the side of the mountain, and rolled onto the path, long red hair tumbling and whipping about. The head finally came to a stop, its open, lifeless eyes staring straight at me.

"Oh, God!" I pulled back into my hiding place, stomach churning. The horrible sight was imprinted in my retinas for several sickening moments. I tried to think of something else, anything else: home, my cozy bed, the hospital with its long, sterile halls, my patients smiling happily, anything to erase that blank stare from my mind.

The sounds of battle continued all around me.

Damn, why didn't I know how to fight? I felt useless.

"I got him," Cylea shouted, then there was a grunt of pain, followed by a *thud*.

"There are two more. Over there," this from Kryn.

"Careful!" Arabis cried out.

Another grunt.

"He's down!"

No!

Unable to stop myself, I stuck my head out again. Jeondar was on the ground, an arrow protruding from his stomach. His face was contorted in pain, teeth bared, as he tried to push with his legs to hide behind a nearby boulder. Another arrow whizzed down and hit his leg.

He screamed in pain.

Without thinking, I let go of the horses' reins and ran toward Jeondar.

"Daniella, stay back!" Kalyll shouted, but I was running at full pelt, my legs and arms pumping as I zigzagged, hoping to avoid being hit. Several arrows sailed too close for comfort, but they missed me. I skidded to a stop next to Jeondar, my boots kicking back gravel.

"You're going to get yourself killed," he chided, as I hooked my hands under his arms and started pulling him behind the rock, his uninjured leg pushing, helping me with the bulk of his considerable weight.

"You're welcome," I said between grunts.

Another arrow zoomed by his already injured leg. It sliced through his trousers, but only grazing him, then inserting itself into the ground. With one last effort, I managed to pull him entirely to safety, falling flat on my butt. I scrambled to a kneeling position and quickly assessed his injuries. Dark blood stained his tunic, quickly blossoming. I checked the leg injury next. It was bleeding, but not profusely. Not the priority.

I placed my hands over his stomach wound.

He twisted in pain. "Take it out!"

"No. It might make things worse. Stay still," I ordered. "I need to assess your injuries first."

I closed my eyes and concentrated, trying to ignore the sounds of battle. I did my best to construct that mental picture of his injury and the exact position of the arrow. Once more, it was hard not having a visual aid. It took great effort to get a rough idea of his internal injuries, though not as much as last time. Based on the image I formed, I was confident I could pull the arrow out without further injury. My eyes popped open.

"So?" Jeondar demanded.

"I'm taking it out. Don't move."

He gritted his teeth.

I placed a hand around the wound and grabbed the arrow with the other. Without preamble, I yanked it out.

Jeondar growled, but I immediately got to work healing him, mending veins and tissue. When I was done, he exhaled in relief and threw his head back.

"Now your leg."

I started evaluating the second injury. This time, it didn't take as long, and within a few minutes, the arrow was out and the wound repaired. He sat up, looking a bit woozy. He'd lost blood, but not so much that he would pass out.

"Thank you," he said. "You've now saved three members of the Summer Court. What would we do without you?"

I couldn't help my bitter retort. "Remain untouched by the low-born?"

Jeondar cocked his head to one side. "It's not like that, Dani."

"Isn't it, though? But never mind."

I moved away from him and peeked around our hiding spot. I was trying to assess the situation. Jeondar jumped back into the fray, picking up his sword on the way.

"Really?" I called after him. "Do you have a death wish?"

The sound of clashing metal drew my attention to a ledge about fifty feet up a very steep section of the mountain. Kalyll was up there, sword-fighting against a massive male at least two heads taller than him. As they exchanged blows, they teetered precariously, sending rocks sliding down the almost vertical slope.

It took me a moment to notice that the others were just standing there, watching Kalyll fight. I glanced all around and realized that they'd taken care of everyone else, and the male fighting Kalyll was the last one left.

Hesitantly, I walked into the open, my eyes glued to the fight taking place high above. How had Kalyll even gotten up there?

"Will no one help him?" I asked, more to myself than anyone else.

Kryn shrugged. "He can take care of himself." He turned around, looking uninterested, and started poking at a fallen enemy, as if searching for clues.

"What an asshole," I said under my breath. "But what do I care?"

Except, despite myself, I did care. I couldn't take my eyes off that ledge, couldn't stop imagining Kalyll tumbling off, breaking his neck on his way down. He couldn't shadowdrift, not at this hour.

Kalyll's opponent lifted his sword high and brought it down as if he intended to chop the prince in two. My heart jumped into my throat as Kalyll leaned toward the cliffside and, through some impossible maneuver, ended behind his attacker. Wasting no time, he slammed his sword's pommel into the back of his attacker's head.

"What?!" Silver exclaimed. "Just kill the bastard."

The blow should've knocked the male unconscious, but it merely slowed him down. He blinked, looking dazed, then whirled on Kalyll, setting his left foot too close to the edge. He teetered for an instant, then toppled. The prince tried to take hold of one of his windmilling arms, but he missed, and the large male rolled down the mountain, the sounds of cracking bone echoing throughout.

I averted my eyes as he reached the bottom, landing in a heap of broken bones.

"Dammit!" Kalyll cursed and started descending, easily finding footholds.

My healer instincts had me rushing toward the injured male. Silver ran ahead of me and got there first. He kneeled in front of the male, reaching a hand behind his back and coming up with the dagger.

"No," Kalyll and I both yelled at the same time.

When I came around Silver, I found he had the tip of his dagger pressed to the male's neck.

"Stop. I want to question him," Kalyll ordered as he jumped onto the path and came running.

With a snarl of disappointment, Silver reluctantly pulled the dagger away and sheathed it. He stepped away as I fell to my knees, immediately assessing the injuries. One leg was twisted at an unnatural angle, and one hand was mangled out of shape.

Kalyll settled next to me. "Is he alive?"

I nodded. "Barely. Internal injuries. Broken... everything." There was a rib that had cracked and punctured his lung. His breathing was weak and wet-sounding. After healing Jeondar, my power was at half capacity at best, but perhaps I could heal the worst of his injuries and his enhanced Fae healing would do the rest. But who was I kidding? My healing magic couldn't remove broken ribs from punctured lungs. That had to be done by surgery.

"Can you save him?" Kalyll asked.

I shook my head.

The male opened his eyes. They were an intense violet color that reflected the extent of his pain. I took his unbroken hand and held it in mind, knowing that these were his final moments. I wanted to turn away, but I made myself hold his gaze, trying to convey a sense of peace and easing his pain with my skill.

"Who sent you?" Kalyll asked him, leaning forward, trying to get in the male's field of vision, but those violet eyes were locked on mine.

"Be—" he managed in a watery voice.

When he exhaled his last breath, I gently placed his large hand on his chest and walked away, fighting against the emotions crowding my chest, making it feel as if it would explode.

Kalyll approached me and placed a hand on my shoulder. I took a step forward and shook him off. I didn't want or need his attempts at comforting me.

Silver was the first one to break the silence that ensued after the male expired. "I think he was going to say Belasha."

"That can't be," Arabis said. "She wouldn't try to harm Kalyll. She wouldn't."

I turned and started walking back toward Dandelion, trying to ignore their discussion. I didn't want to hear any of it. I just wanted to stick my head into a hole in the ground and forget about everything.

Silver huffed. "So she says, but you know she hates Kalyll and always goes against him in everything."

"That's not necessarily true. She just... disagrees with him. Besides, she wants peace," Arabis argued. "It's the reason she married King Elladan. Why would she make an alliance with the Summer Court just to turn around and try to have the Seelie Prince murdered? It makes no sense."

Silver shrugged. "I'm sure it makes sense in her mind."

"What I can't understand is how they were able to track us?" Cylea said. "I wiped the trail clean. I left no signs at all. No one knows where we're going, and even if they do, there are several paths to Mount Ruin, this one being the most unlikely of all. So how in the name of all the gods did they find us?"

Kalyll rubbed the back of his neck. "I was wondering the exact same thing."

Silver ran a hand through his short hair and stared at the ground as if it would provide the answer.

I reached Dandelion and ran a hand down the length of her neck. It was meant to comfort her, but maybe it was more soothing to me. A headache pounded in my temples, and I reached for one of my saddlebags. In the list of ingredients for The Sage Crystal that I'd given to Kalyll, I'd jotted down a few extra things, including headache powders. Headaches were tricky to self-treat, especially when they were brought on by strong emotions.

I searched inside, taking a few things out, but not finding what I needed. Nerves and frustration getting the best of me, I unhooked the saddlebag and dumped its contents on the ground. One particular item that shouldn't have been there immediately caught my eye.

"What the hell?!"

Everyone turned to me, wearing matching frowns, while all I could do was gape.

CHAPTER 31

T hey all stepped closer and looked at the mess I'd made.

"What is it?" Arabis asked, her blue eyes roving over the spilled items on the ground.

I pointed at the necklace I'd worn to the Summer Solstice Ball. "That sneaky little pixie."

Jeondar leaned down and picked up the luxurious piece of jewelry. "This?" He squinted at it. "It…"

"What's the matter?" Kalyll asked.

"It looks like… one of my mother's necklaces, except…" Jeondar shook his head, looking confused.

Kryn's eyes slid in my direction, narrowing to slits. "It appears somebody has wandering fingers."

"It appears so." Silver jumped on Kryn's bandwagon.

"How dare you?!" I stood up straighter.

Kalyll put a hand up to silence Kryn, who had been about to say something else. Jeondar held the necklace up against the light, squinting at it. The action distracted everyone. He pondered for a moment, then cocooned the necklace between his hands. A thin layer of heat built around it. We all watched, confused. A moment later, a gooey mixture leaked through his fingers and dripped to the ground. When he held the necklace up for everyone to see, it had changed. It wasn't silver with diamonds anymore. It was gold with onyx jewels.

"Yes," Jeondar said. "This was my mother's, and this... this is how they were able to track us. It was made by a Ye'narian master. My father gave it to my mother as a birthday gift. Whenever she went anywhere without him, he wanted her to wear it. Of course, she thought it was the stupidest idea ever. First, it's conspicuous. Second, queens don't wear the same jewelry to every important event." He took a step toward me. "You were wearing this at the ball. I thought it looked familiar, but the coloring threw me off. How did you come to be in its possession?"

Everyone was staring at me again.

"I'll tell you how," Kryn said, but a stern look from Kalyll shut him up again.

"Larina put it on me when she was helping me get dressed," I said. "She said it was a gift from the former queen."

Silver snorted.

Kryn blew air through his nose. "Ridiculous tale."

"That's enough, Kryn." Kalyll hissed between clenched teeth.

They exchanged charged glasses that left me feeling horrible. They were good friends, and my kiss with the prince had driven a wedge between them. I couldn't understand exactly why, but I still didn't want to be responsible for it.

After their little glaring match was over, I thought Kryn would stomp away, but his curiosity proved more powerful than his anger, and he stayed to listen.

"Go on, please." Kalyll inclined his head.

I wanted to punch him in that beautiful, tasty mouth of his. He could stick his diplomacy up his ass. I wasn't buying it now that I knew what he thought of me and my kind. No amount of respectful posturing would ever erase that knowledge.

Reluctantly, I explained myself, not because Kalyll asked me to, but because I wasn't about to let this bunch think I was a thief.

"I had no reason to distrust Larina, so I wore the necklace because I didn't want to offend her. Then the morning we left, she said she wanted me to have it. Of course, I said no. She insisted, said the necklace looked beautiful on me, and she could never wear it, anyway. Even though it felt terribly rude to refuse her gift, I did. Adamantly. She seemed to understand and finally relented. The thing is... she packed my bags. It's obvious she slipped it in and that she's working with whoever is trying to hurt Prince Kalyll." I added the tile to his name and said it with as little emotion as I could. It felt cold on my lips.

From the way a muscle jumped in his jaw, it was clear he'd felt the chill.

"Thank you, Dani, for explaining." Jeondar nodded once, then addressed the others. "Belasha is in possession of all my mother's jewelry. I suppose Larina could have stolen the necklace, but it's more likely that the queen ordered her to give it to Dani."

Kalyll cursed under his breath. "She certainly had me fooled. Despite everything, I thought she was on our side."

"Do you think she suspects... about you?" Cylea asked.

"Everyone suspects something is afoot." Kalyll paced, staring at the ground. "But if my enemies knew the truth, they wouldn't keep it to themselves. They would shout it off the top of Mount Ruin, and the entire realm would hear of it. So no, I don't think anyone has figured out I'm a shadowdrifter."

Jeondar unsheathed a dagger from his belt and started digging a hole in the ground. "We can't take this with us. Maybe one day, if any of you come back this way, you can claim this buried treasure."

He threw the necklace in the hole and covered it. I hoped someone worthy and in need would find it instead of one of these entitled jerks. They deserved to encounter a rattlesnake instead, if they had those here.

Disgusted by it all, I picked up my saddlebag and started putting everything back in. Kalyll leaned down and picked up a bundle of hemlock.

"I don't need your help. I can take care of it." I bit out the words.

"I want to help."

Next, he went for the small pouch of headache powders at the same time I did. His fingers brushed mine, sending an electric jolt up my arm. I recoiled. We stared at each other for a long moment.

"Daniella," he said my name with such a feverish longing that my anger almost melted away.

If he was some Fae elitist, how could he look at me that way? Why did it seem as if he felt the same things I did?

But whatever the answer, it didn't matter. Soon, I would be back home, and this would be nothing more than an unfortunate bleep in time, an unwanted detour that I would easily sweep under the rug.

Yeah, keep telling yourself that, and maybe you'll believe it, Dani.

It took all of my willpower to look away and continue gathering the rest of my things. When we had picked everything up, I extended the saddlebag in his direction so he could deposit the items he'd retrieved. Then I turned away, doing my best to ignore his presence, even though I could sense him standing behind me. He felt like a brewing storm ready to unleash its pent-up energy on me. He took a step closer, so close that I could feel his warmth along my back and his breath on the nape of my neck. His breathing was audible, ill-restrained, as if he was fighting something back. Anger perhaps? But I didn't find out because a moment later, he marched away without a word.

I was both relieved and mad. I hated myself for wanting him. Because I did. Very badly. It seemed he wanted me to. At least his body did, even if his mind told him otherwise.

Maybe there would be a cold stream up the mountain pass where I could jump in and draw out this awful want. I could only hope.

An hour later, we were still on the same mountain pass, barely starting to see the other side of the range. The sun was nearing the apex of its daily trajectory, and soon we'd have to stop so Kalyll could take his elixir. We were riding at a clipped pace, trying to make up for the lost time to ensure we would arrive on time. Taking a detour through North Crosswood had eaten away time, and today was the first day of the new moon. We had to hurry.

I kept praying there wouldn't be any more mishaps, nothing to keep us from getting there in time. I would go crazy if I had to wait in Kalyll's company until the next new moon.

Arabis made a signal when it was time to stop. There was nothing but rocks and small patches of weed around. Though the sight of Mount Ruin in the background was the most majestic thing I'd seen in Elf-hame. The mountain was enormous, its peak topped with clouds and dappled with snow. The air blowing from it was so fresh it seemed to pierce my nose. It was the sort of sight that made you believe in gods.

Patting Dandelion's withers, I dismounted. The others also got off their horses. Kalyll approached with a weary expression. He couldn't like this any more than he liked becoming a bellicose brute or a monster for half the day, though at least this way, he didn't have to worry about killing anyone. I reached for the saddlebag that contained the implements and ingredients to make the elixir. It felt strangely light, and when I reached inside it, I discovered why.

It was empty.

I gasped.

"What is it?" Kalyll asked, noticing my reaction.

Mouth hanging open, I extended the open bag toward him. "It's empty."

"What do you mean, it's empty?" He snatched the bag from my hands and peered inside.

"The marsh flower, the hemlock... it's all gone."

"What?!" Arabis joined us and so did the others.

Once more, like with the necklace, they were all staring at me accusingly. I took a step back, shaking my head. Fear settled in the pit of my stomach at the way Kryn was glowering. He seemed ready to kill me.

"I didn't do that," I said.

Kalyll glanced up at me, doubt in his beautiful cobalt eyes, which was all it took to drive me over the edge.

"You all think I would sabotage my chance of getting the hell out of here?" I demanded. "I'm not stupid. This only complicates things for me. I want out of this nightmare that you're putting me through. And the worst part of everything is you." I pointed a finger straight at Kalyll.

He flinched and had the decency to look embarrassed.

"And do you know what all of that means?" I asked, savoring the words I was about to throw in their faces. "It means you have a traitor in your midst."

Now, the suspicious glances moved away from me. They all watched each other surreptitiously, questioning their loyalty. Had they been traveling with an enemy all along?

The saddlebag dropped from Kalyll's hand. In one swift motion, he whirled on Kryn, grabbed him by the neck, and lifted him off the ground. "You did this."

Kryn's feet kicked. Kalyll's eyes darkened and black veins webbed around them.

"I... didn't," Kryn croaked.

Arabis was at the prince's side, trying to use her power. "Let him go. You're going to kill him. Your best friend."

Kalyll continued to choke him.

Jeondar and Silver tried to pry him away, but Kalyll was too strong.

Arabis turned to me, her eyes pleading, begging me to get Kalyll to stop.

I took two steps forward and held Arabis's gaze. *Now, you deem me important?* I asked her silently.

"Please."

Kryn's lips were starting to turn blue, and his eyes were rolling backward. He was an asshole, and he hated me, but that didn't mean he deserved to die.

Jeondar and Silver got out of the way as I lifted a hand and placed it on Kalyll's rock-hard bicep. "Let him go, Kalyll." My voice was gentle, beseeching.

By degrees, he tore his attention from Kryn and looked at me.

"Just let him go."

In the next instant, he dropped Kryn, who collapsed to his knees, coughing and gasping for air. Kalyll pulled at his hair and let out a growl of frustration, clearly fighting against his demons.

"I have to leave," he spat suddenly, then jumped onto Stormheart and was gone, speeding down the mountain pass at a breakneck gallop.

Cylea ran a few steps. "Kalyll!" She stopped and turned around. "What do we do?"

"All we can do is continue on our way," Jeondar said. "Let's hope he doesn't come after us tonight. He'll rejoin us in the morning. I'm sure."

"But if the beast takes him too far?" Cylea shook her head.

"You know we can't keep up with him," Jeondar said. "Not even under normal circumstances. Our best bet is to do what I said."

I picked up the saddlebag from the ground, apprehension sinking its claws inside my chest. I knew I hadn't disposed of the ingredients, which meant there really was someone in the group who could stab either of us in the back at any moment. I frowned, wondering why they hadn't done it already. Who could it be? And why?

"Dani." Jeondar came up behind me.

I jumped and had to bite back a scream. I took a deep breath, readying myself for his accusation, and faced him.

"Do you have any idea who might have done this?" He glanced sidelong at the saddlebag.

So he didn't think *I* was responsible? How refreshing.

"I don't know," I answered. "It could have been anyone. It was all there at dawn."

He nodded, looking conflicted. "I can't decide whether or not Kryn could have done it out of mere anger."

"He wouldn't have," Arabis came up behind Jeondar. "You know that. Kryn loves Kalyll. It was either Cylea or Silver."

I scanned Jeondar's face. Arabis had been quick to point a finger elsewhere. Did he think that was cause to suspect her?

"What are you three talking about?" Silver asked loudly, causing Cylea and Kryn to glance our way. The latter was standing by his horse, rubbing his neck.

Jeondar squared his shoulders. "We're trying to figure out who threw away the ingredients for Kalyll's elixir."

Silver narrowed his eyes and exchanged a glance with Cylea. "Shouldn't all of us be part of that conversation?"

"Indeed." Jeondar nodded. "Did anyone notice anything?"

No one did.

"I still think it's the human," Kryn said.

"Fuck you, asshole." I flipped him off.

"But do you have proof?" Jeondar asked.

Kryn shrugged as if proof was something inconsequential when it came to a Fae accusing a human.

Cylea smoothed her blue hair and asked reluctantly, "What if... what if Kalyll did it?"

"Why would Kalyll..." Jeondar began but couldn't finish.

"I mean... that *thing* overpowers him sometimes, even in the morning," Cylea added.

I shook my head. "But afterward, he always remembers what he does."

"Not always," Cylea said.

Jeondar thought for a moment. "It's true. There's been a few times when he couldn't remember short stretches of time."

It would've taken Kalyll a matter of seconds to dispose of everything, but still, we had no proof, and I didn't like it one bit, especially when I noticed the way the others seem to favor this explanation. They'd been friends for a long time, and they didn't want to believe that one of their own was a traitor. It was easier to blame the dark forces that controlled the prince.

There was nothing else to do but keep going. We had to get there by dawn. We traveled quickly but warily, especially when we reached the craggy foothills of Mount Ruin, where dried trees and outcrops provided plenty of places for someone to hide.

Without towing Kalyll, we actually managed to make good time.

"We're here," Jeondar announced when we reached the mouth of a large cave right as the sun went down.

Dandelion pawed the ground restlessly as I stared into the large, dark entrance. The remaining daylight managed to barely illuminate a few feet into the tunnel, then the darkness took over, as if past a certain point, light wasn't welcome.

"You have to be kidding me," I said.

"We have to go in there?" Cylea asked, looking as worried as I felt, which only scared me further. It seemed she hadn't known the exact destination either. "That is where the Caorthannach lives?"

"Caorthannach?" I asked. "What is that?"

"She's the mother of all demons," Cylea whispered. "She sends her spawns out into the world to devour us."

Oh, shit!

"Quit trying to scare her," Jeondar scolded her.

Cylea snickered and urged her horse forward.

"Why would she make up something like that?" I asked no one in particular.

Jeondar stopped his horse next to mine. "She didn't make it up."

"What?"

"Don't worry about it." He waved a hand, then called the others. "Let's make camp."

Everyone worked, setting up quickly in front of the cave, someone always keeping watch for Kalyll, though we saw no sign of him, which was a relief but also a source of concern. The sky was moonless and dark, our space illuminated only by the fire, which did nothing to breach that barrier that seemed to delineate this realm from the utter darkness that lay inside the nearby cave.

After a quick meal of dry fruit and meat, I settled on top of my blankets, trying to decide whether to turn my back on the cave or the open space in front of us. What if this Caorthannach or one of her spawns crawled out of the cave? What if Kalyll or the queen's men came to attack us? Fretting, I did neither. I just lay flat, rocks poking my back, and counted the stars to distract myself.

It was near dawn when he came. I was awake, but it didn't matter because I didn't see or hear anything. One moment, I was on top of my blankets. And the next, I was in his arms as he ran away from the camp.

CHAPTER 32

W e rushed past hundreds of trees at a prodigious speed. The trunks blurred by, looking like nothing more than wavering reflections. Darkness streamed around us, transparent ribbons caught in a draft. The name shadowdrifter made more sense than ever.

I clung to Kalyll's neck, afraid we would crash as he dodged the obstacles that stood in our path. I tried to find comfort in his leather and rosewood scent, but my heart only pounded faster.

He stopped shortly, but I knew we were far enough from the others that if I screamed, they would not hear me.

Kalyll set me down gently. The ground beneath my feet was supple, covered in soft moss. A circle of trees created a barrier around us, and what looked like fire sprites floated above our heads, casting a warm glow. The scent of flowers impregnated the air, and the chirping of bugs sounded faintly like a melody.

Prince Kalyll Adanorin stood in front of me, shirtless. His thick arms rested at his sides, and his large chest gleamed with sweat as it rose up and down. His wide pecs gave way to a well-defined abdomen that seemed to defy all the anatomy classes I'd ever taken. No one had that many abs or a "V" as perfect as that. Corded veins traced paths over his smooth, golden skin. His hair was loose, one strand cutting across his handsome face.

He was a work of art, all perfectly sculpted sinew, and male beauty.

A tremor went through him, that ill-contained darkness trying to break out. I told myself he was in control, but I knew he was hanging by a thread.

I glanced toward the sky. Dawn was near. All I had to do was stall him.

"Are you all right?" I asked, doing my best to sound calm.

He didn't answer, just went on looking at me with predatory hunger.

"We were worried about you." I turned away from him and paced around the circle. His shirt was on the ground, which meant he'd meant to bring me here, to this secluded, magical spot. I knew what he wanted. How could I not when the heat between my legs meant I wanted the same thing? Was it possible he'd thrown away my ingredients to bring this about?

Either way, this couldn't happen—not with him in this state. Or in any other, for that matter. It would just be a good fuck. Somehow, I knew it would be good. Mind-blowing even. Maybe so good that it would ruin me for life.

So I knew I shouldn't, couldn't. For my own sanity.

"You don't want this, Kalyll," I said, my voice shaking. "In a few hours, when you're rid of this curse, and you're nothing but Prince Kalyll Adanorin of the Seelie Court, you'll be glad nothing happened here with me."

He moved closer, stopping a foot away from me. Raw, animalistic energy rolled off him. I felt it in my skin, waves of shivers that coiled tightly and turned into desire.

Kalyll chuckled. "Is that what you think?"

"Yes. I'm just a human, remember?" The way he'd spat the word... It still hurt.

"A very tempting one."

His cobalt eyes tracked the length of my body, making the shivers coil tighter still and spiral down straight to my core. He reached out, took my hand, and raised it to his mouth. He planted a hot kiss on my palm, his tongue tracing a circle there.

My knees wobbled.

"A very delicious one," he rumbled. "I've had a taste, and I want more. The beast *and* the prince."

He took another step forward and wrapped a hand around my waist, pulling me to him. "I know you want this, too."

I clenched my teeth, the only form of refusal I could muster.

"Don't fight it." He brought his nose to my neck and inhaled me. "I can smell it on you. The want. Your arousal saturates the air, and it's driving me mad."

Damn, oh damn, my traitorous body.

His own body quaked in evidence. He was fighting to restrain himself, and I knew one small sign from me, and he would give in.

Would it be so bad to give in? Would it be so terrible to be irresponsible for once? Me, the older sister who always did the right thing?

Yes, it would be irresponsible. YES, IT WOULD!

But why not live a little? Why not share a moment of perfect bliss?

I took a yearly remedy of my own creation that would protect me from pregnancy. There would be no illegitimate children that proper heirs would later want to murder to protect the crown. So why not let this gorgeous prince take me and fuck me out of my mind?

And in the process, prove to him that this human could also ruin him.

I raised a hand to his naked chest and pressed it to his heart, which was pounding hard and wild. I traced the edge of his pec with my thumb, a feather's kiss. The way he shivered under my touch made me bold, made me act like never before.

"I want more too," I said, fighting the blush that threatened to bloom in my cheeks. "I think I like what you have to offer."

I let my hand slide down his abdomen, enjoying the dips and valleys. I stopped at his waist though I wanted to keep going and discover more, but why so fast? If I did this, I would enjoy it.

We might both regret it later, but right now, neither one seemed to care.

His mouth crashed against mine, and in an instant, we were lost in a wild mess of lips and tongues and teeth. He tasted like tart berries as he kissed me with powerful strokes of his tongue, sending the most delicious jolts of pleasure through me, turning my blood to lava.

I was enthralled, practically off my feet as I tried to keep up with the savage way he was devouring me. He growled with my bottom lip trapped between his teeth, and I moaned, even as the bite caused pain. We gasped for air with every swipe of our tongues, and he became my oxygen, my lifeline. Our hands slid over each other's bodies, touching everywhere we could.

The firmness of his body felt like heaven against my fingertips as they traveled the length of his naked back. There was nothing at that moment that marked Kalyll as a prince, and me as someone out of his league. It just felt like a male and a female who had been yearning for each other for days and were finally together.

His mouth traveled down my neck, and he barely came up for air. He was like a starving beast finally offered a meal. He cradled my ass and lifted me up. I wrapped my legs around him as he pressed me against a tree, the bulge in his trousers rubbing me in the right place.

"You want this, don't you?" he growled, rubbing again.

"Oh, yes!" I cried out, running my tongue along the column of his strong neck.

He whirled and dragged me to my knees on the soft grass. Heat flooded my insides as he looked at me, and I turned to putty, ready to be made into any shape he wanted. In one quick motion, he removed my tunic, then disposed of my bra like an expert.

Possessively, he pulled me close, his warm torso caressing mine, one of his hands squeezing my breast as he kissed my lips.

He was driving me crazy, but I could do the same to him. Finger trembling, I undid his pants, fighting with the string. When I was done, I slipped my hand inside and was welcomed by his large, throbbing length. My hand couldn't even wrap around his girth, and I couldn't help but imagine how delicious he would feel inside of me. He threw his head back, eyes growing darker as I caressed him.

With a growl, he dropped me to the ground, and I let out a gasp when his mouth sucked on my nipple. My hips writhed against him as he bit, his hand finding my other breast, massaging it, and pinching the sensitive bud as I moaned.

"Oh, God!"

Kissing down my stomach, he dragged down my leggings. I stared up at the fire sprites as Kalyll buried his face between my legs, nuzzling against the moisture there. I felt I should be self-conscious, but it only felt right, so I allowed myself to fully enjoy it.

"You're so wet," he whispered, his fingers pulling my panties and everything out of the way. I was totally naked as his wild gaze devoured me.

Unapologetically, he leaned down between my legs again, his broad tongue swiping upward to my very center while I moaned in delight.

"You taste so good." He lapped hungrily as I squirmed, ready to melt and soak into the ground or evaporate into the air. It felt so right. Everything he did was perfect.

"I'm going to come," I panted.

He stopped, the bastard. "We don't have much time, and I need to fuck you now."

So unprincely of him, but even his dirty talk was spot on. Impossibly, I got wetter still. I latched my ankles around his waist and pulled him closer.

"I'm ready."

He pressed against my core, draped my legs over his shoulders, and thrust, impaling me in the most delicious way possible, sinking himself to the hilt. He roared like a crazed beast. His black gaze locked with mine as he plunged once more. I should've been afraid of how savage he looked, but I only felt elated, whole. He went hard, pausing for an instant when he was seated all the way in, then pulling out and slamming in again.

My fingers dug into the supple moss. He filled me so tightly that I felt tears in my eyes. He picked up speed, hitting an untapped spot deep inside me. It was bliss and a little torture all at the same time. He slammed into me over and over again, unleashing a frenzied rapture such as I'd never felt before.

I cried out, the orgasm rolling in waves as he kept the hard speed. I stared into his face, at the expression of wild pleasure shaping his features. He groaned and trembled, and I reminded myself that *I* did this to him. *I* drove him wild. When he finally came, the entire clearing practically rattled at his bellowing roar. He became but a male in my hands, laid bare and vulnerable.

I stared up at the prince, a million emotions crashing into me: delight, contentment, more desire. Sitting, I wrapped my arms around him and kissed him. His heart thumped alongside mine, and we held each other for a long time. I squeezed my eyes tightly, the moment slowly unpacking itself.

What have I done? Sex had never been this good, and I knew that no one, only Kalyll, would ever be able to top tonight.

CHAPTER 33

Kalyll lay next to me, naked and god-like. His powerful shaft—which had been inside me, thrusting and pleasuring me just moments ago—rested against his lower abdomen, impressive even at rest. I tore my eyes away and ignored the thrill for more in my core.

He rolled onto his side, nostrils flaring, and peered at me with bedroom eyes. "I can oblige, my lady."

Witchlights, could I hide nothing from him?

I peered toward the fringes of the clearing, judging the light. "I think we have to go."

He rolled on top of me and nibbled on my breasts, giving each his undivided attention. His dark blue gaze stayed on me as he sucked. There was a fringe of darkness still left there, but I felt the prince was more present than he'd been so far, and still... he wanted me.

I threaded my fingers through his silky hair.

Beautiful, wild man. What if you could be mine?

"We need to go," I blurted out, realizing I was in dangerous territory. "If we're late, the other ones are going to kill me."

He buried his face in my neck and groaned. "If the rest of the realm could just disappear."

Was that what he really wanted? For everyone else to disappear so he and I could...?

Don't go there, Dani. Just don't.

It took all my will to plant my hands on his chest and push him away. He didn't fight me. In fact, he looked as resigned as I felt. It was time to go. We'd come here for one reason and one reason only, and that reason—whatever it was—waited for us in that cave.

I was dressed a moment later, each garment I replaced feeling like an extra barrier between us, like the brick walls going back up.

"Ready?" he asked.

I nodded.

"I have just enough time to take us back." He lifted my arms, placed them around his neck, then lifted me off the ground. "It's a convenient power. It'd be nice to keep it." He smiled crookedly, making me unsure of whether or not he meant this.

Once more, he moved like a shadow traveling on the wind, the forest becoming nothing more than a river of shadows. I didn't know how else to explain it.

A moment later, he was setting me on the ground. My mind whirled as I tried to get my bearings, but all I could tell was that the spot where he'd deposited me wasn't as beautiful as the one we'd just left.

He pushed a strand of hair behind my ear. "No matter what happens after this moment, I want you to know that I don't regret anything."

His words touched my heart. I believed him. The way we'd devoured each other, the connection we'd shared, was something I would never regret, even if the others decided to judge us. I had no idea why they hated me. Perhaps their reasons were valid. Perhaps they would make sense if they explained them to me. Perhaps not. Either way, I couldn't help how they felt about me. If they thought I was less because I was human, that was their problem, not mine. Let them judge all they wanted. I would take what Kalyll and I had shared and cherish it for as long as his memory was vivid in my mind.

A smile stretched his lips, and I figured he must have seen the resolve in my expression, the fact that I held no regrets either.

"Let's go." He extended a hand toward a gap between two trees.

I walked ahead of him, trying to mentally prepare myself for what lay ahead, both the known and the unknown.

Five minutes later, I spotted the others, all of them waiting, shoulder to shoulder—Kryn in the middle, arms crossed. Their expressions were cold, unyielding. With their enhanced senses, they'd heard our approach. It was clear.

We stopped in front of them. I held myself with dignity under their cold scrutiny.

"It's about time you showed up," Kryn spat.

Kalyll ignored the comment. "Everyone ready?"

"You would let her delay you, fail in your quest?"

"No one has failed. I'm here. On time."

"What about your duty?"

"That conversation, right now, that's what would make me fail." Kalyll walked past the others, holding himself like the powerful royal that he was.

His message to Kryn was clear: I owe you no explanation for my actions. I am your prince.

Kalyll entered the cave. The others stared at me. I was no princess, not theirs or anyone's, but I walked forward as if I was, my steps confident, my attitude a raised middle finger to their obvious disdain for me.

In a few days, you'll be home, and their hatred will be the last thing you'll ever think about.

I knew it because the memories that would haunt me belonged to Kalyll and me.

I've had a taste, and I want more. The beast and *the prince.*

My insides shivered as the words echoed in my mind, and it was an effort to focus on the moment. At least until the gaping mouth of the cave stood in front of me. I froze.

I couldn't see Kalyll. The darkness had swallowed him, or maybe the darkness had become him. If I stepped forward, would he swallow me in turn?

Jeondar came behind me, a lit torch in hand.

I took one step forward into the puddle of light the flame created. I stopped again, even when Jeondar matched my step, and the light advanced with me.

"I'm right behind you," he said, assuring me that the glow of his torch would be my protection. It was a slim comfort, but it was better than nothing.

Ahead, Kalyll's silhouette guided the way. I don't know how long we walked, turning right and left, climbing and descending, but we finally came to a large space with a high ceiling.

Thousands of stalactites dripped from the top toward the stalagmites below. They gave the appearance of many teeth ready to open just to snap shut again. They dripped with water, which made splashing sounds as it hit the ground.

Kalyll planted his feet and squared his shoulders, tight fists at his sides. The others formed a line behind him, while I stood awkwardly off to the side, unsure of my place. Everyone stood tense, looking ready for a fight. Whatever they expected to find here could not be good.

My heart began hammering out of control. Whatever was about to go down in this place was the reason I was here. If only what the damn Envoy had told Kalyll could've been shared with me, but all I knew was that this was the place where I was supposed to use my healing powers. I was supposed to cure the prince here, but I had no idea if I would be able to.

"Caorthannach," Kalyll shouted the name and it echoed through the space.

The only response was the dripping sound of the water.

"Show yourself, Caorthannach. Come and take your curse from me."

There was a skittering sound, like hundreds of claws clicking on the hard ground. My insides turned to mist at the sound. I peered into the darkness beyond the rock formations. Shadows scurried about like ink blotches without true substance.

Everyone except Kalyll unsheathed their swords. They zinged, the sharp metal sound reverberating throughout. What good could those be against shadows? Wouldn't light have been a better weapon? I took a step closer to Jeondar, moving further into the circle of the torchlight. His normally calm expression was tight, full of worry. He offered me the torch, and I took it, held it with both hands in front of me. I wanted to turn away from the approaching entities, but I was hypnotized by my own terror.

The shadows skittered closer. How their insubstantial shapes could make that horrible sound, I didn't know and didn't want to find out.

"You insult me by sending your spawn," Kalyll spat. "Come out and face me. You know who I am. You know you mustn't trifle with me."

A couple of the creatures reached the edge of the torchlight, and they immediately stopped being only shadows. I nearly screamed when Caorthannach's spawns took shape.

The dark blotches were still there, reflected on the ground and the rock formations, but when touched by the light, the creatures casting the shadows were suddenly visible. They were hideous, humanoid in shape, with sparse strands of greasy hair sprouting from their pale scalps. Their spindly figures crawled on all fours, all bones with blue-gray skin hanging loose about their frames. Their eyes were completely black, and they wore no garments. Sharp, black claws at their hands and feet were responsible for the awful skittering sound. More and more appeared, their dark eyes fixed, their rotting mouths half-opened. They looked hungry, starved actually.

"You will soon be like them," an eerie female voice called from the depths of the cavern. "Just like once, they were like you."

Oh, God!

"I will not. I am Prince Kalyll Adanorin, Dragon Soul, Defender of the Realm. I will never serve you."

"But you already do. I feel you every night. The deaths you cause feed my power."

Anger rippled through Kalyll.

"I feel you now," the voice said with delight. "Your anger festers. It is pure. Tasty."

Whoever was talking—Caorthannach, I supposed—sounded gleeful.

"Take this curse away or face my wrath," Kalyll growled.

High-pitched laughter filled my ears. She was mocking him, showing no hint of fear at the threat, and her dismissal resonated with me because how could seven Fae warriors, no matter how dexterous, defeat the dozens of spawns that hid in the shadows?

"Have it your way." Kalyll unsheathed his weapon and attacked.

Moving like a tornado on a path of destruction, he sliced his sword from side to side, cutting down everything that stood in his way. Rock fragments and pale limbs flew through the air. Caorthannach's spawns barely had any time to react before Kalyll was there, tearing them to pieces. Loud screeches of pain tore through the creature's mouths, and as they hit the ground, their bodies turned to black shadows and disappeared completely.

More spawn advanced from the depths of the cave, their skittering claws announcing their approach.

Jeondar, Kryn, and the others jumped into the fray, the former dolling out orbs of fire, turning the creatures into lumps of coal that quickly flatten into patches of gloom, then were gone.

Three spawns came at Arabis all at once.

"Look out!" I screamed, my heart jumping into my throat.

Moving on lithe feet, she seemed to dance out of the way, her sword sweeping with her like a ball gown flowing with her movements. She cut two spawns in half. Their bodies fell with a wet *thud*, then vanished. The third one overshot her and as it spun around, it received the brunt of Arabis's Susurro skill.

"Your brethren are your real enemies. Attack!" she commanded, her voice like a physical slap.

The spawn turned on one of its own and pounced, sinking sharp claws into its belly and pulling out its innards as they both screeched.

Silver used his elemental power, freezing the creatures as they flew at him, then shattering to smithereens with a blow from his sword.

Kryn and Cylea delivered their own deadly blows, moving across the ground with ease and tremendous agility. They worked in unison like a well-oiled machine of death and ruination, crossing each other's paths and never once getting tangled or disoriented.

But it was Kalyll that left me speechless. He was something to behold. He fought with such assurance, with such undivided attention and deadly accuracy, that he made the others look like clumsy toddlers.

He was like... the God of War.

Caorthannach had been wrong to laugh, and I had been wrong to doubt, especially considering what I'd heard about the prince's indomitable reputation, and what I'd seen with my own eyes in the past days.

The last few plumes of darkness dissipated as Kalyll slew the last of his foe.

"You can't avoid me forever, coward," he yelled into the darkness. "Come out or I'll come in there and find you." He twirled his sword, which hissed its own threat.

Caorthannach cackled, then the sound abruptly morphed into the spawn's skittering. Goosebumps broke all over my skin as my fear multiplied to match the incoming blitz. If before there had been dozens of spawn, now it sounded as if hundreds had crawled from the depths of hell itself.

The creatures streamed like an army of incensed fire ants. My heart sank to my feet, fearing that, today, Kalyll and his crew would discover their limits.

CHAPTER 34

I held the torch in front of me and pressed my back to the stone wall. I wished for a real weapon and the skill to wield it, but I was helpless to defend myself. I was the only one of my siblings useless in a battle. Lucia had telekinetic powers. Toni was a werewolf with sharp teeth and claws, and Leo was a mage, who was only restricted by his imagination in the sort of attack he could fling at his enemies.

But all I could do was heal. My skill couldn't be used to harm—something that never bothered me until now.

If only I could reverse the way my skill worked, I could suck what little life these zombie-like creatures possessed and vanish them into nothingness.

As the others fought, I retreated the way we'd come, ensconcing myself in the narrow tunnel, where no more than one spawn could attack at once, and I hoped to be able to fend them off by brandishing the torch.

The others fought in the open, cutting down their enemies one after the next, but there were too many of them, heedless of their lives, obeying their master blindly. They piled on top of Kalyll until I couldn't see him under the horde.

"No!"

A voice inside my head urged me to run, to escape, but it was small, too cowardly to make a convincing attempt.

I was about to run to attack the horde with the torch when Jeondar directed a stream of fire in the prince's direction, setting half the spawn on fire. As they shrieked, Arabis commanded them to attack their own. The spawn turned on each other, the ones that were burning, sharing their blaze with the others until they all disintegrated into piles of ash that quickly disappeared. Kalyll emerged unscathed from the melee and ready for more. He stood back to back with Kryn, and they moved like the blade inside a blender, whirling and cutting, slicing and pulping.

The six were like an entire army, a fearless axis of power that seemed unstoppable. They complimented each other perfectly and appeared to have a sixth sense that told them when one of the group needed help.

The battle seemed to go on forever. For every spawn they killed, another one crawled out of the darkness to replace it. There seemed to be no end to their number and no way for Kalyll and the others to keep their strength. But their stamina was unlike anything I'd ever seen, and they fought on even as others would have collapsed.

Impossibly, the stream of spawn slowly turned into a trickle until no more could be seen behind the rock formations, and the Fae warriors stood panting, ready for more.

I gaped. Not one spawn had broken their ranks and made it to the tunnel where I stood on wobbling legs. They seemed to have defeated Caorthannach's entire force.

Kalyll took a moment to make sure I was all right. His gaze met mine as he glanced over his shoulder, and I swear I saw relief on his face. His clothes were torn to shreds and deep gashes bled profusely in his arms, legs, and torso. It looked like every square inch of his body was injured, and it was the same for the others.

I ran out of the tunnel, ready to help. This had to be why they'd brought me. They'd known the battle would be brutal. I went to Kalyll first and quickly assessed his worst injuries.

"Let me—"

He shook his head. "Save your energy. There's worse to come."

What? Worse than this? They were all torn to pieces. Their smaller wounds were closing thanks to their fast healing abilities, but some of the cuts were deep enough that I feared they would bleed to death if we didn't do something quickly. Still, they all stood firmly, ready for more.

Kalyll took a step forward, limping. "If you have more of your spawn to waste, we'll be glad to dispose of them."

No more chuckles came from the depths of the cavern. This time, it was an angry growl.

"You could have released me when I first asked you," he said. "It would have cost you one servant. Instead, now you've lost hundreds."

"Damn you and all your descendants," that eerie voice called, charged with frustration.

"Come out," Kalyll ordered, "or I'll come for you, and you'll lose more than your spawn." When no response came, he cracked his neck and started walking forward.

Something red glowed behind the many stalactites and stalagmites. Kalyll stopped and watched as the light moved closer.

A moment later, a female figure stood tall and proud, caged by the many rock formations that stood around her. She was tall, nearly seven feet. Her naked body was gray and cracked as if she were made of ancient stone. Through the cracks, her essence was revealed. It looked like molten lava and was the source of the red glow, which also escaped through her eyes, nostrils, and mouth. Hair like fire cascaded around her shoulders, framing a face that was like a shard of glass, angular and with high cheekbones. She also had horns sprouting from her forehead, and sharp claws that glowed like hot knives.

Demon.

She was a demon.

I had seen this glow before. After coming across an ancient tome on how to heal demons and studying it in depth, I'd once healed the Prince of Hell from a mortal wound, and his insides had looked exactly like this. This creature didn't belong in this realm, but somehow she'd crossed the veil, made her home in Elf-hame, and figured out a way to cause trouble.

"Take the curse away," Kalyll demanded.

Caorthannach bared pointed teeth and grunted. "Fine. You know what to do."

Kalyll sheathed his sword and instead pulled out a dagger from his belt. Without hesitation, he plunged it into his chest and drove it downward, creating a ragged wound down his sternum.

I gasped in horror and dropped the torch. "No."

The others stepped forward as if to brace their prince, but before they reached him, some sort of force took hold of Kalyll, elevating him in place.

Caorthannach beckoned with a clawed finger. Dark energy began flowing from the wound Kalyll had created. Blood and blackness oozed out of the Seelie Prince, while his legs and arms hung limply as he floated in midair.

Now, it was finally clear. I was here to heal Kalyll Adanorin from *this* wound. A tear streaked down my cheek as his face contorted in agony.

I shook my head, refusing the weight that suddenly settled on my shoulders. This was too much. What if I couldn't save him? He was already weak. If he died, I would never recover. Failure would haunt me for the rest of my life.

As Caorthannach pulled a long wisp of darkness from him, Kalyll dropped. Kryn and Silver were immediately there to hold him up. The cowardly demon retreated back to where it'd come from.

"This is your time to shine, healer," Kryn said.

I rushed to Kalyll, my hands already glowing with healing energy, my senses assessing the damage. He was still breathing, and his heart was still beating, if only weakly. The dagger had nicked his heart muscle, and I was sure that anyone else would be dead after enduring what he had, but not my strong prince.

I had no time to marvel at how quickly I was able to determine his internal injuries. Instead, I started healing his heart muscle, knitting the damaged myocardium layer. As I worked, I perceived a swirl of darkness still lingering around his heart. I could tell it apart from the prince's essence and knew it didn't belong there. I also knew how to get rid of it. I'd learned it on that same ancient tome.

"Can you save him?" Kryn demanded.

"Yes, yes, I can," I responded with certainty. I'd healed worse wounds before, and one way or another, whether or not I wanted it, I was vested in Kalyll. I would give my all to save him. It was a scary thought, but it was true.

Behind the prince, Kryn nearly slumped with relief, while Silver's reaction seemed to be quite the opposite. I perceived the moment he made the awful decision. I would have cried out a warning in time if I hadn't doubted my instinct, but I hesitated because Silver was Kalyll's good friend, wasn't he?

Too late, I reacted. "No!"

With my healing magic deeply intertwined with Kalyll's body, I felt the moment Silver plunged the dagger into Kalyll's back, the sharp, lethal weapon going straight through the prince's heart.

Time slowed to a crawl.

Tangled with Kalyll as I was, I felt the wound as if it were my own. The air was driven from my lungs, and I barely had an instant to inhale sharply before I was back, mending the old and new damage all at once.

I was faintly aware of the others pulling Silver away as they shouted in rage and incredulity. Kryn pulled out the dagger and slowly deposited Kalyll on the ground, and I fell to my knees with him, working frantically, pushing all my healing energy forward in a desperate effort to repair the terrible damage to the arteries and heart muscles.

I worked on knitting everything back, but the certainty I'd had just moments before was gone. I would not be able to save him. He was already slipping away, his heart going dormant.

"Why? Why?!" Arabis shouted.

"No, no, no." I repaired another tear, and sealed one of the pulmonary arteries. I was doing everything humanly possible, even though deep down inside I knew it was all for naught.

"Kalyll, brother." Kryn was clutching the prince's shoulder, his face etched with utter panic. "Hang on. Hang on."

I shook my head.

Kryn noticed. "Save him. You have to save him."

"I can't."

"You must!"

"There... is one way, but..."

"It doesn't matter what it is, just do it," Kryn ordered. "Everything depends on Kalyll's life."

I had started ushering out the portion of black energy that still remained inside the prince's body. It was meant to be flushed out, meant to be expelled, so that Kalyll could be purely himself again. But as his life ebbed, all his goodness slipping away, I pulled the evil back in and invited it straight into his heart.

The demon energy was resilient and twisted. It defied any sense of goodness or right and wrong. It was the energy of Midnight Mages and taboos, the verve of morbidity and necromancers, the only thing that could defy death.

My healing energy also tangled with it, shaping it, coaxing it into the right places. In an instant, Kalyll's heart was repaired, made whole by light and dark. The wound in his chest closed with a wet sound, and so did the rest of his injuries.

Kryn reared back, his eyes wide with amazement. Relief flooded his expression. He stared intently into his friend's face, waiting for signs of life, but none came.

"What's wrong?" he demanded.

I saved my strength and instead of responding, cupped my hands on top of Kalyll's chest and started pumping. He was a large strong male, and it took all I had to apply the necessary chest compressions to jump-start his newly healed heart.

Kryn watched me as if I were crazy. He was about to say something when finally Kalyll gasped for air. His eyes sprang open, and for an instant, they were dark all around, but then they cleared, and he sat straight up, gulping for more air and pressing a hand to his chest, feeling for the wound.

I slumped down, my head spinning, my vision blurry. I had only enough time to feel a burst of joy at seeing Kalyll's beautiful eyes once more, then I lost consciousness.

CHAPTER 35

W hen I woke up, I was wrapped in furs, lying down inside the small tent. I blinked, trying to dispel the sluggishness that clung to me like a wet blanket. It took a moment for my thoughts to realign themselves and for the memories of what had happened to rush back and hit me like a tsunami.

I sat up, panting, my eyes roving all around. I started to crawl out of the tent, but before I went too far, the flap opened and Kalyll walked in. I froze. For a moment, we just stared at each other without saying anything.

He was the first to say something. "How do you feel?"

I sat back, crossed my legs, and shrugged. My thoughts felt lethargic, which normally happened after an intense healing session. "I'll be all right. How about you?"

He nodded. "I feel great. It's nighttime and..." He patted his chest, then put his hands out as if to say, *Look at me. I'm in control. No more beast.*

I swallowed thickly. I had to tell him about what I'd done in order to heal him. There was no way of telling how the darkness I'd weaved into him would affect him. Would it manifest? Was he strong enough to overpower it and never know it was there? Was I really asking myself that? The male was stronger than anyone I'd ever met.

Kalyll pointed at the spot in front of me. "May I sit? I wish to talk to you."

I scooted backward to give him room.

He settled in front of me, also crossing his legs. "How could I ever repay you? You haven't only saved my life, but have also spared my realm much strife—more than you can imagine."

It wasn't as if I'd been given a choice, but I figured it was too late for recriminations. Instead, I said, "Silver?"

A wave of sadness washed over the prince. "Our Sub Rosa circle had a traitor, one who will pay for his crimes."

"He was the one who threw away the marsh flower and hemlock."

Kalyll assented.

"Is he working with Queen Belasha?"

"No. Surprisingly, Queen Belasha is on *our* side. We've just encountered an envoy she sent to protect us. Her emissary explained everything. She *was* responsible for the necklace. She instructed Larina to give it to you, to ensure that when we left Imbermore the necklace was with you, so she could keep track of us. Our secrecy worried her. She was afraid for our safety. At least that's what Captain Nataar, her envoy, says. She sent a small force after us when the necklace stopped moving. Earlier, she'd received some disturbing news from her spies relating to Silver. Apparently, he was spotted in Gleelock Alley, meeting with Lyanner Phiran, who has, after our departure, been confirmed as an Unseelie spy. The party that attacked us in the mountain pass was sent by him and, by extension, the Unseelie King."

My head spun with all the information. Silver, who had been Kalyll's friend since childhood, had betrayed him. He'd even traveled all the way into that cave, risking his life, to get a chance at murdering the Seelie Prince when he was the most vulnerable because otherwise, Kalyll had simply been too powerful to take down.

"I'm sorry you lost a friend," I said, knowing the words were inadequate at best.

"I am too. What's more, we fear what information he must have shared with Phiran. You see... there is more than one reason why I wished to hide my predicament from everyone. It would have been bad enough for the court to find out that their prince and future king turned into a monster every night. *The cherry on top*, as you say in your realm, would be finding out that I'm not... my father's son. That the heir to the Seelie throne is a bastard, the love child of a deceiving queen."

I gasped, unable to help my reaction. "I'm sorry. I..."

"No offense taken, but I see you realize the magnitude of my dilemma."

I knew enough about the Fae to understand that purity of blood in their royal lines was paramount.

"The shadowdrifter curse was passed down to me by my biological father. It takes time to manifest, and it wasn't until it did that I learned the truth about my parentage. My mother had hoped that the curse would spare me, but we weren't that lucky. She confessed the truth when she spotted the symptoms she'd been watching for my entire life."

I could only imagine how hard it was for Kalyll to hear the truth.

He continued. "I have no hunger for the throne, Daniella. I would gladly step down for my brother if only he weren't utterly unsuited for the job. You see, Cardian is a frivolous man. Not only that, he is cruel and thinks of nothing but himself. I fear what would happen to my people if he were ever in charge. He would terribly love to be king, and if this knowledge reaches his ears, I don't even want to imagine what he would do. Not now when we teeter at the brink of war against a man so similar to him. Imagine the destruction Cardian and King Kellam Mythorne would cause, blinded by their selfish pursuits."

"I see," I said, for the first time fully understanding why he could justify sacrificing one person's freedom. My small losses were nothing compared to what he feared for his realm.

One life, your life, is nothing compared to that, he'd said to me a month ago. I'd believed him to be a bad person and thought someone virtuous could never do something bad for a good reason, but I'd been wrong.

He went on. "I know none of these things justify taking you from your home, but I hope you can understand me better now."

"I do."

He smiled. "You're the bravest of us all, Daniella."

"Me?"

"You give so much of yourself, without regard for your own life. You give openly with kindness in your heart and life at your fingertips. You are... the most amazing person I've ever met."

A knot formed in my throat. He couldn't be serious. Was he? I wanted to reach out and touch him, but something in his expression stopped me.

"There is one more thing I must say to you," he added.

He was already crestfallen, but whatever he was about to say seemed to weigh more heavily on him than everything he'd already shared.

"I wish at all costs to prevent a war. Mythorne is a despicable man, and I would like nothing more than to rid our land of his blight, but that would only cause the death of innocent people. So in order to smooth things over and create an alliance, I've entered into a contract with the Fall Court." He paused, his gaze breaking from mine.

After a long moment, he told me the rest. "I am engaged to marry Kryn's sister, Princess Mylendra Goren."

My heart had no business taking a tumble. My feelings had no reason to be hurt. There was no slight. Kalyll owed me nothing, was nothing to me. And yet, his words felt like an arrow straight through the chest and caused a wound that no amount of healing power or dark energy could mend.

That was when I realized that my feelings for Kalyll had, at some point, changed.

You idiot, heart! What have you done?!

I don't know how I held myself together, but despite the deep ache in my chest, I took the news without giving my distress away.

"That's why they were all mad at me," I said, choosing to focus on the least distressing aspect stemming from this news. "They thought I would jeopardize this... contract."

Kalyll was engaged to a Fae princess who would help him prevent a horrible war. Of course, the others had a right to be upset with me. Of course, a common human sharing a tryst with their prince would be cause for anger in a situation like this.

"Daniella." Kalyll reached for my hand, but I pulled away.

I would not be able to bear his touch without falling apart.

"I barely know her," he said. "And what I do know of her suggests we have nothing in common. I didn't wish to marry her before and now—"

"Please... don't say anything else." I couldn't take it. I just couldn't. I didn't want to cry in front of him. There were no words that could make this situation better, that could ease the viselike pain around my heart.

He ran a hand over his face, letting out a frustrated sigh. He was biting his lower lip, trying to respect my wishes, even though he clearly wanted to say more.

"I'll go back home," I burst out, "and we'll both get back to our lives. You'll save many people, and so will I."

CHAPTER 36

After my conversation with Kalyll, I remained in the tent, trying to sort out my feelings. I couldn't wrap my head around the terrible pressure in my chest. Ever since Kryn and the others kidnapped me, all I'd thought about was going back home, and now that I would be able to return, I felt no hint of the relief I'd expected. Instead, all I could think about was the way Kalyll made me feel when he was near me, and the way he'd made my entire being soar last night.

Why did I feel this way? Why did the thought of going home scare me when it should be the opposite? And then it hit me, I feared that no one else would ever make me feel this way again, feared that I would never see him again, never inhale his intoxicating scent, never touch his powerful chest and feel his heart hammering under my fingertips.

I feared an empty life.

Pushing up on trembling legs, I stood from the pile of furs and slowly straightened my clothes and hair. I rolled the leather strip Kalyll had given me between my fingers as fairytale ideas flashed through my head: Kalyll breaking his engagement and choosing me, his brother discovering the subterfuge and unseating Kalyll, the once-prince leaving Elf-hame to be with me in my realm, and other scenarios each more ridiculous than the last.

None of those things were possible, and it was ludicrous to even contemplate an outcome where he and I could be together.

Our realities were on opposite cardinal points. He was north and I was south, and we'd met in the middle for a bit, but that was over, and now we both needed to get back to our true lives.

Resolved to handle the situation with dignity, I tied my hair and walked out of the tent. Outside, I was surprised to find more tents and several fires casting a warm glow across the night. I glanced around, trying to find Kalyll or anyone in our original party. Belasha's soldiers, I assumed, regarded me with curiosity, probably wondering what I was doing here, how a human woman had come to be part of Kalyll Adanorin's retinue. Did they hate me for being close to their prince? Did they wish they could take my place?

"Dani." Arabis noticed me and walked toward me. "Kalyll says you're feeling better."

I nodded.

"And he... explained everything."

I nodded again, unsure of how to feel about her. She had been nice to me until she thought I would cause trouble and get in between Kalyll and his betrothed, until she thought my interference would cause a war.

Could I blame her for that?

I guessed not.

I didn't want to be the reason an entire realm went to war and thousands of innocent lives were lost.

"Why don't you join us? You must be starved?" Arabis gestured toward one of the fires. We walked together and, on the way there, I noticed Silver tied to a nearby tree, two males standing guard next to him. His gaze followed me. I expected hatred from him after I'd thwarted his attempt to murder Kalyll, but I saw only regret and sadness in his expression. What was his story? What had brought him to betray his friend? I would probably never know.

Jeondar, Kryn, Cylea, and Kalyll sat by the fire, all eating what looked like roasted meat, flat bread, and fresh vegetables. Cylea picked up a plate that had been set aside and offered it to me with a smile. I took it and sat on a log next to Arabis and across from Kalyll and Cylea. The flames from the fire danced in his eyes as he looked at me, wearing a sober expression.

"It's a novelty, isn't it, Dani?" Jeondar said. "The prince sitting with us at dinner, and all thanks to you."

He lifted a wooden goblet in toast, then drank. The others did the same.

"We can't thank you enough," Cylea said. "He's less of a pain in the ass now." She notched Kalyll with her shoulder.

"You probably prefer me as a beast," Kalyll said. "You've already complained about the additional work."

She bobbed her head from side to side. "You have a point. All the planning meetings and talk about strategy and the need for counsel do get in the way of fun. I hope you won't be so overbearing when we get back to Imbermore. The last time I didn't even have time to go shopping."

Everyone rolled their eyes, including Arabis.

"Like you need another dress," Kryn put in.

"How long will it take to get back to Pharowyn?" I asked, poking at my food with a two-prong fork.

"Eager to get back home, I see," Kryn said, wearing the biggest smile I'd ever seen on him, especially directed at me.

"I am," I said, returning his smile. I had no intention of letting him see my true feelings about my departure.

Across from me, Kalyll lowered his gaze to the fire and shifted in place. I tried not to read anything into his reaction. If he felt the way I did, even just a little, I didn't need to know it. Things were hard enough already.

"Then you'll be happy to learn that you don't have to go all the way back to Pharowyn to cross back into your realm." Kryn pulled something out of his pocket and offered it to me.

I took it, a wooden coin with the carving of a snake in the middle. How appropriate.

He continued. "It's a transfer token. You use it to get back. You can even keep it as a gift from me for saving my prince. All you have to do is hold it tightly in your hand and think of home, then you'll be there."

A transfer token. Very few people in my realm possessed one of those. The majority of those who had permission to travel between the two realms did so through the use of uniquely assigned runes that needed to be traced to specific locations to gain access. For my rune to work, I had to go to Steinberg Bridge and trace it on the wooden railing. It was a pain, so I'd always wanted a token, but now that it was in my hand, I wanted to fling it into the fire. I thought I'd have a few more days with Kalyll, but instead, they were kicking me out.

Maybe it was better this way.

I set the plate down on the ground and stood. "No time like the present, I suppose."

Kalyll jumped to his feet, looking alarmed. "Must you leave so soon?"

"I'm afraid so. The sooner I get back, the sooner I can put my life back together."

He lowered his head, looking embarrassed and apologetic for the damage he'd caused.

I turned to Jeondar. "Do you still have my belongings?"

"Certainly." He rose and walked away.

"Prince Kalyll, there's something I must talk to you about before I leave."

His attention bounced back from the fire and focused on me. He inclined his head.

"In private, please."

Kryn watched me with narrowed eyes. He probably thought I was about to throw myself at his prince and beg him to let me stay. Either way, I didn't care. He could think what he wanted. He would soon be out of my sight, after all.

Jeondar returned with my messenger bag. I took it and turned to the group. "I wish you all the best."

Looking stern, Jeondar took my hand and pressed it between his. "If you ever need anything, I am your humble servant. There will never be a deed too big to repay you for what you've done."

"Thank you, Jeondar. You are an honorable male."

"Um," Kalyll appeared uncertain, something I'd never seen. "In the beginning, I said that you would be compensated."

I shook my head forcefully. "No, please."

He put both hands up. "I know. I know. I'm sorry."

Arabis and Cylea walked over and hugged me.

"We are so very grateful," Arabis said.

Cylea gave me a radiant smile. "Come back and we'll party all night."

I had no words for them and only a head nod for Kryn to match his. Slinging the messenger bag over my shoulders, I walked away from the fire, Kalyll following me. When we were far enough from everyone's earshot, I stopped and stared into the dark forest that surrounded us, unable to face Kalyll.

He placed a hand on my shoulder and I startled. I turned, and it took all my strength to stand in front of him without breaking into tears. He waited. I tightened my fist around the token.

"There is something you must know," I began.

Kalyll took a step closer, looking eager, making me wonder what he imagined my words would be.

"It's about something I had to do when I healed you."

"Oh."

"When Silver stabbed you, it was too much for my healing powers. I tried, but you... you died."

From the surprised look on his face, it was clear Kryn hadn't told him how dire things had gotten.

"I had no choice," I went on. "The only way to save you was to use some of the dark energy still left in you. I had expelled most of it, but I pulled some back in order to repair your heart. It was the only way."

He rubbed the back of his neck, looking concerned. "What does that mean? Will I still...?"

"I don't know what it means. Hopefully nothing. You're strong, and maybe it will little less than affect your temper every once in a while. Maybe you won't be able to tell the difference."

He grunted, looking as if he were considering the worst-case scenario.

"It shouldn't be as bad as it was before," I said. "I mean... look at you, no hint of the beast. Unless you feel something?" I put a hand to my chest to suggest there may be some unwanted emotions there.

"What I feel has nothing to do with the dark forces that plagued me before. I—"

"Good." I cut him off, aware that if I let him go on, it would destroy me.

"Daniella," he said my name like a plea, "allow me to say one more thing."

I nodded once.

"When I implied that Kryn shouldn't worry because you're a human, it wasn't because I think less of your kind. I'm not a bigot. It was because a Seelie Prince may never have a serious... association with anyone who isn't Fae. It's not a statute of my making, nor one I can change, but believe me, I think it's the most dull-witted thing anyone ever came up with. I think you're my equal, and whatever stardust you're made of, it came from the same galaxy as mine."

My heart literally quivered at his words.

He reached for my hand, but I knew that if I allowed him to touch me, I would become undone, so I pulled away and held up the token.

"It would be best if I leave now. I'm sure you would agree."

A muscle jumped in his jaw, and he shook his head. "I can't say that I do, but I understand it's necessary." He took a step back and pressed a fist to his chest. "Daniella Sunder, it's been an honor. You are a remarkable female, and you will forever be remembered."

Tears pooled inside my eyes, and before they managed to spill, I clenched the token in my hand and thought of home.

The world seemed to run down, the night melting to the ground and spreading in a large puddle. Only darkness surrounded me, and for a moment, I panicked, but then the puddle climbed up again, color returning and shaping itself into the walls and furniture.

I blinked and tears streamed down my cheeks, just as I recognized my living room. My joints became unhinged, and I fell to my knees and cried like a baby. I don't know how long I kneeled there, letting my emotions take over, but when I stood, my nose was stuffed up and my eyes swollen.

Absentmindedly, I placed my messenger bag on the sofa and padded to my bedroom. A lamp was on, casting warm light over my bed and the pile of books on the night table. I caught a glimpse of myself in the full-length mirror on the closet door and barely recognized the person staring back. My skin had acquired a darker bronze hue after so much time spent on horseback. My Fae-made clothes made me look like I didn't belong in this realm. Angrily, I pulled the tunic over my head and threw it to the floor. I did the same with the boots and leggings until I was left in my bra and panties.

My legs wobbled as I turned off the lamp, climbed into bed, and curled under the covers. I tried to find comfort in the fresh scent of my clean linens and my comfortable pillow, but it was no use. The tears kept coming, and there was nothing I could do to stop them.

It will get better. Just give it time.

Time would be the only thing that would heal this pain, this sense of loss. Kalyll had never been mine, but my heart didn't understand that. Inside, I felt as if something precious had been ripped away from me.

Finally, I cried myself to sleep, and only then I found relief.

I awoke from a dead sleep, my eyes springing open and going wide. A hand was pressed against my mouth, caging the scream that rose to my lips. Adrenaline punched me in the chest, and I tried to fight back, but my attacker straddled me and held me down.

My eyes roved around desperately as I kicked and tried to free my arms. A guttural growl rumbled in my attacker's chest. I stilled, and for the first time, tried to focus on his face. Long hair hung down, framing his obscured features. The scent of leather and rosewood flooded my senses.

I whimpered.

He growled in response and slowly removed his hand.

"Kalyll?"

He got off the bed and threw the covers aside. Light from the window illuminated his face as his gaze devoured me.

I bit my lower lip and trembled at the sight of him. It was not Kalyll, not really. It wasn't the beast either. It was something in between, a male with bloodshot eyes, long fangs, and claws.

"What are you doing here?" I asked in a trembling voice.

"You're mine."

My skin pebbled as his deep voice burrowed deep into my bones.

"Kalyll, please, this isn't you."

He grabbed my wrist and yanked me out of bed until I was standing in front of him, pressed against his hard body, his arm wrapped tightly around my waist.

He pressed his cheek to mine and whispered in my ear. "This *is* me, pure and unadulterated, and nothing and no one will keep me from what I want. You're coming with me."

With one quick motion, he squeezed a pressure point in my neck and I went limp. My head spun as unconsciousness threatened to overtake me. He scooped me in his arms and held me tight.

"Sleep," he said, and I knew no more.

GET BOOK 2

A CAGE SO GILDED

Made in United States
Troutdale, OR
10/12/2023

13601178R20174